A HALF-HEARTED
HEARTED

MELANIE JOY

TWO STEPS
FORWARD PRESS

Two Steps Forward Press

Copyright © 2025 by Melanie Joy

If you would like permission to use material from
the book (other than for review purposes),
please contact info@twostepsforwardpress.com.

This is a work of fiction. Names, characters, places, and
incidents are products of the author's imagination or are
used fictitiously and are not to be construed as real.

First Two Steps Forward Press edition / May 2025

ISBN 979-8-9925898-0-1 (paperback)
ISBN 979-8-9925898-1-8 (ebook)

This book is a work of fiction and is not intended to diagnose, treat, or provide guidance for mental health conditions, including suicidal thoughts or behaviors. If you or someone you know is struggling with thoughts of suicide or self-harm, please seek professional help. Suicidal ideation, depression, and other mental health conditions are treatable, and support is available.

For immediate assistance:

In the United States: Call or text 988 (Suicide & Crisis Lifeline).

Outside the US: Visit befrienders.org to find a helpline near you.

for healers

Contents

1

A Deadly Awakening

Day 1: Saturday

I*'m dying to kill myself, but I want nothing more than to live.*

If Emma weren't feeling so sluggish, her thoughts would be racing. Her psychological condition makes no sense. It's like those paradoxical Zen koans, those riddles that mean nothing but are supposed to hold the answer to everything. Most people who are suicidal are in such pain that death seems the only way out. But Emma isn't in pain—unless you count the distress caused by feeling compelled to end the life you want to keep on living. She's not depressed, and she's in excellent mental health. At least, she was before this morning.

It's as though while she was sleeping, she contracted some strange virus that infected her will to live, disabling her survival instinct. And now she's crossed an invisible emotional line that she can never cross back over. Like when you suddenly just know that your relationship has run its course, and you can't stand staying in it for another second. Or when you realize you've got to quit your job, or move from your home, or change your hair color.

Not doing so feels implausible, profane.

Emma looks up from the online Saturday edition of the *New York Times* after obliviously rereading the same blurb for five minutes. Sunlight glints off the damp, budding trees outside the bay windows of the bedroom, and the mirror next to the curtains reflects her tumble of shoulder-length auburn hair, gray roots just starting to re-emerge, and the soft lavender pajama top that makes her green eyes pop.

Leaning back against her pillows and cushioned headboard, she takes another sip of coffee from the mug she bought from a local potter at the New England Artisanal Fair. The nutty organic brew has the perfect amount of oat creamer, and its velvety warmth flushes out the chill of the early-April morning. Sip, swallow, sigh. The familiar rhythm of decadent simplicity.

Beside her, the ivory duvet moves to a similar beat. It undulates with each knead of a fluffy orange paw, the movements accompanied by a steady purr.

Everything is just as it was yesterday at this time. And yet it's all so different. Each of Emma's usual creature comforts is failing to deliver. The world seems somehow tainted, ominous. It's like that lingering sense of impending doom after a nightmare whose contents you forgot but whose haunting emotions you just can't shake.

But it wasn't a nightmare that led to this. Surely Emma would recall a dream so bad it left her yearning to take her own life. It's like she's being pulled toward suicide by an irresistible siren song. The urge to kill herself is so strong it feels like a mission—something that, if not acted upon, will itself kill her.

Maybe she's experiencing the health anxiety that sometimes follows a professional development seminar for clinicians, in which scary new insidious psychological disorders are unveiled. She did just finish an online course on rare and bizarre mental health conditions she'd never heard of—like Alice in Wonderland syndrome, where an individual perceives parts of their body to be growing or shrinking, and zoanthropy, where someone believes they've turned into an animal and starts whinnying or chirping or rolling in mud. At one point she actually googled to make sure the syndromes were real. She'd thought the course would be interesting enough to prevent her from surreptitiously playing Candy Crush while listening to the lectures, which always left her feeling guilty. In hindsight, she should probably have enrolled in something more benign.

Still. She's not delusional. Before this morning she was feeling just fine. So what went wrong between yesterday and today?

Yesterday was, by all accounts, a perfectly normal day. Better than normal, in some regards. She saw her usual Friday clients and one even had a breakthrough of sorts. She finished her tedious billing paperwork early and treated herself to dinner from her favorite Vietnamese takeout joint, The Dancing Buddha, which for once didn't give her something other than the #73 chicken curry and rice that she always orders. She did, however, get home to find that she'd gotten the #39 pork dumplings instead of the #36 shrimp ones, but appetizer mix-ups are far less upsetting than main course ones. She ate in front of her guilty pleasure, Netflix's *Love Is Blind*, and then turned in early.

The only unusual thing that happened was that she felt nauseous after eating, and almost had to vomit. But the feeling had subsided by the time she went to bed, and given that there's probably a five percent chance of getting food poisoning from a greasy fast food restaurant and she hadn't gotten sick once in the past decade of orders, she figured she was actually ahead of the curve.

Could the culprit be that natural hormonal supplement she started taking two weeks ago for perimenopausal symptoms, which had been recommended by her thirteen-year-old niece who'd learned about it on TikTok?

Or maybe it's not the hormones, but the mere fact that she's lived in a woman's body for over four decades. Nearly half a century of frantically juggling the needs of others while dropping the balls of your own, all the while making sure to keep a smile on your face so your resentment never shows. Emma has talked to enough middle-aged women to know that if there were ever to be a hashtag that captured this demographic, it would be #I'mDone.

The purring amplifies, and Emma glances ruefully down at Annie. The cat's name was chosen by a family that hadn't thought to check his sex and she had kept it, not wanting to mess with his identity. Golden eyes stare out of a cloud of orange and squint repeatedly, in the ultimate expression of cat love. Emma's stomach clenches and her eyes start to burn. If she kills herself, Annie's life will be over.

She adopted Annie four years ago from the local no-kill shelter. Her heart had lurched when she'd seen the trembling ball of fluff curled up in the far corner of a dark cage, his wide eyes glazed in terror—a state he'd apparently been in since arriving at the shelter a year earlier.

Annie had originally lived with a girl who'd loved him, and he'd been happy and well-adjusted. But the girl's parents, who suffered from addiction and other mental health problems, dropped him behind the shelter when the girl was away visiting her grandparents during her Christmas break. The shelter workers found him three days later lying on his side in a tiny carrier, starving and almost frozen to death, covered in his own excrement. They learned of his story the following week, when a neighbor called to check on him after finding out that he'd been left there.

It took every device in Emma's psychological toolkit to finally gain Annie's trust, to help him heal and become the playful, loving feline he is today. He's even become a "velcro cat," sticking to her wherever she goes. But, like many individuals with attachment trauma, Annie carries invisible scars. Emma is the only person whose presence doesn't cause him to regress to the flat-eared, shivering ball he once was. He'd never recover from a second abandonment.

Annie isn't the only one for whom Emma's untimely death would have catastrophic consequences. She has a full caseload of clients who have confided in her their tragedies and traumas, their anguish and despair, their secret shames and private ambitions. Emma is well aware that there's nothing more sacred than being trusted with someone's vulnerability, and few things more devastating than violating that trust.

Then there's her father. Her regular visits are possibly the only reason the grieving old man hasn't succumbed to the metastasized prostate cancer that's been ravaging his body for the past three years. And although his death would bring relief, an end to his suffering, it would be tragic if it came before he had a chance to release the regret that's gripped him even more tightly than the illness.

And what about her younger brother, Nick, who's relied on her advice and guidance since the two of them were old enough to stop drowning each other's dolls in the unflushed toilet? Or Rachelle, the long-limbed pansexual barista covered in unintelligible tattoos, whose polyamorous relationships would surely implode if not for the free therapy she gets from Emma every time the psychologist treats herself to her weekly latte? Or Jonas, the local postal carrier who has bipolar disorder and who—

Emma shakes her head. She needs to snap out of this. She's never been one to indulge her worries, and she doesn't plan to start now. She needs a change of scenery to ground herself and recalibrate. Throwing back the covers, she slides out of bed, pads to her vintage walnut armoire, and pulls on her gardening clothes.

ONE OF THE NICEST THINGS ABOUT LIVING IN ARLINGTON IS that, unlike many other Boston suburbs, it's actually suburban. In place of sprawling apartment complexes are spacious Victorian and colonial homes, as well as quaint Cape and ranch houses, on quiet tree-lined streets.

Emma was fortunate enough to have bought her two-story, two-bedroom colonial before the real estate boom that made most of Massachusetts unaffordable. When she purchased it after her divorce ten years ago, though, it was the yard that had attracted her. The little plot of land behind the house was just what she needed to recharge her introverted batteries and reset her sensitive nervous system so that she could maintain a life dedicated to helping and healing.

The weather has been as unpredictable as ever this time of year. Yesterday it sleeted; today the sun warms her back through her light sweatshirt, and the thawed earth sinks beneath her clogs as she leans over to pull up emerging weeds.

"Looks like our little hypocrite is at it again!"

The weathered face in the adjacent yard is framed by wispy gray hair that stands out as though charged with static electricity. The only thing preventing the septuagenarian from looking like a rogue dandelion is the pilled winter hat sitting askew on his head.

Walter chuckles at his cleverness, as though it's not the millionth time he's repeated that same joke, and shakes his finger at the pile of weeds next to Emma. "I thought you knew better!"

"Ah, you caught me," Emma replies with feigned guilt, as though she hasn't repeated that same line a million times. And so the conversation will go. Emma will keep weeding her garden, and Walter will keep pointing out the contradiction in nurturing certain kinds of plants while killing those that have been arbitrarily designated as weeds, asking her, "Who gets to determine which plants should live and which should die?"

Emma's heart sinks as she imagines Walter having nobody to chide or to indulge his eccentric commentaries.

As far as she can tell, she's the only person Walter banters with.

"By the way, Emma, Charles is looking forward to lunch tomorrow." At the sound of his name, a plump white chicken comes clucking toward the lanky man. He hops nimbly past the widespread clutter (or "collectibles," as Walter calls it), his neck jerking back and forth, and cocks his head sideways to look up at Walter expectantly.

Like many people Emma encounters, Walter often expresses his feelings and needs as though they were someone else's. When you don't risk showing your true self, it's safer. At least in the short term.

"Well, you can tell Charles to rest assured that *Pasta alla Emma* is already in the making." Emma ekes out a smile, despite the vice grip squeezing her heart at the thought of Walter being left to dine alone.

Charles has taken an interest in a decaying birdhouse lying on its side on the ground, pecking at it as though it's going to peck back. It's one of countless birdhouses in varying states of disrepair that Walter has "collected." In fact, he's amassed a plethora of items, like barrels and bottles and rye sacks to make the experimental microbrews that he now has enough of to rehydrate the state of California, as well as a tower of rotting durian he's planning to ferment and turn into "Stinky Schnapps." But his greatest passion is all things bird: bird houses, bird baths, bird feeders, bird binoculars... bird everything. Except cages. Walter would never want to see anyone in a cage, least of all someone with wings.

Which is why Charles ended up living with him. Three years ago, Walter was at the Global BirdPeople convention (GloB), which is like a Star Trek convention for bird lovers. Rather than speak Klingon, though, people go around imitating bird calls. And instead of dressing up like their favorite Starfleet character, they don a costume of their favorite avian, sometimes with families dressing up in tandem, parents prancing about like proud storks dragging their egg-ensconced children behind them in a giant, makeshift diaper.

At the convention, Walter met a woman who was looking for someone to adopt her pet chicken, who she'd been keeping in a cage since she'd sold her suburban house and moved to a small apartment in the city. So Walter ended up coming home with Charles, who's proved to be a faithful companion.

Emma finds some solace in the thought that the old man wouldn't be completely alone if she were gone, as her gaze lands on the upturned tines of a pitchfork on the ground and she fantasizes about falling on it, chest first.

The fresh air, scent of moist earth, and Walter's familiar, good-natured chatter somehow have no effect on her suicidality. Killing herself feels like an imperative, a non-negotiable.

If one of Emma's clients reported the same symptoms, she'd refer them to a suicide intervention center immediately. Suicidal ideation—thoughts of killing yourself—is never to be taken lightly and not something people should try to deal with on their own.

If she reaches out for help, though, she'll be forced to take a break from seeing clients, something she hasn't done in years because there's always been someone in crisis. Plus, she wouldn't want to burden others with the worry that she's unwell.

Maybe she simply hasn't fully recovered from the tainted food she consumed last night. In which case, the best thing to do is to approach her suicidality like it's a bout of food poisoning, and just wait it out.

But Emma is all too aware that deeper urges usually find a way to fulfill themselves. She just hopes that hers won't make her do something stupid.

2

Sick and Sicker

Day 2: Sunday

An amorphous, cloudlike sphere skids across the rustic hardwood floor. It's followed by the erratic lunges of Annie, who is wholly consumed by the chase-and-smack drama he's created. The crumpled tissue is but one of many littering the bedroom, which is still dark despite the late morning hour. It was a long night.

Emma drags herself out of bed and takes shaky steps to the bathroom. As she brushes her teeth, propping herself up with one hand on the sink, she recoils at the swollen, crimson nose and chafed nostrils protruding from the pallid face in the mirror. But it's her eyes, sunken and haunted, that make her heart stop.

She's sick. Physically, and mentally.

Just two days ago she was in perfect health. What the hell is wrong with her?

She did recently spend an evening at Nick's place for her twin niece and nephew's thirteenth birthday party, when her brother told her that he and the family were all recovering from the flu. The timing of her own illness would make sense if they'd been contagious. Maybe they felt suicidal, too.

The steps down to the kitchen creak in time to the jolts in her aching joints and the throbs in her pounding head. Fixing herself a cup of coffee, Emma taps Nick's number.

"Hey. What's up? How're ya doing?" Nick's baritone voice, like his six-foot-two-inch frame, rarely fails to stand out. But now it's obscured by shrieks, bangs, and barking in the background. Who needs their own children when their sibling has enough kid energy to keep the entire extended family overstimulated?

"Hey, I'm good. Just a little under the weather." Emma instinctively raises her voice so Nick won't have to struggle to hear her over the clamor, and her throat feels like it's being sliced by a thousand tiny razors. She plunges into a coughing fit and hits mute.

Emma has the rare ability to hone in on other people's psychological and emotional experiences, as well as a natural desire to be helpful and the intuition to know what to do. So she automatically calibrates herself to maintain interpersonal harmony and connection, even when it's not in her best interest to do so—and often she only catches herself after the fact. Being highly relational is Emma's superpower. And her kryptonite.

She takes a sip of coffee, and the warm liquid quiets her coughing.

"Jeez, Em. Sounds like you're more than a *little* under the weather. When'd you get so sick?" Nick's speaking at a normal volume now. Thankfully, the family circus seems to have migrated to a different part of the house.

"I woke up in the middle of the night last night with a

cough and sore throat." And worsening fantasies of killing myself.

"Do you have a fever? What are your other symptoms? Maybe it's what Marina and the kids and I had last week." Nick can always be counted on to try to help diagnose and fix a problem. He's a genuinely nice guy, one of those rare individuals who has no hidden layers of darkness that emerge once the other layers have been peeled away; no scary, heavy baggage that's going to get stuffed into your personal knapsack to shock and burden you one day. What you see is what you get. Plus, he inherited the same sense of conscientiousness as Emma.

"I've got a fever, but only 100.5. It's my throat, head, and chest. And I've got body aches. Is that what you guys had?"

"Yeah, sounds pretty much the same. Jeez, sorry. You probably caught it from us."

"It's not your fault." Although it would have been helpful if Nick or Marina had thought to prevent the kids from licking Emma's nose and cheeks, pretending to be giving her canine kisses. "And I'm fine, really. Just one thing—did you guys have any weird symptoms?"

"Weird? Like what?"

"Just any symptoms that aren't usually part of a cold. Like… a rash? Or swollen toes. Or maybe… a strange mood?"

Nick barks out a laugh. "None of the above. Why?"

Because I want to kill myself more than anything in the world.

"I was just wondering." As soon as Nick smells a problem, he'll be sniffing around trying to root it out, and the last thing he needs, on top of his demanding jobs as co-director of a high-maintenance consulting company and co-founder of a high-maintenance family, is to worry about her. Plus, as two years his senior, *she's* the one who's supposed to worry about *him*.

Pivoting, Emma asks if Nick has returned their father's calls.

"You know the answer to that, so why do you always have to ask?" This is the one topic that puts an edge in Nick's voice.

"C'mon, Nick. Dad was so disappointed. It was the twins' thirteenth birthday party, and I'm sure they would have loved to see him. And he doesn't have much time left. This would have been the perfect opportunity to finally put an end to so much heartache."

"Seriously? He actually thought he'd be invited? We haven't talked in over five years. What the hell does he expect?"

A loud bang is followed by a child wailing. "Hey Em, I gotta run. Call me later to let me know how you're doing, 'kay?"

"Okay!" Emma yells, and falls into another painful coughing fit.

LIVING IN NEW ENGLAND IN APRIL IS LIKE LIVING WITH A partner who has an untreated mood disorder. One day they're beaming and wrapping you in their warmth, and the next day they're storming and flooding you with their wrath.

The bitter wind whips Emma's hair across her face and licks the exposed areas of her neck like an icy tongue. She pulls her scarf tighter and lowers her head as she climbs the three steps to Walter's side door.

"The Sunday lunch special, *Pasta alla Emma*, is here!" Walter guffaws. "Oh, and so is Emma!" More laughter.

Emma holds out her bag of food but stays on the stoop. "I seem to have caught a cold and don't want to get you sick. So what do you think about eating in the Pavilion?" The Pavilion is a raised, rickety platform with a makeshift wooden "pillar" on each side. In nice weather, Walter likes to sit there and savor his skunky microbrews, as though it were his personal throne.

Walter's watery, gray blue eyes look past Emma at the gathering clouds and flailing branches. "Well, sure, Emma, if you really want to. But you're welcome to come in. My immune system's as strong as a well-fed albatross!"

Emma's attempt to suppress a cough fails and she falls into a spasm. Her condition seems to have worsened since she spoke with Nick earlier in the day.

"Or, uh, maybe you'd rather go back to bed? I reckon it can't be good for you to be out and about, especially in this weather." Although Walter left South Carolina for Massachusetts forty years ago, he still sometimes speaks Southern.

Emma wills her chest and throat into stillness. "No, no. It's fine, really. I mean, *I'm* fine." There's no way she's going to cancel on him last-minute and leave him to eat alone.

After gathering plates, cutlery, and paper linens from the kitchen, the pair head to the Pavilion, settling into wobbly chairs at the table and starting in on Emma's rich, tomatoey concoction. Walter has placed broken chunks of sandstone and muddied bird figurines on the napkins and tablecloth, using them as makeshift paper weights, but they barely suffice against the gusting wind.

The thickening clouds above are getting darker and Emma shivers as she forces herself to take another bite of the pasta she can't taste. Chewing slowly, she readies herself for a long afternoon. Like dog years, time in the Pavilion doesn't follow the usual laws of nature. For every hour you're in it, only five minutes have passed in the outside world.

"… but the lyrebird, now *that's* a whippersnapper! Did you know that lyrebirds can mimic the sounds of other kinds of birds so perfectly that they actually fool the birds of those species?" Walter seems impervious to the raw turbulence of the afternoon. In fact, he's opened his coat and his face is flushed. He's in his element, holding court. Sharing his favorite kind of collectible: facts.

"Wow." Emma hopes she sounds engaged. "So lyrebirds are like the deepfakes of the bird world."

"Ha! You could say that. And did you know turkey vultures are also pretty shocking, but not because they're so clever, but because they're so foul?" Walter sucks a large wad of linguine into his mouth, leaving sauce in the corners of his lips.

Emma winces. She always forgets about Walter's compromised social skills, including his lack of etiquette.

"Turkey vultures, see, they eat dead animals. They're vultures. But—get this"—suck, slurp, stain—"those rotting carcasses in their stomachs are their self-defense!" Swallow. "They projectile vomit on potential threats—hurling their regurgitation up to ten feet!" Walter laughs as he mercifully wipes his face.

Emma sees an opening to take her leave. But before she can say anything, Walter starts chuckling as he looks down at the chicken who's approaching him. Charles chuckles back.

What?

Emma's head is throbbing and her ears feel like they're stuffed with cotton. Maybe what she thought was a chuckle was actually a cluck. Or maybe she's had an auditory hallucination.

Leaning forward, Walter obligingly lifts Charles onto his lap. The chicken settles down as if in a cozy nest, head lolling to the side and eyes slowly closing as his person strokes his chin.

"So chickens, chickens are like little people. Really. They're as intelligent as some toddlers. They can recognize more than *a hundred* different faces, and even remember them after a long time has passed. Faces of chickens *and* of humans!" Walter smiles down at Charles.

Emma tries not to look at the chicken, for fear of having another seeming hallucination. She doesn't know how she'll keep it together if she suddenly sees Charles with the head of Barbara Walters or Snoop Dogg or Greta Thunberg, or wearing a nose and glasses set.

"They're self-aware. And I bet you didn't know this, but chickens dream! And hens talk with their chicks while they're still inside their eggs! And the chicks peep back from inside the eggs, and—"

Emma's violent coughing breaks through Walter's discourse and he blinks at her, clearing the facts from his mind's eye to finally focus on the person across from him.

"I'm so sorry," she chokes out between hacks. "I—I really think I should get going now."

EVEN THE FLANNEL PAJAMAS, FLEECE SLIPPER SOCKS, AND thick cotton bathrobe Emma put on after a steamy shower haven't driven out the chill. Maybe the chamomile tea she's steeping will do the trick.

What she really needs to drive out, though, is her death wish. Or *the* death wish that's gotten lodged inside her. It's not *her* wish. Not really. It's as though a strange new part of her was suddenly birthed, another Emma, Suicidal Emma, who's hellbent on killing her. She feels like she's being terrorized, stalked by a predatory entity she can't evade. She's been oscillating between mortal terror, which arises when she thinks about death and dying, and grief, which is triggered by her thoughts of the imminent loss of her life and the actual loss of her will to live.

As she's giving her tea bag a final dunk, the phone rings. It's Shana.

"Hey, lady! So sorry to bother you to talk shop on a Sunday evening, but I've got a little favor to ask, and it's time sensitive. How ya doin'?"

Shana rents the office across from Emma's on the first floor of an old Victorian house in the center of town, and she's the best psychiatrist Emma knows. Although Shana can and does treat a range of clients and problems, she specializes in Black adolescent girls. Like most clinicians, Shana's mission is autobiographical.

"Hey, I'm good. And you're not bothering me at all." Emma musters what she hopes is a normal, non-suicidal voice. Shana is like a heat-seeking missile for emotional undertones.

"Whoa. What's wrong? You sick? Your voice sounds awful."

"I've just got a cold. I'll sleep it off tonight."

"Yikes. Yeah, here's hoping. Anywho, so, Theresa surprised me with a seven-day vacation the second week in August, when she gets her annual leave. For our anniversary. It's so sweet. *She's* so sweet."

Shana's wife is an epidemiology rock star who works for the World Health Organization and is often referred to as the Greta Thunberg of the public health world. Suddenly recalling chuckling Charles, Emma shudders.

"So... I wanna tell Theresa yes, but when I think of Autumn, I feel terrible."

Fourteen-year-old Autumn is Shana's highest-risk client—a trauma survivor who regularly self-harms. When Shana's away, the girl becomes extremely anxious, and Emma is the only stand-in clinician she's willing to talk to. Autumn has had two breakdowns already, and a third one could cause irreparable damage.

"Of *course* I'll cover for you." As soon as the words are out of Emma's mouth, she realizes her mistake, and she tries to push away the image of a shattered Autumn wandering the drab halls of a group home after learning that her stand-in therapist has killed herself.

"Thank you *so* much. I totally owe you one. Jamaica, baby! Here we come! And you take care of yourself. I know you wanna see clients tomorrow, but you gotta take care of *you*, especially if you wanna be there for your people. Stay in bed and do a Netflix binge. And then it's *your* turn to go on vacay, which you haven't done in years." Shana chortles. "Doctor's orders!"

Officially miserable, her fever at 101 and her suicidality at about the same level, Emma climbs the hardwood stairs to the bedroom. She's desperate to be unconscious and hoping to sleep off whatever bizarre illness she's contracted.

But before she reaches the top, the buzzer rings, making her jump. With a groan, she turns back to see who it is.

WIND AND RAIN LASH THE NAKED TREES BEHIND THE USPS delivery woman. She's standing in the open doorway beside a large, soaked box, awaiting Emma's signature. The inside temperature is dropping by the second as Emma fumbles in the closet next to the entrance, digging for the two packages she wants to hand to the driver to take back with her.

As she pulls out the first package, a loud explosion erupts from the back of the house. Emma startles, yelping and dropping the box on her foot. And before she's even had a chance to turn around, a terrified Annie darts out the front door and disappears into the night, heading straight for the traffic jam in the road ahead.

3

The Suicidal Shrink

Bob Marley's "One Love" has been looping for what must be fifteen minutes, but Emma's arm is too heavy to reach over and hit the snooze button on her phone. She stares helplessly at the nightstand through burning, slitted eyes. Usually pristine, it's now strewn with balled up tissues and cough drop wrappers. An untouched mug of tea and a half-empty glass of water linger next to the thermometer, which displays a punitive 101.5.

The bed is arrestingly still, a silent indictment. Poor Annie is still in hiding after his ordeal last night.

Emma had fled after the cat into the tempestuous downpour, shouting and zigzagging behind him as he dodged in and out of traffic trying to cross to the other side. The storm had downed a tree on the main road that runs parallel to Emma's, causing near-gridlock on her normally quiet street.

Her desperate search-and-rescue mission lasted for more than an hour. She found the sodden, terrified cat huddled in a corner under the porch steps of the house across the street. He was shaking, his skinny tail curled tightly around him. His tiny, skeletal frame, usually hidden beneath his optimistic shock of fur, was exposed in all its raw vulnerability. Her voice breaking as she cooed his name, Emma gently lifted him and carried him home.

The blast had come from next door. Walter, it turns out, has a massive collection of pyrotechnics, an interest derived from his years in the navy when he was responsible for sending out emergency distress signals. He'd been experimenting with a new Morse code when he accidentally tripped one of the explosives.

Walter apologized for the incident, but Emma blamed herself for the fallout. She knew better than to leave the door open and unattended. The robust, clear-headed Emma of last week would never have let that happen.

By the time she went to bed, she was feverish and coughing relentlessly. She set her alarm for 7:00 a.m. so she could contact her Monday clients with sufficient notice in the event that she'd be too ill to go into the office.

Which she is. So she'll offer to see them on Zoom rather than in person. She doesn't want to expose anyone to her strange flu, especially the severely depressed clients who are more vulnerable to suicidality. What she does want is to slip back into unconsciousness. But her clients need her. She simply doesn't have time to be sick, physically or mentally.

One love. One heart. Let's join together, and—

Groaning, Emma turns off Bob Marley's sentimental proclamations.

The room lurches as she steps out of bed. Steadying

herself, she makes her way cautiously toward the kitchen, where she'll start caffeinating so she can be coherent by the time she talks to people.

A half hour later, at 8:00, she's ready to start making calls. Unfortunately, the caffeine hasn't had much of an effect, other than making her wound up and anxious on top of feeling dull and exhausted.

"Thanks for checking in, Emma, and for being so available. But you really don't sound well. We're fine canceling this week, really."

Jenna, one half of her Monday morning couple, is usually the contact person for the duo. Like Emma, she's highly relational, which is one reason she struggles so much in her marriage to Alexander, who has ADHD and is somewhere on the autism spectrum. It's also one reason the relationship works.

"It sounds worse than it is." Emma never lies, on principle and just because she can't. Her ex-husband—who's an honest guy himself and who Emma has remained on good terms with—used to tease her for being unable to conceal even the slightest transgression. And she's not lying now: she feels awful, but her voice is *really* awful.

"Well, Alexander and I didn't have any major incidents last week. I mean, he did bring home twenty apple tree saplings that he planned to grow on our *eight-by-eight-foot* balcony, because he thought I'd love being able to harvest our own fruit. And I traced a fruit fly outbreak to a drawer full of used tea bags and banana peels he'd been saving to start a compost, which he'd forgotten about. And then there was the filthy rag he'd used to mop a spill off the apartment stairwell that I found in the clean dish rack. But we were able to talk about everything without it getting too heated. I'm actually proud of myself; I stayed pretty calm. And he didn't tell me he thought I was being controlling. So all in all I think we did pretty well, and we're fine. Fine enough for now, anyway."

Jenna's pride is punctuated by subtle notes of pain, the pain of someone struggling to hold onto affection for their beloved partner. One of Emma's goals for the couple is to help them—especially Jenna—rekindle this feeling. Losing the light warmth of affection for the person you love, which often results from repeated relational breaches that haven't gotten fully resolved, is heart-wrenching. Dr. Xi, Emma's favorite professor in grad school, used to say that without affection, relationships feel flat, disconnected, and empty, and partners don't have the emotional resilience they need to ride out the inevitable waves of triggers and conflicts and annoyances. Affection is the vital glue in a relationship, yet it's often only noticed once it's missing, as Jenna and Alexander have been learning.

"That's great to hear, Jenna. Good work." Emma mutes her phone while she momentarily hacks. "And thanks for being so understanding."

There's no point in insisting on a session today. Not only would Alexander have a hard time focusing in two dimensions—three is already enough of a challenge—but the conversation would be too complex and loaded to skillfully carry out online.

AFTER A LUNCH OF BLAND MINESTRONE SOUP AND MORE useless coffee, Emma braces herself for her afternoon appointments. Her cozy home office, with its soft caramel armchair, tidy desk, and array of eclectic throw rugs, somehow feels claustrophobic. And the orderly Ikea bookshelves seem tilted, the walls askew.

Emma flips open her laptop, squinting at the glare of LED light, and fights the urge to hit "resume" on yesterday's search for "quick and painless ways to kill yourself." Instead, she opens Zoom and admits her first client.

"Thanks for seeing us on your day off. We really appreciate it." Olivia often misses critical elements of a communication. Part of Emma's job is helping the woman course correct, but today she has neither the bandwidth nor the desire to do so by pointing out that she's not on vacation.

"So, a lot's happened with us since we last saw you," Olivia continues. "We were on the cusp of breaking up." The attractive woman in her mid-thirties with straight black hair, wide espresso eyes, and light brown skin is sitting next to a suitcase.

"Did Karl have another one of his episodes?"

"Pff! 'Episode' is putting it lightly. I was literally ready to pack my bags—and I told him so." Olivia looks at the steel-blue carry-on suitcase standing on the sofa beside her, smirking.

Emma cringes. She'd been working with the pair for a year, and they had almost gotten to the point where Olivia could stop talking about packing her bags, which was Karl's biggest trigger. It incited his jealousy so much that he snapped into becoming the perfect partner again. Until he wasn't. And so the cycle went.

All relationships follow the cycles of connection, disconnection, and reconnection. Emma has often explained to Olivia that what's most important is not how couples connect or disconnect, but how they *re*connect. When reconnection leads to true insight and genuine behavioral change, the relationship can deepen and grow—or end, if that's what's best for both parties. This has not been the case with Olivia and Karl, because Olivia hasn't been ready to let Karl go.

"But he's been *amazing* the past couple of days, and we're planning a vacation to Cancun later in the year." Olivia beams at the bag.

Olivia started therapy in order to work on her relationship with Karl—who, it just so happened, turned out to be a suitcase. Olivia has objectophilia, a condition where someone falls in love with an inanimate object, like a train station or a light switch or, in Olivia's case, a piece of luggage. "Karry-on Karl" is the object of Olivia's affection, and—according to current psychological perspectives on objectophilia—Olivia won't be able to move beyond her attachment to the bag until she's worked through some of her deep-seated relational issues.

"Okay, Olivia. Let's strategize about ways to prevent Karl from having another meltdown if he has to be checked at the gate again."

It's going to be a long session.

EMMA'S LAST CLIENT OF THE DAY IS, THANKFULLY, ONE OF her least demanding, and he often likes to end early since his energy wanes quickly. Today, though, he'd asked to meet at 7:00 p.m. since he had earlier commitments, and since the Monday night support group that Emma facilitates and he attends was canceled due to her illness.

Seventy-eight-year-old Arthur is a congenial great-grandfather with a Roman nose, a slight New York accent, and neatly combed strands of white hair. He started therapy last year after discovering that his daughter had been hospitalized for depression following a suicide attempt, and he'd never even known she was unhappy. "Can you imagine? All those Thanksgivings, Christmases, birthdays, extended family field trips to desalination plants"—Arthur's family had a thing for desalination plants, and there was nothing Freudian about it as far as Emma could tell—"and not a peep. I never knew *squat*. All because she didn't think I'd understand. And she knew I'd just try to find a 'quick fix' like I always did."

Most of the session today is spent communicating with the top right corner of Arthur's forehead, with occasional stomach-lurching swings showing the edge of the ceiling or the floorboards.

Arthur tells Emma how he cried last week at his great-granddaughter's christening and, rather than feel ashamed of his sensitivity, he took pride in it. "It's like Brené Brown says. It's the power of vulnerability." Because his phone has fallen onto his foot and Emma's mic is muted, Arthur doesn't notice her violent coughing fit.

Thirty-five minutes into the session, he swings his camera up to his cheek and outer eye and announces he "got what I came for!" and would like to wrap up. His image flips sideways in a final, nauseating salute.

Feeling bile in the back of her throat, Emma lets out a breath she didn't know she was holding and gratefully ends the call.

After sitting at her desk with her head in her hands for nearly half an hour, waiting for the queasiness to pass, Emma trudges to the living room to take her temperature. 102. Out of habit, she takes her emotional temperature. Her suicidality has gotten worse as well.

Maybe NyQuil will cure her.

Pulling on her winter parka and flipping up the hood to protect her head from the relentless, windswept rain of the continuing storm, Emma steps into the inky black night. She climbs into her gold four-door Toyota Corolla that's parked in front of her house and heads off to the drug store.

Streaks of light from street lamps and oncoming traffic dance across the deluged windshield, threatening to morph into a bizarre hallucination. Thankfully, the store is a mere five minutes from her house, on familiar roads.

As she nears the main intersection of the four-lane road, she slows to stop at the yellow light, rather than rush through it to avoid the long wait for the green arrow to turn left into the store parking lot. She switches on the radio to distract herself from her pulsing temples and morbid fantasies, turning up the volume so she can hear the music over the hammering rain and rapid whoosh of the windshield wipers.

She's flipping between stations to find something that doesn't sound abrasive when she pulls forward through the red light. And obliviously turns in front of an oncoming pickup truck.

At the sound of a blasting horn and screeching brakes, her head jerks up and she slams on the gas to pull forward out of the way, careening into the parking lot entrance. She crashes into the fire hydrant on the side of the entryway, snapping her head forward and wrenching her neck.

Stunned, her car alarm blaring, she raises her eyes to look in the rearview mirror. The pickup truck has pulled over just behind her, and its furious driver is scrambling out.

If she'd been a fraction of a second slower she'd have been hit.

Clearly, Emma is no longer safe from herself.

4

SOS

❖

Day 5: Wednesday

Emma almost always has to explain to her clients how important it is that they reach out for help when they need it. She encourages them to appreciate that nobody can or should try to be an island unto themselves and that, as relational beings, humans are naturally interdependent. Unfortunately, it's taken a near-death experience for her to start following her own advice.

She sips her morning coffee and sets the heavy mug on the white Ikea desk that matches the bookshelves and cabinets lining the eggshell walls of her home office. Staring at her open laptop, she readies herself to consult with her personal psychologist: CouchGPT.

The cursor at the end of her query blinks at her methodically, an unfeeling, robotic eye, and her finger hovers over the "enter" key. There's still time to stop herself from learning something that could make matters worse. You don't have to be a mental health professional to know that symptom surfing is a high-risk behavior.

But at this point, she doesn't have a choice. After the "accident" two days ago, it's impossible to deny that her own psyche has become her adversary. And a war with the unconscious is always a losing battle. If Emma doesn't get a hold of herself, a lot of innocent people will have to pay the price: her clients, her family, Annie, other motorists…

The driver who almost crashed into her had been livid. He charged over to her car and banged on the window beside her lolling head, demanding that she open it. Normally she'd know better than to do the bidding of a screaming male in the throes of road rage, but she was too shaken up to think straight.

The prematurely lined face of a heavy smoker, eyes bulging and small mouth tight with fury, leaned into her personal space, oblivious to the violation. "What the HELL, lady?! What were you *thinking*?! You SAW me, you had to have seen me, so WHY the HELL did you go pulling out right in front of me?! You trying to get us both killed?!"

He was half right.

Emma tried to croak out an apology but when she opened her mouth, nothing came out. Not that it would have mattered.

"I'm gonna SUE your ass! Got that? I'm gonna take you for ALL you GOT!"

The man made a show of striding to the back of Emma's car to take a photo of her license plate, before stomping off back to his truck. "Bitch."

Emma had been expecting the slur—it was inevitable—but she nevertheless cringed.

Narcissistic misogynist.

Even in her compromised condition, Emma caught herself engaging in a mental process she advises her clients to avoid: reducing someone in your mind to nothing more than a behavior or quality. Ironically, she always uses the example of driving to make her point. The driver who cuts you off becomes "the jerk driver," rather than someone who's got hopes and fears, who's loved and lost, someone who may be rushing to the hospital to see a loved one in need—or someone who's triggered, even selfish. Reductive thinking shrinks someone into a one-dimensional caricature, erasing their being. And, Emma often points out, it disconnects you from your empathy, your humanity. Not surprisingly, it's a big Relationship Killer.

Fortunately, Emma's car wasn't badly damaged. She had it towed to the body shop that night and will pick it up later this morning.

Now, after two nights of disturbing and incomprehensible fever dreams and sweat-soaked sheets, her temperature is finally back to normal. Her other symptoms are also pretty much gone, except for a lingering headache. The only symptom that's gotten worse is her suicidality. And it's clear that no amount of NyQuil—other than an overdose—is going to cure it.

The office door creaks as Annie pushes his way through. Emma pivots her swivel chair in his direction, savoring the sight of him restored to his fluffy, contented indoor self.

She's finally getting the hang of turning her chair or torso rather than her head, thanks to the neck brace she's been wearing. She'd held onto the old brace she bought after the last time she got whiplash, when she'd ridden the

Wicked Cyclone roller coaster at Six Flags. She'd known better than to volunteer for a fifty-five mile per hour ride with three inversions, but she hadn't wanted to disappoint her nephew, who, at ten years old, bounced off the ride buoyant rather than broken.

Emma swivels back to face her computer, pausing to free the bottom of her full-length cotton cardigan that got stuck beneath a wheel of the chair. The cursor stares back at her soberly. Waiting. Before she loses her nerve, she hits "enter." Her heart pounds and the blood rushes to her head as the pulsating black dot appears, indicating that the bot is about to answer.

Nothing could have prepared her for what comes next.

The bot lists the usual contributors to suicidality, which Emma is familiar with—but a few paragraphs later, she stops short, seeing *SOS*.

The full bullet reads *Sudden Onset Suicidality*.

With trembling hands, she clears her original search and types in "What is Sudden Onset Suicidality?"

The black dot hovers, beating, the bot gathering information that will change the course of Emma's life. Or death.

Sudden Onset Suicidality, or SOS (sometimes referred to as Sudden Onset Suicidality Syndrome, but whether it's a syndrome has been debated), is a rare condition in which an individual in sound mental health suddenly and without explanation feels a strong urge to commit suicide.

Ohmygod ohmygod ohmygod.

The condition was first recorded in 1768 by Dr. Matthieu Garnier, a French gynecologist who had diagnosed a patient with postpartum depression but later determined that she had what he termed "Suicidal Madness Syndrome." Since then, SOS has been reported by several other physicians and researchers, including an Egyptian psychiatrist who treated three patients in the late 19th century, a Guatemalan internist who treated one patient in the early 20th century, a Canadian entomologist who diagnosed herself with the condition while studying the plague flea species responsible for spreading the Black Plague, and—

Impatiently, Emma scrolls down to the next section.

When it was first recorded, SOS was considered a form of madness. Today, whether it is some kind of psychosis is disputed. Regardless of how it starts out, in many cases SOS appears to lead to insanity. People with SOS often become delusional and lose their grasp on reality as the condition progresses.

Ohmygod.

Only 210 people have reportedly developed SOS. Due to a lack of research and awareness of the condition, it's likely that this number is much higher. People who develop SOS may simply not know that they have it. Or they may have killed themselves without reporting the condition.

Because of limited data, no known cause or cure has been determined. Causal factors and purported cures are entirely anecdotal, based on what survivors have reported. Available data suggests that determining the cause is the key to the cure, as survivors have all reported to have eliminated the causal trigger.

Reported causal factors include:

- *significant, unresolved relationship issues*
- *a parasite found in the water supply used by the Quechua tribe in the high Andes*
- *being in close proximity to individuals who are either actively or passively suicidal; such "suicidal contagion" may be especially relevant to individuals high in empathy*
- *getting hit on the head by a rock during a meteor shower, which causes microabrasions on the scalp enabling stardust to enter the bloodstream*
- *excess consumption of underripe plantains—*

CouchGPT has no bedside manner. Shaking and in a cold sweat, Emma scrolls past the rest of the list.

Based on current statistics, SOS is a fatal condition, with a 94% suicide rate, but—

Oh. My. God.

Stricken, Emma slams the laptop shut. She's read enough.

This can't be happening. Maybe this whole chat has been a hallucination.

Getting hit by a rock during a meteor shower? Unresolved relationship issues? Suicidal contagion? So, is she supposed to believe that her family's ongoing post-traumatic feud is killing her? And what's she supposed to do about her potentially suicidal clients? They're depending on her to save them, not nudge them closer to death. How can she possibly do her job if she's preoccupied trying to determine whether someone is unconsciously suicidal?

Rubbing her temples, Emma takes a few deep breaths to regain her composure, then lets out a sound that's a half-snort, half-sigh. CouchGPT is *not* a mental health professional, despite her relationship with it. It's a bot, simply reporting unfiltered and uncensored information from the psychological Wild West that is the Internet.

Inserting herself further into her father and brother's messy dysfunction, scanning her clients for suicidality like a mammogram looking for a tumor, wasting precious time checking her scalp for stardust—all of these things would get in her way of doing the one thing that makes her life worth living: helping others. If she follows the bot's advice, she could end up feeling even more suicidal.

On the other hand, if she doesn't follow it, she could wind up dead.

5

Family Feud and a Molotov Cocktail

Emma absentmindedly covers the sharp knife in front of her with the white cotton napkin she pulled out from under her fork. Sunlight slants through the wide window of the bistro, casting a beam across the pristine fabric with its concealed weapon, like a spotlight on her dangerous secret.

At 1:15, the spacious, modern dining room of the trendy hotspot is starting to fill up with its usual clientele of professionals, along with a smattering of tourists. Nick is predictably late and has predictably forgotten to update Emma on his ETA. She had hoped Ritalin would make Nick's life less chaotic. Or at least make interacting with him less chaotic. Emma is an outlier in her family, which is riddled with ADHD. She's often wondered whether she'd been some kind of Tasmanian Devil in a past life—a neurodivergent cyclone pulling everyone into exasperating pandemonium—and this lifetime is payback.

"Hey!" Nick is making the final, hurried strides to the table, tucking his phone into the back pocket of his fitted Levi's. "Sorry I'm late." He says this as though it's an aberration. "My meeting ran over and then I got a little sidetracked."

Nick had suggested he come to Arlington to have lunch with Emma since he had to be in neighboring Cambridge in the morning for a meeting. Emma welcomed the opportunity to spend time with her brother—a familiar and comforting presence despite his tendency to space out and lose track of time—especially given her disturbing session with CouchGPT yesterday.

Nick pauses before sitting in the chair he just pulled out, his eyes and mind finally focusing. "Whoa, what happened to you?"

My unconscious tried to kill me.

I tried to kill myself.

I pulled in front of a narcissistic, misogynistic pickup truck driver in a suicide attempt and now I'm probably going to get sued.

"Oh, nothing serious. I just had a little fender bender. It only takes a tap to get whiplash." Technically, this is not a lie.

"How's your car?"

"My car's fine, too." Emma forces a little laugh that she hopes is convincing.

"Oh, good. It sucks to be without wheels. So what've you been up to, besides playing bumper cars?"

"Not much. The usual. Sessions with clients. Had a session with my own therapist yesterday." Emma has never felt the need to tell Nick that her therapist is a bot. "The usual. How about you? How's the fam?"

"Good. Busy. It's a lot. But good, yeah."

Both of Nick's children also have ADHD, as does their dog; the only one who's been spared the condition is his wife, Marina, who got lucky—or not. "Busy" and "a lot" are Nick's norm. So conversations that require a beginning, middle, and end have to take place when he's out of the house and away from the rest of his family.

Emma decides to seize the moment. "I'm heading to Warmer Planet to visit Dad later today." The care home had gotten its name before there was widespread awareness of climate change and the board didn't want to change it. "I know you still feel like you need more time, but he's not doing well and I don't know how much longer he can hang on."

"Really, Em? *Really*? You're the shrink. So how do you not get that Dad and I are never going to be okay, no matter how much you try to play mediator?"

For the first couple of years following the trauma that drove Nick to cut off communication with their father, Emma had actively tried to facilitate a reconciliation. But once it became clear that her exhaustive attempts to heal the family risked damaging her own relationships with her brother and father, she'd stepped back.

"I thought we'd agreed to drop it. And then you brought it up on Sunday, and now today. What's gotten into you?"

I've come down with a rare condition that may drive me to commit suicide if I don't heal a significant unresolved relationship issue.

"I just think it's time, is all. If you won't do it for Dad, or the kids, then do it for me. It's killing me to see you two like this."

Literally.

Nick's usually kind hazel eyes are unfeeling, and his relaxed, attractive features have tightened. Even his soft wavy brown hair seems to have stiffened. "Emma, *no*. Okay? What he did was—is—unforgivable. Everyone who knows what happened agrees. Please. Just stop, okay?"

As if on cue, the server approaches, a platinum-haired trendite with impossibly tight skin and unnaturally dark brows who could be any race, age, or gender. "Are we ready to order?"

Emma has never been able to figure out why customer service staff always use an inverted version of the royal "we." She's hypothesized that it's a form of narcissistic infantilization, in which customers are perceived as young children who are extensions of the server-parent. *Are we ready for a nap? Did we spill our juice?*

After a brief exchange with the patronizing server, Emma turns back to her brother. "Look, Nick—" She flinches as a sudden pain pierces her temples.

"Em? Are you all right?"

Emma grabs her head, gasping.

"Em? Are you okay?"

"Do you have any ibuprofen?" She already took four hundred milligrams for what had started out as a dull ache. Two hundred more will hopefully do the trick.

"Yeah, here." Nick pulls out a handful of pills from the pocket of the gray puffer coat that's hanging over the back of his chair. He sorts through Ritalin, Vyvanse, aspirin, cough drops, and more, and hands her an Advil.

The stereotype is true. Americans really are like walking pharmacies.

"Thanks." Emma tosses the pill in her mouth and chases it with a gulp of water. "Anyway, I just want to say—" A loud slurp from the table beside them cuts her short. A portly, middle-aged businessman with an unapologetic combover has lifted his bowl of noodle soup and is pouring it into his mouth.

Nick and Emma exchange glances and stifle a burst of laughter—or, in Emma's case, a would-be grin, which is as close as she's able to come to good humor. "Imagine if Marv were here," they say in unison.

Emma started dating Marv about a year ago and the relationship lasted six months. Marv was by all accounts a great guy, and he and Emma had often gone on double dates with Nick and Marina. Things started to get wonky when Marv's misophonia—a painful condition that makes people highly sensitive to certain types of sounds, notably eating sounds—took a turn for the worse.

When they first started dating, Marv's misophonia hadn't posed much of a problem, especially since Emma was a natural at modifying her behavior to ensure others' comfort. Apart from the rare slipup when she produced an audible slurp or smack or sip, Emma never triggered him.

But when Marv's worsening symptoms drove him to get involved in an online community, things went downhill. As is often the case, social media became a forum for deepening divisions, rather than a platform for increasing understanding. Originally meant to empower sufferers and raise awareness of a real and debilitating condition, stopthesmack.org became a mechanism for polarization. "Smackers" were derided and restaurateurs who refused to serve all drinks, including wine and beer, with straws were under constant threat of getting tagged with the pejorative #stopthesmack.

After being accused of creating "smackfests" and told that she didn't provide a safe space for him, Emma realized that she and Marv had irreconcilable differences. And that she needed a break from the dating scene, which she had just been getting ready to end when she came down with her unfortunate condition.

"Poor Marv." Nick shakes his head at the memory, his eyes dancing.

Emma is grateful that she and Nick can end their conversation on a note of shared reminiscence rather than on one of discord. She shouldn't have let her problems—and her ongoing desire to honor her father's wishes—get in the way of respecting Nick's boundaries. "I hear you, Nick. I'll let the thing with you and Dad drop. I promise."

It was absurd, anyway, to think that healing her family's rift would somehow heal her suicidality.

THE SUN HAS JUST SET AND THE CLOUDLESS SKY IS A PALE, dusky gray when Emma pulls into the parking lot of the Warmer Planet care home. The set of interconnected buildings, peppered with curtained windows, looks like a small hospital that's trying to masquerade as a hotel. Emma parks in her usual spot and proceeds through the sliding doors of the main entrance.

"Hi, Emma. He's been expecting you." Amala, the receptionist-nurse from Jamaica with a loud voice and a soft heart, greets Emma with a smile that belies the concern in her dark eyes.

"Hi, thanks. How is he?" Emma's stomach flutters. His condition has been precarious for weeks.

"It's not one of his better days. I think it's the pain. But he's coherent, and in a surprisingly good mood. Your visits always do him good."

The blood drains from her head as Emma forces aside the image of her father's stricken face upon hearing that his only daughter has died. Taken her own life. Swallowing, she makes her way toward his room.

"Emma!" Her father's familiar grin greets her from the simple bed in the small, stuffy chamber that's become his forever home. Even now, with cancer tearing through his body like vultures scavenging carrion, he looks at least fifteen years younger than his age. His thick, wavy hair that he passed down to Nick is still not fully gray, and the only lines on his face are those etched from a lifetime of smiling.

"How's my favorite palindrome?" It didn't matter that Emma wasn't named Emme or Amma. By the time her father learned he'd mistaken the meaning of the term, he'd already gotten attached to it.

He sits up a little higher, leans forward, and peers at her, his smile fading. "Emma, honey, what've you done to yourself?"

How could he know that she's to blame?

"You have an accident or something?"

Phew. "Hi Dad," Emma answers warmly, heading toward the thermostat on the far wall. "Do you want me to turn the heat up? It's chilly in here."

Her father's expression hasn't changed. "Yeah, sure, whatever you want. You gonna tell me what happened?"

His Massachusetts accent always gives off a subtle mobster vibe.

"I'm fine, Dad. It's just whiplash. I had a fender bender on Monday, that's all."

"Some Masshole rear-end you?"

Masshole, vernacular for Massachusetts—usually male—driver, is a stereotype that lives up to its name. "You could say that."

Her father snorts and rolls his eyes, mercifully dropping what could have become an interrogation. Everyone knows Massholes are ubiquitous. Yet nobody thinks of themselves as one, including her father, one of the worst offenders.

Emma turns back from the thermostat, hangs up her coat, and sits in the plain, upholstered chair by her father's side. She takes his hand gently. "How're you feeling, Dad?"

Her father, once a paragon of invincibility, the man who the heavy hand of adversity never seemed to touch, turns toward her with a vulnerability that makes her eyes sting.

"Don't you worry about me, sweetie. I'll be okay. It's your brother I'd be worried about."

Emma had always thought of her father as a somersaulter, someone who tumbled through life as though it were one giant circus act. He was adventurous, daring, and capricious, qualities that make for a great explorer. But not necessarily a great parent.

When Emma and Nick were young, they admired and adored their father. His were the broad shoulders they sat atop as he skied down the steep icy slope behind their homestead. It was his solid hands that tossed them high in the air and were there to catch them just before they hit the pavement. His unending luck kept them believing that, as he always insisted, everything would turn out fine.

Unflappable optimism and unfaltering luck, though, can lead to unchecked narcissism. Their father's chronic good fortune helped spare him the suffering that would have motivated him to grow. Emma and Nick had paid the price for this, and now he is paying it, too.

"I hate to see you like this, Dad. You have enough to deal with without worrying about Nick. He'll be all right. I'll make sure of it. Just save your energy to take care of yourself."

"Nick'll get on with his life, sure. He already has. But he's never gonna be 'all right' if our family feud doesn't get resolved—if his father dies and he doesn't get the apology he needs."

"You've apologized, Dad. A million times. Nick believes you that you're sorry." But Emma knows what her father means, and she knows she's just trying to take away some of his pain in the only way she can. Nick won't find resolution and free himself of the resentment that's been eating away at his heart until he truly understands just how sorry their father is, as well as why the older man made that unfortunate choice five years ago and how he's changed since. With understanding comes empathy, and with empathy comes healing.

"I just want him to know. I want you both to know before I'm six feet under, that I'm sorry. Not just for what I did to Nick's family. I wasn't there for you two, way before that. I left you alone when I shouldn't have, I didn't protect you like I should have. And then five years ago… my god, I almost *killed*—" His eyes are suddenly bloodshot, and he turns away.

Nick isn't the only one who needs resolution.

A sob builds in Emma's chest, and she barely manages to prevent it from escaping. Her father sees himself as no more than a perpetrator, when it's his victimization that's the deeper cause of all the heartache. Like so many people, especially men, he was raised in relational ignorance. He was never taught the value of cultivating healthy connections with others and himself. In fact, what he learned was the very opposite: to move through life as a rugged individualist, invulnerable and untouchable. Alone.

"Dad, don't do this to yourself, please," Emma whispers. They've had this conversation many times, and it always ends the same way.

"And what about the twins? They were eight when they last saw their grandpa. They always loved having me around. They're missing out on their last chance to be with ol' Pops."

"I'll talk to Nick again, I promise."

Despite what Nick believes, their father *has* changed. The tragedy, which was the wakeup call he needed to finally stop drinking, combined with the natural mellowing of age and the humility that comes from facing one's mortality, has eaten away his relational armor. Plus, the television in the corner of his room, which he keeps on all day for its comforting background noise, has been stuck on the Oprah Winfrey channel for the past eighteen months.

Emma remains by her father's bedside until he's drifted off to sleep. She hopes she'll be able to stay alive long enough to keep her promise.

Yet her chest is heavy with grief, not only for her father, but for herself. Losing her will to live feels like losing a life partner. And her deepening sadness is mingling with her worsening suicidality, like a Molotov cocktail.

6

A Spark Falling Dimly

Day 7: Friday

"If I weren't depressed, I'd be mentally ill."

Ricardo looks like he's just stepped out of the pages of *GQ*, with his classically handsome features and smart outfits. Even his smell is polished, just the right mix of cologne and man. Only his taut face and darkly ringed eyes betray the struggle beneath the surface.

Emma's office is lit solely by a brass torchiere in the corner of the room and an off-white porcelain table lamp. It's bright enough to see well, but dim enough so nobody feels exposed. The plush, forest green carpet, warm-hued throw cushions, and soft sofa and chair swallow sounds, making voices seem hushed. A large bronze vase with calming lavender rests beside the tall Victorian windows, the scent wafting over Emma as she struggles to stay focused. Friday sessions are always a challenge and today is no exception, especially since she's still drained from her emotional visit with her father yesterday. Thankfully, Ricardo is her second to last client.

"Seriously. I just read this quote from Jiddu Krishnamurti that really hit home: 'It is no measure of health to be well adjusted to a profoundly sick society.' I mean, just *look* at the world. Look at humanity." A flush tinges Ricardo's light brown complexion.

Ricardo, who usually sees Emma every other week, started coming for therapy five months ago, after he'd been laid off from his job as legal counsel for an environmental justice nonprofit organization and he'd slipped into a severe depression. He'd been told by the executive director, a well-known activist in the climate and social justice spaces and who Ricardo had idolized, that his layoff was due to funding cuts. But Ricardo, a highly experienced lawyer in his late thirties, learned that the organization had actually decided to restructure in order to save money and had replaced him with a less expensive employee fresh out of law school.

Ricardo had been shocked and devastated by the deception and betrayal, particularly since it was carried out by an activist he'd deeply admired. As he commented nearly every session, "If Kaleem Decheran, a model of integrity, could do something like this, what hope is there for the rest of society?"

Shifting his large body on the sage green sofa, Ricardo sets his water bottle on the vintage mahogany coffee table between the couch and Emma's matching chair.

"Entire families are getting their limbs blown off in Ukraine and Gaza, prisoners are being tortured to death in Myanmar and lots of other places, girls are being genitally mutilated all across the East." Ricardo's expression is haunted. "California, Canada, Australia, *everywhere*, is going up in flames, people are being macheted to death in Sudan, rape gangs are storming through Haiti. Misery—violence—is the *norm*."

Outside the window behind him, a large shadow plunges downward—a crow diving straight toward the ground, like a kamikaze pilot. Do birds also kill themselves? Aghast, Emma yanks her focus back to her depressive client.

"And *look* at us. We have enough resources, enough money, enough technology and knowledge and skills to reduce global suffering by probably ninety-eight percent if we wanted to. How fucking depressing is *that*?"

Could Ricardo be even more depressed than Emma had thought? Depressed enough to be suicidal? And therefore putting her at risk of "suicidal contagion," as CouchGPT had described?

Emma flashes back to the sobering images from the World Health Organization in 2020, graphic simulations of Covid's spread that showed aerosols spraying from mouths and noses, sending their viral particles far and wide.

After instinctively nudging her chair back several inches, in the interest of social distancing, she gets up and opens the window. She barely stifles a groan as the effort sends a fresh spike of pain across her temples.

Thankfully, Ricardo has worked himself up so much that he either doesn't notice her odd behavior or doesn't care. "And what are we doing? We're *shopping*—we're glassy-eyed, Amazon-surfing, mall-crawling overconsumers. We're *binge-watching stupid TV*. We're taking the whole freaking family to Disney on polluting planes to go on polluting rides and scarf down huge plates of polluting junk that's served *on* plastic, *with* plastic, and *in* plastic. And we get all twisted into self-pitying, self-righteous pretzels because our new toaster doesn't perfectly match the handles of our kitchen cabinets or our smart TV is taking too long to load or we didn't get enough likes on our selfies. We're totally caught up in our own little worlds, destroying the one we all share." The veins along Ricardo's neck pulse like drum beats in a revolutionary march.

He has a point. Emma wouldn't blame him if he were suicidal. But how can she possibly assess him for suicidality? It's like an active alcoholic trying to determine whether someone has a drinking problem.

Ricardo soldiers on. "The world's fucking insane. If you're *not* depressed, you're part of the insanity."

Emma nods supportively. "I know what you mean, and I really understand where you're coming from."

More than he realizes. By Krishnamurti's account, Emma's suicidality is a sign of psychological success, the pinnacle of human development, the ultimate refusal to conform to the dysfunctional norm. If he had his way, Krishnamurti would have her dash to the roof of the gray Victorian that houses her office and fling herself off it as soon as Ricardo's session ends, and—

Blinking rapidly, she rubs her sweaty palms against her thighs and pushes the dark fantasy out of her mind.

"It's like there's no solution." Ricardo's tone has a finality to it, a certainty. He's been selling himself on his depression for weeks. "People suck." His moral outrage is palpable, as is his sadness for a world he cares so much about and yet feels so helpless to heal.

Emma's heart swells. Most people react to anger with anger. But Emma understands the pain of this emotion, how profoundly disconnecting it is, and how it's often a cover for more vulnerable feelings, such as grief and fear. How isolated and lonely Ricardo must feel to be so misanthropic. Like a tiny spark flung far from the fire of humanity, burning itself out as it falls dimly toward the ground. "People do some really sucky things, for sure. The problem is, when you lose sight of the goodness in people, it's hard to respect them, among other things. And without respect, you can't feel connected with people."

The usually astute Ricardo looks at Emma uncomprehendingly.

"Meaningful connections are the foundation of healthy relationships," Emma continues. "Relationships with others and also with yourself. And healthy relationships are essential for healing depression, and for healing most kinds of psychological suffering. At their core, healthy relationships reflect the practice of love, of treating—and being treated by—others with respect and compassion. This leads to a greater sense of connection. And security, too."

Emma sits up a little straighter. Maybe she hasn't lost her touch.

"I can't, I *won't* believe in the 'goodness' of people who think of no one but themselves, doing stupid shit and dragging the world to hell in a handbasket." Ricardo's tone is high-pitched and acerbic, like he's been sucking on a dirty helium tank. This is especially disturbing since his voice is usually pleasantly mellow and full-bodied, like a perfectly aged wine.

"I know it's hard to reconcile the fact that good people can do bad things—"

"*Hard* to reconcile? It's impossible," Ricardo interrupts, uncharacteristically rude.

Emma decides to change tack. "Ricardo, listen. I'm with you. I get it, I really do. Let me just ask you something. What do you imagine you would lose if your depression suddenly went away?"

Sometimes people cling to things that hurt because on some level they believe that it's more painful to let those things go. Like holding onto a relationship that's not good for you out of fear you'll feel worse without it.

"What do you mean, *lose*? I'd give anything not to feel this way. It's the reason I come here every week. And honestly, my *depression* is what's making me lose things. I'm burning through my savings and won't be able to pay my mortgage much longer, my career is essentially over, and—" Ricardo's voice catches.

He pauses, taking slow, deep breaths, like a living sculpture trying to maintain its statuesque composure. "I'm sure Jesse's going to leave me if I don't get my shit together. He hasn't said as much, but I… I just can't feel connected. With anything. Activism, myself, and worst of all, him." Ricardo and Jesse have been together for seven years. Jesse proposed to him six months ago, which Ricardo said was the happiest day of his life. His eyes glassing over, he looks down at the carpet.

Clients pay Emma to usher them through the turbulent emotional waters of their inner worlds. And yet they often try to conceal their feelings from her, ashamed of the vulnerability she's been hired to help them embrace. They hold back tears, swallow down fear, and apologize when the emotions happen to break through. How many times has Emma explained to clients that apologies are for when we do something wrong or harmful, and crying doesn't fall into either of those categories? It's like not wanting to take off your underwear in front of your gynecologist, and then when you do, saying you're sorry for being naked.

"I can imagine how painful this is for you, Ricardo, I—"

Emma is interrupted by Ricardo's loud exhale. He deflates like a balloon, sinking deeper into the thick cushion beneath him. "The messed up thing is, I'm almost more afraid of Jesse staying than I am of him leaving."

"So if your depression goes away, you and Jesse stay together. And that's more upsetting—scarier—to you than if you stay depressed and he leaves?"

"Yeah. No. I mean, I don't know. I'm such a mess. I just don't know what to do."

"Well, try to imagine that you're not depressed, and you stay engaged to Jesse. You end up marrying him. What does that look like?"

"I just can't go through this again. I wouldn't survive another betrayal, another disappointment like what happened with Kaleem. It would destroy me." Now that Ricardo's anger has run its course, the sadness beneath it has surfaced. He hangs his head in despair.

"So if you weren't depressed…"

"If I weren't depressed, I'd be all sloppy in love with Jesse again, and probably diving right back into activism. I'd be a sitting duck."

Emma is suddenly overcome by a vision of Ricardo as a dashing mallard wearing suave aviator sunglasses, bobbing up and down in the calm waters of life, oblivious to the fact that he's about to get shot by a predatory human who sees killing as a game.

Ricardo raises his head and meets Emma's eyes, bringing her back to the session.

They both know he's just had an important insight. His look is beseeching, desperate yet hopeful that his therapist can do what he's hired her to do: help him find the way through the complex labyrinth of his tormented psyche.

"What do I do?" His voice is barely above a whisper.

"You're already doing it. You're asking the hard questions, and grappling honestly with the answers. It's a process—learning to trust again, to have faith, given what you've seen and experienced. Ultimately, you need to learn to trust *yourself* again, to trust that you'll be able to withstand the disappointments and betrayals and traumas that come with being alive. A big part of our work is to help you build up your resilience, your ability to maintain self-connection and a sense of 'okayness' in the face of adversity, so you can be like the ocean of life rather than the waves crashing on top of it. So that you can be a functional person in a dysfunctional world."

"That sounds almost Buddhist."

"It is Buddhist. The Buddha was one of the first psychologists."

Emma would smile if she weren't so miserable. Ricardo's taken a big step forward today.

"Ricardo, I have an idea. What do you think about volunteering somewhere? Finding meaningful work, ideally that's hands-on so you can see the direct results of your efforts. You'd be around like-minded people, and you'd be helping people in need. So it's all-win."

"If you'd suggested this thirty minutes ago, I'd have thought you'd lost your mind."

He wouldn't have been fully wrong.

"But maybe you're right. Maybe doing the only thing that's ever really made me feel like there's a reason to get out of bed in the morning makes sense. I can't make any promises, but I'll think about it."

***

EMMA SLUMPS ON HER ROLLING STOOL BEHIND THE DESK IN the corner of her office, relieved to have made it through the session. In these few minutes before her final appointment of the day, she needs to recoup her energy and talk to her insurance company, since the infuriated misogynist is trying to sue her for emotional damages. Apparently, the fact that he flew into a rage and threatened her, an injured driver, while hurling bigoted epithets at her didn't make a difference in his ability to file the suit.

As she dials her insurance agent, Jamal Jones, she holds her breath.

"Ms. Parkland, hello." Jamal's tone is professional-friendly. "You're right on time, as usual. How're you doing today?"

Emma ekes out a fake laugh. "That depends on what you have to tell me."

"Well, then, you're doing just fine." Jamal returns the good humor. "It turns out Mr. Todesco was on his way to commit a crime when you pulled in front of him and stopped him in his tracks, so to speak."

"Oh!" It's the best Emma can come up with.

"He'd borrowed the truck from a friend and was on his way to crash it through the garage door of his ex and their two children, who he knew would be in the space working on some project. He had explosives in the backseat and was planning a murder–suicide."

"Oh!" Emma's head starts to pound again, as a wave of hysteria wells up inside her.

"So, Ms. Parkland, you almost killed yourself, but you saved three lives. I guess that makes you a hero!" Jamal laughs. "But next time, try to find a safer way to be of service."

7

Little Miss Meme

"**S**o I explained to her: 'You can't love others until you love yourself.'" Emma's supervisee, Melissa (or Missy, as the young woman often refers to herself), announces this with the smug confidence of youth. And of someone used to getting most of their information from TikTok.

Perched on the same cushion Ricardo had occupied just an hour ago, Missy's raised chin, straight back, and disconcerting optimism are the antithesis of Ricardo's dejected brooding. She's like the manic to his depressive.

Missy is a walking generator of platitudes and pseudo-truisms, like "opposites attract" and "just listen to your heart," which have been floating around unchecked since they went viral centuries ago and which continue to cause a lot of damage. Emma has lost count of how many clients have fallen prey to such bad advice. These kinds of phrases were probably made up by people who, at the time, thought they were being wise. And the sayings caught on because others found them pithy and profound, without actually thinking about whether they made any sense. Even many mental health professionals don't question the validity of these psychobabble-proverbs. So the psychological misinformation they spread is rarely countered.

Emma has spent countless hours doing damage control. Opposites, she's explained, are more likely to repel than attract. Most people are drawn to like-minded others, which is why, generally speaking, neat-freaks and slobs don't turn each other on any more than conservatives and progressives do. And *don't* just follow your heart. Making a decision based solely on emotion—checking your critical thinking at the door—is one of the reasons people get stuck in all sorts of dysfunctional situations, like abusive relationships. Emma has also often pointed out that believing you can't love others before you love yourself actually gets in the *way* of loving yourself. Many people learn to love themselves through loving and being loved by others, as new parents and lovers can attest. She'd come to this last realization after her own therapist, who she'd seen during the final months of her marriage, explained that love isn't just a feeling; it's a behavior. When we practice the behavior of love, we become better at it, and can apply it to all our relationships. So there's no reason one particular kind of loving has to come first, just like there's no reason you have to be able to braid your own hair before you can braid the hair of others.

"And you know what?" Missy enthuses, pulling Emma back to the conversation at hand. "This triggered something deep inside her." The intern's wide blue eyes brighten, the color rising in her soft, porcelain cheeks.

With her ash blonde ringlets framing her round face, she looks like the doll Emma had when she was a child, which she was oddly frightened of. "She started crying, talking about how her husband is drinking again, about his anger management issue, and about how he'd gambled their mortgage away without telling her and still doesn't think he was wrong. She was really worried their marriage wasn't going to survive so many hurdles. But I reassured her: 'Love conquers all.'"

Little Miss Meme. The name had popped into Emma's head during their first meeting and it stuck. She doesn't feel good about it, but it's too late to unthink it.

Little Miss Meme has been seeing Emma since she started her internship, which is part of her master's degree and licensure requirement, a few months ago. Like all interns, she's required to have weekly supervision in which she is mentored by a licensed practitioner. Right now, she's Emma's only supervisee. Emma stopped taking new interns after her client caseload exceeded maximum capacity and she'd had to start scheduling sessions at 7:00 a.m. and staying late in the office three days a week to accommodate all the people who needed to see her.

"It sounds like you feel good about the conversation," Emma offers supportively. "I'm just wondering whether you think it's possible that 'loving' and 'conquering' are contradictory terms? And that if the marriage does end, that could mean that love has in fact succeeded?"

Hearing her own words, Emma breathes a sigh of relief. It was touch and go for a minute; she didn't know if she'd be able to bite her tongue and avoid telling the intern that condescendingly spewing out cliches is not in her clients' interests. Emma knows that Missy means well and is simply young and naive, more annoying than malignant. It's just that her patience is wearing thin. Her headache hasn't responded to the handful of ibuprofen she downed after Ricardo's session, and she's starting to feel like she's coming apart.

"Um, yeah." Missy blinks a few times, smooths the front of her Laura Ashley puff-sleeved shirt, and stares at Emma blankly.

"Like we talked about: love is not just a feeling. It's also an action. A verb. When you love someone, you act in their best interests. You treat them the way you would want to be treated if you were in their position. Love is nonviolent. Conquering, which is exercising power and control over someone or something, is a form of violence."

"Okay, yes, I see what you mean." Missy nods thoughtfully. "And so then if they break up, that's also love because like you said before, sometimes the loving thing to do is to end a relationship."

Emma smells a meme in the making. It's striking how Missy seems unable to avoid Memespeak. Maybe it's a generational thing. Maybe all communication will be reduced to nonsensical banalities at some point. At least the intern seems to be understanding Emma's point now.

"Right," Emma replies. "The job of a couples counselor is not to protect the *relationship*, but to protect the *integrity* of the relationship. To ensure that the relational dynamic is healthy. Sometimes that means supporting the end of the relationship."

Even if it's the end of the relationship you have with yourself.

Emma's heart clenches and she shoves the troubling thought away.

The letter opener lying on her desk across the office catches her eye. The cold metal gleams invitingly in the early-evening sunlight streaking through the window. Emma makes a mental note to get rid of the blade as soon as the session ends.

"So I got a new patient on Wednesday, Jim, and you won't believe it." Missy has already moved on to another story. "It's going to be intense. Jim's a really tough case."

No matter how many times Emma explains the importance of using person-centered and non-stigmatizing language—the person sitting across from you isn't a *case*, but an *individual*; they're not an *anorexic*, but a *person with anorexia*; they're not a *patient* who's sick and needs you to figure out how to cure them, but a *client* who has commissioned you to work with them on their process of self-discovery—Missy can't seem to remember it.

"Jim's a schizophrenic." Missy pauses for effect, as though waiting to see if Emma's taking in the magnitude of this announcement. Interns don't usually work with clients who have serious mental illnesses. The recent dearth of mental health professionals, though, has been changing this.

As she smiles and nods blandly to encourage Missy to continue, Emma tries to keep her eyes away from the tempting saber on her desk.

"*And* he's got a trauma history. A *major* trauma history. He was *tortured*. By his own mother!"

Missy's all lit up, like a sparkler at an Independence Day celebration held high in the air being waved in time to "The Star-Spangled Banner."

"Seriously. I can't believe my luck!"

Missy, fresh out of school, is hungry for suffering, starving to be needed. But her cravings will no doubt cause the opposite outcomes of what she wants. Emma has been trying, unsuccessfully, to help the intern understand that the degree to which you can help others heal depends on the degree to which you can stay connected with your empathy, compassion, and—notably—humility.

"As they say, 'the harder the struggle, the more glorious the triumph.'" Little Miss Meme states this with the moral certainty that you can only have if you spend most of your time scrolling social media.

Trying to ignore the throbbing in her head, Emma considers the possibility that she's too weary and wrapped up in her own mess to continue working with a supervisee who needs this level of hand-holding. She'll talk to the university and see if it's possible to refer Missy to someone who's better able to give her the guidance she requires. And she'll mention that a co-therapist should work alongside the intern with some of the more challenging clients.

Missy pivots again, this time to tell Emma that she's concocted a new type of intervention, or at least a major variation on a theme, which she's certain will cure one of her "patients" of what had seemed to be an impossible problem.

Missy has been working with a family of five for about a month. The middle child, a girl, suffers from triskaidekaphobia, fear of the number thirteen. Being exposed to the number brings on a full-blown panic attack, so the girl avoids anything that might expose her to it, such as watching television, using social media, and going to Chinese restaurants that have numbered menus. She wears blinders, as well as dark sunglasses and headphones, to reduce the chances she'll inadvertently see or hear the number. Thankfully, though, as long as they're careful, the family is still able to take vacations since a lot of hotels don't have a thirteenth floor and most airplanes don't have a thirteenth row, a carryover from more superstitious times and which has surely encouraged the development of the phobia in susceptible individuals.

Since the girl came down with triskaidekaphobia two years ago, the family has done everything possible to accommodate her, and has been largely able to cope with the problem. They've been hoping she'll eventually grow out of it. However, her thirteenth birthday is coming up in three weeks, and the girl is terrified. She believes she'll end up phobic of herself, having become the very trigger of her fear.

"Missy, have you considered that if you feel responsible for healing others, you might also feel responsible for having harmed them if they don't get better?"

Missy shifts in her seat, as though repositioning her body will rearrange her mind. "What do you mean? I mean, I didn't cause the triskaidekaphobia. But I *can* heal it. So I don't see the parallel."

"When you believe you have the power to heal others, then when they don't get better, you can feel like you've failed. As therapists, our job is to help clients help themselves, to act as a bridge between them and themselves, connecting them with their own, internal wisdom and resources. People aren't projects to be completed. They're not problems to be solved. They're human beings, doing the best they can to make it through their lives, and they've come to us to help them along in that process."

Missy nods but says nothing and leans over to take her coat, signaling that she knows the session is about to end. There isn't time for her to explain her Grand Plan for healing the twelve-year-old, and Emma cautions her to hold off on the intervention until after their next super-vision session so they can discuss it first.

"I hear you, Emma. But 'nothing great is ever achieved without risk.' I'll let you know how it goes!" And Little Miss Meme bounces out of the office before Emma can pull herself together to respond.

THE SETTING SUN IS CASTING A DEEP, GOLDEN GLOW ON THE blade lying on Emma's desk. Like a medieval sword in a radiant halo, it beckons her to carry out the heroic deed that is her calling. Her destiny.

Appalled, Emma snatches up the offending weapon. She holds it in front of her, arm outstretched, to keep it as far from her body as possible.

As she strides across the room to toss it in the bin, her toe catches on the carpet and she trips. With a violent lurch she hurtles forward, yanking her neck out of align-ment and falling onto her dagger, which sinks deeply into her chest.

8

Wakeup Call

Day 8: Saturday

S oft fur brushes against Emma's ankles as Annie makes figure eights around her slippered feet. The gentle caresses, rustling the bottoms of her airy linen pants, are in stark contrast to the shooting pains in her upper chest and the aches in her neck and head. It's as if the top and bottom of her body belong to different people.

Emma reaches for the bottle of ibuprofen next to the open laptop on the desk of her uncharacteristically disorganized home office and takes two pills, grimacing as she washes them down with her morning coffee. She moves her cursor so the screen lights up, to obscure the reflection of her bandaged shoulder and hard, plastic neck brace—but not before sticking out her tongue at herself, sneering in contempt.

She really has become her own worst enemy.

Emma had managed to Uber to the hospital last night before she lost too much blood. The attending ER nurse—a no-nonsense, nonbinary New York transplant—told her she was lucky because the stabbing was high and far enough from the center of her chest to have just missed her lung.

Emma isn't sure whether the miss counts as good luck.

She was sent home encased in what seemed like an entire roll of bandages that stretched around her ribcage and over her shoulder, like a giant, deformed girdle holding her together. She was also given a new neck brace since her old one had come undone and her neck had made a sickening snapping sound during her ungainly tumble.

Was it really only three days ago that she last sat in this same chair, naively expecting her bot-shrink to comfort and guide her? It's odd how time seems to move at an abnormal speed during challenging experiences. It crawls during the event, but then when you look back, you feel like the time has sped by.

She looks at the pulsing black dot of CouchGPT, which is just as it was last time. Unemotional. Unflappable. Uncaring.

With a deep inhale, she clicks to repeat the investigation she prematurely aborted on Monday. "What is Sudden Onset Suicidality?"

She holds her breath.

The dot beats slowly, systematically, menacingly, in time to the throbbing of her wound. Text appears, and Emma reads the opening paragraph line by line as each phrase is typed out.

Sudden Onset Suicidality, or SOS (sometimes referred to as Sudden Onset Suicidality Syndrome, but whether it's a syndrome has been debated), is a rare condition in which an individual in good mental health suddenly and without explanation feels a strong urge to commit suicide.

Exhaling, she scrolls past the sections she read on Wednesday and begins ingesting what will either be her remedy or her ruin.

SOS is a progressive disease. In all reported cases, it worsened over time. Not only does the feeling of suicidality intensify, but in many cases the delusions—and sometimes hallucinations—worsen. Because the rate of known <u>fatalities</u> from SOS is 94%, it's not possible to determine whether increasing suicidal impulsivity or madness is to blame for most deaths.

A six percent chance of staying sane and staying alive?

An irrational wave of defiance washes over her, and Emma lashes out at her inhuman counselor. "I'm rubber and you're glue! And whatever you say—"

What the *hell?*

Of the 210 people who have reportedly developed SOS, thirteen have survived. The purported cures for the condition are all based on survivors' self-reports. In all instances, determining the cause of the condition has been essential to finding the cure.

Of the causal factors identified, three are believed to be especially relevant, as they were reported by multiple survivors:

- *significant, unresolved relationship issues (with four survivors reporting success once they'd repaired the problem)*
- *suicidal contagion (with three survivors reporting success after eliminating the factor)*
- *a growth in the brain in the region known as Brodie's*

> *Brain Bridge (with three survivors reporting success after eliminating the factor); this factor should be considered only if the suicidality has been accompanied by headaches*

Aghast, Emma grabs the bottle of ibuprofen and tosses two more down her throat.

Resisting the temptation to slam her computer shut as she did the first time she read about SOS—and this time to also throw the machine against the wall—she reads on.

Some survivors have reported developing childish outbursts. This kind of regression to silly, infantile behaviors—such as sticking out one's tongue and chanting immature insults—increases suicidality because it leads to inappropriate public displays of preposterous, humiliating actions which, if unchecked—

Emma's widened eyes brim with tears and a wail builds in the back of her throat. Her face reddens as she thinks of Karry-on Karl, who—speaking through Olivia—jumps at any chance to take her down. He'd have a field day taunting her and depicting her wearing a giant diaper during their sessions.

With a whimper, she continues reading. The words before her, distorted by her tears, seem to twist and swim on the screen.

Since depression has not been identified as a causal factor, antidepressants aren't a recommended treatment protocol. Not only do these medications often take weeks to have an effect—longer than most sufferers can afford to wait—but their side effects could exacerbate the suicidality.

Emma blinks to clear her vision. The article just got shorter. What happened to the paragraph about turning into a spoiled brat? It was just above the last paragraph she read.

She scrolls through all the text, and that section is gone. Apparently she's more at risk of hallucinating than she is of regressing to the terrible twos. She isn't sure which is worse.

With a dry mouth, she reads on.

There has been some speculation that SOS is an adaptive condition. It's been hypothesized that a small percentage of the human population may be genetically predisposed to developing it. The theory posits that the suicidal gene is triggered when the number of living humans reaches a certain threshold, to ensure population control. As such, the number of individuals who develop SOS would increase with population growth. However, this theory lacks empirical support.

Will 23andMe one day have a section for SOS?

There has also been speculation that suicide clusters—groups of suicides or attempted suicides that occur near the same time in a given community—may contribute to the development of SOS, suggesting that the condition itself may be contagious. However, there are no known reports of SOS-induced suicides occurring within a suicide cluster.

Emma swallows, and scrolls down to read the last section of the article.

Currently, there is only one living researcher who has been working to find a cure for SOS: Dr. Hans Müller.

The cursor in the blank question box below the final line blinks impartially. It could just as easily be awaiting a query about how to safely bleach your nose hair as about how to avoid killing yourself.

Emma types in "Who is Dr. Hans Müller?" Keeping her eyes fixed on the screen, she takes a sip of lukewarm coffee.

Dr. Hans Müller is an Austrian national who received his MD from the Medizinische Universität Wien and graduated top of his class, with specializations in internal medicine, infectious diseases, and epidemiology. He then did his residency at the Charité Hospital in Berlin, after which he became the Medical Director of the Traumatic Injury Unit, where he worked for twenty-five years.

Emma envisions a brawny Arnold Schwarzenegger boasting a white coat and dark sunglasses, a stethoscope hung heroically around his neck. The Terminator of SOS.

Dr. Müller is widely regarded as a brilliant scientist who's an "out-of-the-box" thinker. He was twice nominated for the Nobel Prize in Medicine for his breakthrough discoveries treating rare and insidious diseases. At once a consummate empiricist and an open-minded investigator of phenomena not explained by science, Dr. Müller took an interest in Sudden Onset Suicidality, or SOS, in 2014, after one of his patients apparently developed it.

A flicker of hope alighting inside her, Emma reads the final paragraph.

Dr. Müller claims to have compiled and analyzed all existing data on the condition. He's conducted exhaustive searches of people who reported having the hallmark symptoms of SOS, as well as of all hospital and psychiatric databases, to determine the prevalence of the condition. In his last published commentary he stated that he was working on a cure.

Unable to help herself, Emma writes a thank you to the bot.

You're welcome! If you have any more questions, feel free to ask.

There's no turning back now.

THE FIRST ORDER OF BUSINESS IS TO GET RID OF ALL SHARP objects in the house. Emma heads to the kitchen, the most obvious place to start.

Pulling open the cutlery drawer, she grabs a handful of steak knives—only to release them abruptly, with a sharp intake of breath. Viscous blood drips from her palm into the drawer.

Clearly, the rules of engagement have changed.

Holding her hand above heart level, streams of blood seeping into the sleeve of her tan sweater, she hurries to the sink. As she rinses her hand under the faucet, crimson-stained water swirling down the drain, she's transported back to the last time the sink was awash in blood, when—

That's it! Her Knights of the Round Table costume!

She'd bought it on eBay to go trick-or-treating with Nick and the twins a few years ago, and washed the fake blood off her sword in the kitchen sink when she'd gotten home. Although the suit of armor is made of plastic rather than steel, it will at least act as a first line of defense. It even comes with a *cervelliere*, a half-helmet that's short enough to wear without hitting her neck brace. Emma dons the outfit and gets to work.

By the time she's packing the last of the knives, scissors, box cutters, and pruning shears, she's drenched in sweat. She'd forgotten how insulating the suit was.

A knock on the window outside the hallway where she's standing startles her. She rotates her weighty torso to see Walter peering in, his hand over his eyes and a perplexed expression on his face. "Emma, is that you?"

Mortified, Emma pulls off the helmet and lifts up the window. "Walter, hi!" Sweat is streaming down her face and her hair is stuck to her cheeks and chin. "I was just cleaning out some junk, and tried on my old costume."

Walter, an odd duck himself, is easily appeased.

"Yeah, sure. Glad you're all right." He glances quizzically at Emma's bandaged hand. "I just wanted to see if I could borrow your wheelbarrow, and your doorbell doesn't seem to be working."

"Of course! Take whatever you want out of the shed. Anything. And no need to ask!" Emma knows she sounds manic. But she has a busy afternoon ahead of her and really needs Walter to get going. Which, thankfully, he does.

Once she's packed away all the potential weapons and has changed out of her armor, she starts in on her master plan. She sets up a time to meet with her lawyer to draft her will, something she should have done a long time ago. She orders custom stationery with her initials and imagery of a bucolic pasture, to use for her suicide note should it come to that. She sends an email to Amir, her radiologist friend who works at Massachusetts General Hospital, to ask if he can get her an emergency appointment for a brain MRI, explaining that she's suddenly developed intense and unusual headaches. She briefly considers contacting Shana to tell her about SOS, since the brilliant clinician could surely help her hack the problem—but decides against it, since Shana's got a full plate.

Next, she writes out a checklist to help her assess the active and passive suicidality of her clients and others "in close proximity" to her—and freezes when she considers that suicidal contagion may be able to cross digital boundaries, like emotional contagion does. Just the thought of having to forgo Netflix makes her want to kill herself.

Emma then sends an email to Charité, the hospital that Dr. Müller last worked at, asking how she can reach him—to which she immediately receives an autoreply, in both German and English, saying simply that her email has been received and is being "processed." She tries not to fall into catastrophic thinking about German bureaucracy.

Finally, she texts Nick to see if he'll meet for dinner. She's got to help him see the value of talking to their father and putting an end to the tragedy once and for all.

Nick taps back a thumbs up. Then: *maybe this week?*

perfect. [praying hands icon]

k, we can pick time and place later, busy now.

no prob! c u soon

btw em i'm NOT going to talk about dad dying, k? don't even bring it up pls

It's not him dying I want to talk about

Emma deletes that last message.

of course

Getting Nick to be open to talking to their father is going to be harder than she'd imagined. Maybe impossible. Which makes the odds of her survival close to zero.

9

Frozen in Time

Day 8: Saturday

Saturday has always been Emma's favorite day of the week. She has plenty of time for herself, and she knows there's still one more day before the work week starts up. Unfortunately, though, she almost never gets a full day off, since her clients have her phone number and sometimes text her for emergency advice—an unorthodox practice, which is probably why she's started to feel burned out in recent years. She especially regrets giving Olivia such access, since Olivia and Karl often have arguments while on weekend getaways. Like recently, when Karl accused his partner of "dragging him through the mud" even though she'd merely been scurrying to get across a sodden street during a downpour in the Florida Keys. Nevertheless, Saturdays are a chance for Emma to garden and play Candy Crush and love Annie up and recharge her batteries after an intensive week of therapy sessions.

But today has been the second-worst Saturday on record, the first being last week, when she woke up with

SOS. It started with her consultation with the bot this morning when she learned more disturbing truths about her condition. Then she stabbed her hand and hasn't been able to fully stop the bleeding, despite using up all her gauze bandages. And finally there was Nick's refusal to consider a reconciliation with her father, robbing her of her best chance of survival.

Sitting on the chenille, ivory loveseat she'd been thrilled to find last year at a yard sale when she was redecorating her living room and which is blanketed in the final rays of the setting sun, she rereads the text Nick sent a few minutes ago.

btw em i'm NOT going to talk about dad dying, k? don't even bring it up pls

How can she possibly get Nick to change his mind?

Given the tragedy five years ago, Emma can't really blame him for never wanting to talk to their father again. Plus, she still feels partly responsible for what happened. She should never have encouraged Nick to trust their father with something so important. She, of all people, should have known better; the seeds of the incident had been planted long ago.

THE BITING COLD OF A DECEMBER NEW ENGLAND MORNING chewed its way through eight-year-old Emma's consciousness. She awoke, shivering. But she didn't want to move. Not even to pry open her heavy eyelids. She was freezing, but she felt warmer here than she could ever feel inside the house.

The familiar cadence of Blossom's deep breathing and slow, steady heartbeat held Emma like the rocking arms of the mother she'd lost when she was just a toddler. Since then, the pig's love and companionship had been Emma's greatest source of solace. And his friendship her greatest source of joy.

"Emmmmmmaaaa!" Her father's deep voice boomed across the pasture. "Come and get it!" Despite what had happened yesterday, and the fact that she'd snuck out of the house in the middle of the night to come sleep with Blossom, her father's tone was as cheerful as if it were Christmas morning. He never held a grudge. He also never took seriously the ordeals his children had to endure.

There would surely be a roaring fire suffusing the old farmhouse with its warmth, even though it was only 7:00 a.m. And the usual Sunday morning pancakes with chocolate chip smiley faces and hot cocoa would be in the making. But Emma preferred to stay here, smelling the sweet hay, curled up with her sweet pig. Here was safety. Here was respite. Here was peace.

She simply wasn't ready to face her father after what he'd done.

Two days ago, Emma and Nick had gone to visit their maternal grandparents, who lived a couple of hours west, in Springfield, Massachusetts. The children usually visited from Saturday to Sunday, but since Friday was a school holiday they'd gone a day early.

Emma and Nick only visited their grandparents every few months, and just for one night at a time, because the couple lived in a retirement home and were technically not supposed to have overnight visitors. They'd moved to the home after losing their daughter, who had died from a rare amniotic fluid embolism while giving birth to Nick six years ago. The shock had been too much for the couple, driving them to take an early retirement and to give the family orchard, in Acton, to Emma's father. The property came with a petting zoo that included a handful of chickens and two pigs—Blossom, who got his name from the apple tree that he loved to lie under and was still a piglet, and Old Ollie, who died a year later.

Now that Emma was eight, her father—a muscled, second-generation Irish ginger who was good-natured yet brash and whose Red Sox caps, broad "Os," and dropped "Rs" screamed Bostonian—felt she was old enough to take Nick on a bus to Springfield, rather than have the adults drive to meet at the halfway point. Emma's father was never one to be overprotective. Or even protective. He was the kind of person who believed that you teach a toddler to swim by throwing them over your head like a football, as far across the lake as possible. He was naturally risky, naturally optimistic, and naturally confident. This combination made him at once terrifying, fun, and dangerous.

Emma had experienced the usual mix of emotions at her father's latest repeal of a safeguard: anticipation and fear. She and Nick adored their father, who was more fun to be around than most kids their age. It felt like a compliment to their maturity that he didn't hover over them like other parents did. And she trusted him. He was the grownup who always assured them that everything would be all right, which it often was. And when it wasn't, he managed to convince them that it had been. But she felt her stomach flip at the thought of having to be a responsible adult on such a long journey.

Ever the protective big sister, Emma did her best to put on a brave face and reassure her brother that they'd be okay. But her attempts at optimistic reassurance never landed quite the way her father's did.

THE BUS RIDE TO SPRINGFIELD HAD GONE WITHOUT A HITCH. The driver had agreed to make sure Emma and Nick got off at the right stop, and their grandparents—who had been horrified to discover that the children had been put on a bus alone, something Emma's father had only bothered to tell them once the bus had left the station—were reassured by the fact that nothing had gone wrong.

It wasn't until the return trip that things went sideways.

The bus departed on time, at 5:00 p.m. It was due to arrive in Framingham at 8:32—an hour and a half longer than a car ride would have been, due to an alternate route and multiple stops—where the children's father would pick them up and drive them back home to Acton.

Having survived the outbound journey, Emma felt more confident making the trip home and let down her guard. The lights were dimmed in the well-heated bus, and the rocking motion of the vehicle, moving steadily along the Massachusetts Turnpike, lulled her into a trancelike state. She felt cozy, almost safe, as she stared out the window into the black winter sky above the icy trees along the highway. Her eyes heavy, she eventually drifted off to sleep.

When she awoke, the bus had come to a standstill in gridlocked traffic. There had been an accident, and the driver announced that they were going to be delayed by at least two hours. Thankfully, Nick was still sleeping soundly in the seat next to her. Emma told herself there was nothing to worry about, that the worst thing that could happen was that they'd go to bed late, which was something they always begged their father to let them do anyway. Still, the knot in her stomach tightened.

By the time she heard the squeaking of the brakes as the bus slowed to a stop at the depot, it was after 11:00. The station was eerily quiet. The frigid cold had cleared the streets of life, and the only lights were those over the small outdoor bus shelter. Emma and a bleary, dazed Nick climbed out of the vehicle with their oversized backpacks. They wandered around, scanning the empty parking lot for their father's familiar dark blue Ford pickup truck with its light blue panels, which was nowhere to be found.

After about five minutes of searching, Emma pulled Nick by the arm, hurrying them back to the depot to tell the bus driver that they hadn't found their father.

"Wait!" Emma screamed. "No! Stop!" But the red taillights of the bus were disappearing into the darkness.

Nick followed Emma's cue. "Stop! Don't leave us!" His voice broke on the last word, as the sounds of the engine faded into the night.

The driver must have forgotten that he was supposed to make sure the children were safely in their father's care before leaving.

Trembling from more than just the cold, Emma grabbed Nick's hand and walked him toward the unlit station. "Let's see if we can get inside and find a phone to call Dad. Maybe he went back home to wait for us since we're so late." Nick bit his lip and said nothing.

As Emma had feared, there was no getting inside the station, which was closed for the night.

Nick's bulky backpack slipped over his skinny arms and plopped on the ground, and he let out a wail. His face was contorted with anguish, his eyes and mouth wide, as tears mixed with mucus from his runny nose. Emma's heart leapt to her throat.

"He's dead!" Nick screamed. "I know it! He's dead!" Nick's face was bright red, and clouds of hot breath rode the howls coming out of his mouth. He was working himself up so much that he looked like he was going to have one of his fits, where he'd bawl and yell and hyper-ventilate until he passed out. The psychologist the family had seen when the episodes first started said that this kind of reaction sometimes happened when one parent has died, making the child irrationally afraid of losing the other one, even if the death had occurred before the child could remember it.

"C'mon, Nick," Emma said softly. "Let's sit down and play 21 Questions. I bet you'll never guess the new-est riddle I have." She took her brother's listless mittened hand and led him to the covered benches that served as a bus shelter. Because walking the dark streets looking for help seemed more dangerous than staying put, Emma had decided the best thing to do was to wait until the morning when the station reopened. She just hoped they wouldn't freeze to death overnight in what felt like sub-zero temperatures.

The high beams of the Ford pickup flashed as the vehicle bounced over the hill that led into the station parking lot. It was 1:30 a.m. The children were huddled together for warmth, Emma's arms wrapped protectively around Nick.

Emma heard the crank of the emergency brake through the deep thumping of the car stereo as her father pulled up in front of the shelter. He leaped out, his usually smooth forehead furrowed and his mouth a tight line.

"Kiddos!" His features immediately relaxed at the sight of his children, who he must have thought would be worse off.

The children didn't move and sat hugging each other, with Nick's face pressed against Emma's chest. Their father wrapped his powerful, paternal arms around them and rubbed their backs vigorously, as though trying to press warmth into them. "Am I glad to see you two!" His eyes once again twinkled with their usual cheer.

Nick began crying, this time silently. Whether they were tears of relief at being recovered or grief for having been abandoned, Emma never knew. Probably a bit of both.

"C'mon, kiddos. The car's all warmed up, extra hot to melt you two little ice cubes into puddles!" The three of them walked to the truck and climbed in. The engine had been left running and Emma heard the loud heating fan, feeling its blast of warmth as she slid across the wide front seat.

"Sorry I was late getting you guys. I was watching *The A-Team*, and it was great. You guys are gonna love this episode. I'll rewatch it with you when they do reruns, so we can see it together. Anyway, after the show, I *completely* forgot that you guys were coming back tonight. The school holiday threw me for a loop. I know, I'm a total dummy." He chuckled self-deprecatingly at his ineptitude.

Emma and Nick were silent. Defrosting.

"Good thing you don't have school tomorrow!" Their father had the glimmer in his eye that he always got when he was trying to cheer them up.

The children mutely fastened their seatbelts. Either their silence truly escaped their father's notice, or he was pretending it did.

"It's the perfecto combo! No school and you little critters finally get your way—you get to stay up WAY past your bedtime! I bet you planned this whole escapade just so you could go to bed in the 'morning.'" Laughing, their father leaned over and started tickling them and growling in mock indignation. The children squirmed. Nick whimpered. But eventually, their father's silly sounds and absurd complaints resulted in a few giggles.

As they pulled out of the parking lot, Emma caught sight of Nick's anemic smile, and her heart sank. Somehow laughing felt wrong. But so did crying. Or complaining. It was as though what had felt like a trauma was supposed to be an adventure they should be grateful for. Emma didn't know what to think or feel, so she ended up doing neither. She just went numb.

BY THE TIME EMMA WAS HOME AND IN BED, THE SHOCK HAD worn off and her body was flooded with adrenaline. The events of the night played over and over in her mind like a looping horror film. Knowing sleep would continue to elude her, she pulled back her covers and dragged the warmest one behind her as she headed to the barn.

When she crept into Blossom's stall, she threw her arms around the pig's thick neck, buried her face in his bristly fur, and started to sob. Blossom turned his face toward her, his pale blue eyes taking her in, nuzzling her gently, uttering the special, soft little grunts he always made when she was in distress. He nudged his lumbering body closer to hers, pressing his solid mass against her. Emma rested her weight against the one shoulder she could always lean on.

"I love you, Blossom," she whispered into his soft jowl. Blossom's tail swished ever so slightly, and he let out the softest of grunts in assent.

10

Little Messes Everywhere

Day 10: Monday

If Jenna weren't on crutches she'd be sprinting. The slight, stylish forty-seven-year-old hobbles determinedly into the office before Emma even finishes opening the door, sliding with a purposeful thump into her usual spot on the sofa. Pulling her Peet's Coffee thermos out of her metallic, faux-leather backpack, she throws back a gulp like a cowboy swigging whisky before facing surgery.

Jenna pauses mid-swallow, coughing. "Emma, my *god*, what happened to you? Are you okay?" Her shock at seeing Emma's neck brace and bandaged shoulder and hand, as well as the dark rings that appeared around Emma's eyes over the weekend, seems to have snapped her out of her personal misery.

"I'm fine. I had a fender bender."

Jenna's husband, who was trailing behind her, pauses at the door with a quizzical expression on his face, as though he hasn't been attending weekly couples therapy sessions in this office for the past six months. Forty-four-year-old Alexander, with his pale skin and high coloring, looks like a boy accompanying his mother to the principal's office.

"Come on in and have a seat, Alexander." Emma gestures to his usual spot next to Jenna and waits as he tentatively sits down.

Twelve minutes. That's how much time Emma has spent, in total, repeating the same phrase to Alexander and waiting for the same behavior since she started seeing the couple. Thirty seconds every week adds up, and she'll never get those twelve minutes back.

One of the most important data points that guides Emma, or any therapist, is her own experience of the dynamic with a client. In this case, she's having—and not for the first time—a direct, personal experience of what Jenna has been describing over the past months.

Much of the fatigue Emma feels, though, is her own. It's only Monday morning and she's already fantasizing about climbing into bed Friday night and staying there for the weekend. Or until someone finds her body.

Stop. It.

At least she doesn't have to screen these clients for suicidality. She's familiar with their struggle and, though it's been painful and enduring, neither of them has shown signs that they're at risk of killing themselves.

"I really thought we'd turned a corner." Jenna's warm brown skin is already getting flushed and her thick, wavy hair is falling out of its clip. "And now *this*!" She lifts her foot—which is encased in a stiff orthopedic bootie—and gestures furiously at it, her fat gold bracelets, a gift from her Thai grandmother, jangling. "I'm seriously at my wits' end!"

Alexander stares at the leg of Emma's chair in a strange sort of fascination. Even after all these months, Emma still can't quite read him, and she can't tell whether he feels guilty or bored, or whether he's following the conversation at all.

Jenna's slim frame looks almost fragile next to Alexander's stout, muscular one. And she doesn't seem to notice that he's absorbed by a piece of wood while his wife declares a marital state of emergency. Or maybe it's *because* Alexander is mentally and emotionally AWOL that Jenna's so worked up. People tend to turn up the volume when they sense they're not being heard. Their emotions, and often their communication, amp up. So the more Alexander doesn't react to Jenna's distress signals, the louder she calls for help.

With a start, Emma wonders whether CouchGPT is creating the same dynamic with her. Is its dispassionate narration of her potentially fatal condition intensifying her own emotional reaction? Is she in a dysfunctional relationship with a bot?

"I mean, I really thought we'd turned a corner," Jenna continues. "I even told you last week, when you were sick, that we didn't need to see you because things had improved so much. But I was wrong. Here we are again. It's like we take two steps forward and then 1.99 steps back. As soon as I drop my guard and stop hovering over him like a helicopter mother to make sure things don't start to fall apart again, as soon as I start to *finally* catch my breath, the other shoe drops." Jenna is panting, winded from her diatribe. Her almond eyes suddenly becoming moist, she adds more softly, "It's like nothing ever changes."

After years of working with couples, Emma is all too familiar with the despair that accompanies the repetition of a painful pattern in a relationship. All couples have at least one core issue, one pattern that keeps getting repeated. If the couple handles the issue skillfully, over time the pattern repeats less often, and when it does occur, it's less severe. Much of Emma's job is helping couples recognize their patterns and develop the skills to interrupt them. When couples don't know that it's normal for these patterns to repeat, or the issue doesn't improve over time, one or both partners can become despairing. Despair is the feeling of hopelessness, and everyone needs the beacon of hope to guide them through dark times.

For couples like Jenna and Alexander, who are dealing with the added challenge of one partner having a form of neurodivergence—Alexander's ADHD, and to a lesser degree, autistic behavior—healing entrenched patterns is even harder. ADHD makes it difficult for someone to remember and respond to even the most basic of requests, which is why the divorce rate for couples where one or both partners has the condition is nearly double that of the average.

At the shift of Jenna's tone, Alexander seems to come out of his reverie. He turns to look at his distressed wife, his youthful features contracting as his gray eyes start to focus.

"What exactly happened, Jenna?" Emma asks encouragingly.

"What happened is that his messiness landed me in the freakin' hospital!" Jenna spits out, despair ceding the floor back to anger as she remembers the infraction.

"I'd thought we'd gotten the messes under control. I really did. I mean, after all our talks about how I can't stand living in disorder, how it literally *dysregulates* me, throwing my nervous system out of whack."

Jenna's hands are trembling, and she looks like she might start to yell at Alexander. Or cry. Or both. "So the messes had been under control. Under control *enough*. Which meant I didn't have to watch my step in my own home. And then, Thursday night when I got out of bed to pee, I stepped on a roller skate that was in a pile of junk sitting right outside the bathroom door. I twisted my ankle and had to go to the ER. Now I've got to be on crutches for six weeks! I have no words."

Emma is about to express her empathy for Jenna and try to draw Alexander into the conversation when she hears a humming. Did she forget to turn her ringer off?

"But the worst part isn't the fractured ankle. Or the $1,500 hospital bill. Or even the fact that the roller skate had been a filthy garbage pick that Alexander was planning to turn into a plant stand. The worst part is—"

Emma glances at her desk to see her phone lying on it, as always. It's neither vibrating nor lighting up. Maybe the hum is from a car stereo outside? Normally she can tune out this sort of distraction. But her nerves are frayed and the ibuprofen she took this morning is wearing off, so her head and body aches are returning.

"—when we discussed what happened, the next day, and I was trying to get Alexander to understand why I was so upset about the mess, he turned away from me while I was talking. He *literally* turned away. We were sitting up in bed. And then he leaned forward and lay down on his stomach, with his feet toward me so I had to talk to the back of his head and—" Jenna whirls around to face Alexander. "Will you please STOP?!"

And just like that, the humming is gone.

Alexander rolls his eyes upwards and sideways, to stare intently at nothing.

Realizing what just took place, Emma sees an opportunity to finally address Alexander's self-stimulating behavior in real time. When his stimming happened in previous sessions, interrupting the conversation wouldn't have been appropriate. Like when he was repeatedly slapping the back of his hand against the wall behind his head while Jenna was crying about the mushroom farm she discovered he'd started in the bathtub while she was away at a conference.

"Alexander, can you see why humming while Jenna is talking upsets her?"

Rather than look at Emma to respond, Alexander turns toward Jenna and the two lock eyes. He sniggers. And, seemingly against her better judgment, Jenna lets out a little giggle as well.

Despite their very real marital problems, Jenna and Alexander have, in some ways, a remarkable relationship. Although they seem like opposites, with Alexander's neurodivergence and Jenna's high relationality, they have more in common than not. They're both deeply committed to personal growth, intellectual rigor—she's a professor and he's the founder of a successful tech startup, with his neurodivergent brain making him a true innovator and visionary—and humanitarian causes. And they each hold humor as a core value, which enables them to laugh at themselves and their relationship. Emma has always believed that humor is one of the most underrated relational tools. When people can step back enough to see the absurdity that is part and parcel of the human condition, they can take themselves a little less seriously. And humor does wonders to defuse the charge of disconnecting emotions like anger and shame.

"His stimming is really bizarre," Jenna says with a small smile.

Seeming to think he's off the hook, Alexander doesn't respond to Emma's question about his humming. And before Emma can repeat it, Jenna has taken the floor again.

"Look. I get it. I get the stimming, the furious whispering to himself in long imaginary debates, the binge-watching ASMR videos with a package of chilled fruit on his head to keep him cool, the weird hobbies, like making Shrinky Dinks. Some of it's even endearing." Jenna's features have softened but her smile has faded. "But I just can't deal with being in this marital Groundhog Day. It's been eight years. And yes, things *have* gotten better. But 'better' is still me begging for the bare minimum necessary for cohabitating in a halfway decent home." She turns to face Alexander. "Like, just leave a shared space in at least as good condition as you found it."

Which is a good rule of thumb in general. Something to apply to relationships—even to life. When Emma is dead, will she have left the parts of the world that her life touched in the same condition, or better, than they had been?

Jenna is still on a roll. "And if you agree to do something I say is important to me, then don't keep dropping the ball so I have to remind you. Because that's not me. I *hate* feeling like I'm nagging or controlling. I just stop asking for what I want, and then I feel disconnected from you because I'm not getting it."

Alexander is looking at his wife, but his eyes are unfocused, seeming to look through or past her. Emma can't tell if he's listening intently or planning his next messy misadventure.

Jenna seems too intent on her own commentary to notice her husband's strange gaze. Or maybe she's just used to it. "I don't want to have to say 'Alexander, can you please wipe your sticky smears off the refrigerator handle? Can you please not wipe your snotty nose with the clean kitchen towel? Can you please not leave your half-empty glasses all over the house?' Every time I repeat myself I feel a little worse about myself, and us."

"We just have different standards, that's all. I'm not like you." Alexander has finally decided to join the conversation.

Jenna's eyes widen and redden as tears spill over and down her cheeks. Looking suddenly weary, she doesn't bother to wipe them away. "I know. I know." Her voice is small. "And that's what kills me. I don't want to be like this. I don't want to feel so dysregulated, so angry, so exasperated. It's just that I can't help it. It's who and how I am. I can't live in disorder. I can't be around messes. It literally *hurts* me. I've tried to change myself, and I can't." Her tears flowing freely, she adds, "Alexander, the thing is, we've talked about this so many times. And every time, you insist that you 'get it' and things get better—and then as soon as the stars aren't aligned, when you go through a stressful period, they regress."

"But they're a lot better than they used to be," Alexander points out. "Aren't they?"

"Yes, they are. We're past Peak Mess. The big messes are gone. But the little messes are everywhere. And it only takes one roller skate to break me."

Clearly distressed, Alexander frowns and sticks out his bottom lip like a pouting young child. Then he blows raspberries.

"And it all adds up," Jenna continues. "Every extra effort I have to make to do something you haven't done yourself is a cost to me and a savings to you. It's not fair. I'm just. So. Tired."

Jenna turns to Emma. "Can you burn out on a relationship like you can on a job?"

"You can burn out on anything," Emma replies.

Including life.

"But before we go talking about relationship burnout, let's give Alexander a chance to respond to what you've said."

Alexander is looking at his wife, who has started to sob. He reaches over and places his hand tenderly on her thigh. There is such earnestness in his face that Emma's heart goes out to him. To them. Alexander is a sweet man, and he truly loves Jenna and wants the best for her and for their relationship.

At Alexander's touch, Jenna places her hand on his, squeezing it. Her love for him is palpable. She looks into his eyes. "Thank you," she whispers. "Thank you for caring. And for listening. I just… I just don't know what to do."

Emma hands Jenna a tissue, which she uses to wipe

her eyes and blow her nose as her sobs subside.

"I love Alexander more than anything in the world. I'm just… I'm afraid. I'm afraid for us."

Jenna has finally found the courage to give voice to her deeper truth. To the fear that lies beneath all the anger and sadness. The fear of losing the precious bond and affection she holds so dear.

"Jenna, is there anything else you want to say to Alexander?"

Jenna sniffs. "It's hard for me to feel like he loves me. I can't help but feel like I don't really matter to him when he keeps doing things that he knows cause me so much pain. So, it's not just the messes that hurt. It's also what they represent."

Emma turns toward Alexander, ignoring the throbbing in her head that's returned with a vengeance. "Alexander, what do you think about what Jenna said?"

His eyes clear, Alexander replies, "Well, I can understand Jenna's perspective. But the view from the inside is very different."

***

Mercifully, Emma's next client has canceled, so she has a free hour to catch her breath, wait for the new dose of ibuprofen to kick in, and check her messages.

She flips open her laptop to find an email that's just arrived.

From: rezeption@charitéhospital.de

Subject: RE: Trying to contact Dr. Hans Müller, Medical Director of Traumatic Injury Unit

Dear Mrs. Parkland,

We regretfully inform you that Dr. Hans Müller is no longer working at the Charité. He resigned from his post 10 years before and is not in contact since.

Frau Hackner

Emma's nostrils flare. Her American bot has more of a bedside manner than this German customer service professional. She quickly composes an appeal.

Dear Frau Hackner,

Thank you for getting back to me. The matter is of great urgency. If you could please connect me with someone from the Traumatic Injury Department who might know Dr. Müller's whereabouts, I would greatly appreciate it. Please. This is potentially a matter of life and death.

Sincerely,

Emma Parkland

Emma hopes that begging and invoking sympathy will work in Germany like it does in the US. Somehow, she doubts it.

11

Mortal Wounds

Day 10: Monday

They really are a motley crew. As she tries to ignore the hard metal seat beneath her, Emma regards the group members as they trickle into the YMCA fitness studio that doubles as a meeting room. They represent an assortment of traumas and neuroses and unfulfilled wishes, disparate beings united by a common struggle. Like a morbid Island of Misfit Toys.

Emma took over Mortal Wounds when, in a bizarre twist of fate, the founding psychologist stepped on a rusty nail and almost died. With a lump in her throat, she reflects on the cruel irony that she's the facilitator of this Monday night support group, which bills itself as being for those grappling with any death-related issue.

Then again, maybe she's right where she belongs.

Clutching bags and carrying mugs of tea or coffee from the dispensers on the collapsible card table in the corner of the room, the aromas helping to deodorize the tang of sneakers and sweat, the group members make their way past the piles of yoga mats and rollers lining the far wall. They head to the ring of folding chairs, greeting each other and doing double-takes when they catch sight of Emma.

Little Miss Meme scurries through the door just as the last of the members is seated and hurriedly slips into her chair by Emma's side. She's been assisting with the group as part of her training.

Seeing three unfamiliar faces in the circle, Emma is reminded that there are newcomers this week, and with a twinge she wonders how suicidal they may be. So far, she hasn't worried about anyone else in the group. They're here because they're daunted by death, not courting it.

"Hi everyone. It's great to see you all." Emma does her best not to sound like she's lost her way through the very terrain she's supposed to be helping them traverse. "Before we get started, I want to just let you know that even though I look like I've been beaten up, I've just had a fender bender." She's rewarded for her feeble attempt at humor with relieved smiles and a couple of giggles.

"Welcome back—or welcome, if it's your first time— to Mortal Wounds, a safe space for sharing our thoughts and feelings about death and dying."

As always, Emma is touched by the ring of expectant faces turned toward her. Real people, in real pain, who have trusted her with their fears and desires, the soft underbellies that they hide from most of the world. The members are silent, waiting, hoping that somehow, some way, something that is said tonight will relieve a little of their suffering.

"We've got a few newcomers, so, everyone, I'd like to ask you to introduce yourselves before you talk about whatever is on your mind. Who'd like to start?"

"Sure, I'll take a stab at it!" Seventy-eight-year-old Arthur, with his crooked grin and carefully combed hair, is ever the jester, and he's the only one to laugh at his joke. "Hi everyone! I'm Arthur. I'm a proud father, grandfather, and great-grandfather. And I'm here because, at my age, I'm not getting any younger!" More laughter from himself, and a few polite chuckles from the more generous members.

Since starting therapy with Emma after the discovery that his daughter had attempted to kill herself and had never even mentioned to him that she'd been unhappy, Arthur has become a self-professed "self-help junkie." Emma knows from their individual sessions that Arthur continues to grapple with the guilt of not having been there for his family. But his decision to join Mortal Wounds probably has more to do with his desire to throw himself into all things therapy than to grapple with death and dying—especially since this is one of seven different groups he's a member of and because he rarely talks about death, even here.

"Who'd like to go next?"

Silence.

"Okay, ahem, ja." The voice is Olivia's, but the deep tone and German *ja* indicates that the speaker is Karl. Olivia and Karry-on Karl started coming to the group a few months ago, when Olivia forgot her handbag on a plane and was never able to recover it. The handbag had been part of the set that included the suitcase, and the couple decided that Mortal Wounds might help Karl move through his grief.

Emma had hoped Olivia would introduce Karl as her partner before he spoke; she saw the three newcomers startle when a masculine voice with a German accent came out of the slight American woman who'd just moments ago been casually chatting by the coffee dispenser.

"We come here because of my grief, my loss, my sister, who *she*"—Karl can't point, but it almost seems as though he has when Olivia cringes at the reference to herself—"lost. Left behind. Abandoned, like she is *nothing*!" The voice is bitter. Olivia somehow manages to look at once infuriated and chagrined.

The now-pallid newcomers sit unblinking, no doubt wondering what they've signed up for.

"Olivia, do you have anything to add?" Emma has been trying to get Olivia to talk about her own grief, at her sister's death, which is the real reason she's here. Olivia and Karl had been returning from the funeral when the handbag got lost.

Olivia's sleek brown hair slips over her slender shoulder as she turns her body to face the suitcase, which is propped up on the seat beside her. "I'm really sorry," she whispers. She carefully straightens his luggage tag, looking like a wife adjusting her husband's tie. Turning back to the group she replies, "No. Thanks, Emma, but Karl pretty much summed it up."

"'Grief is the price we pay for love.'" Pity tinges Missy's voice. Emma gives the young intern a sharp look, hoping her expression makes it clear that the saccharine sayings have got to stop. Not only are Missy's quips generally unhelpful, but Emma has told her several times not to feed Olivia's delusion by engaging Karl.

Olivia's eyes glisten, and she lays a comforting hand on Karl's back.

The stiff-spined intern goes next. "I'm Missy, and I'm here as part of my counseling psychology internship. I'm assisting Emma. So anything you need, anything at all, feel free to come to me. I'm here to serve." Missy raises her porcelain chin, like a soldier reporting for duty, her eyes bearing the sanctimonious gleam of a martyr.

"Dankeschön."

Emma ignores Karl's response.

"Hi. My name is Gregory." The sixty-seven-year-old Haitian American man, whose narrow, sorrowful face is etched with deep folds, sounds like he's said this phrase hundreds of times. Which he has.

"Hi, Gregory," the regulars reply in unison.

Gregory views Mortal Wounds as his personal twelve-step group. It helps him avoid slipping back into thanatophobia, the fear of death he developed in childhood that plagued him until his early thirties, when both his parents died in a tragic car accident. Being the only child, Gregory had inherited the family coffin-making business, Out of the Box Custom Coffins. In order to step into his new role, he started medication and got short-term therapy, which enabled him to largely overcome his phobia. Mortal Wounds helps keep him "on the wagon."

Gregory's thanatophobia was caused by a traumatic event that took place when he was nine. He'd woken up one night to use the bathroom and heard sounds coming from the basement, where the caskets were stored. Gasping and grunting sounds. Terrified, he'd crept down the dark stairs to the storeroom and flipped on the light. The sounds stopped. He stood there, holding his breath and wondering whether he'd imagined the whole thing, when suddenly his mother sat bolt upright, back first, from within a coffin. She was naked and panting from having held her breath in the hope that Gregory would go away. Her body glistened with sweat and her usually plaited hair was wild and unbound, a giant afro floating like a dark halo around her head. Before his father had a chance to sit up, the boy had fled the scene, screaming and bawling and never to look at a sarcophagus, or his parents, in the same way again.

"I'm so grateful to be here." Gregory's voice is mellow, a slight second-generation Haitian accent softening the edges of his words. "I'm struggling a little this week, feeling a little anxiety creeping back. There's been a spate of suicides in the past couple weeks or so. I didn't mention it before because I was hoping it was a fluke, or that my calculations were off. But it looks like it might be a suicide cluster, and these things always disturb me."

What had CouchGPT said? *There has also been speculation that suicide clusters may contribute to the development of SOS...*

Gregory looks down at his hands. "Anyway, thanks for listening."

"Thanks, Gregory," the group replies.

"Um, Gregory..." Emma usually doesn't ask Gregory questions or give him feedback, knowing he just wants to be witnessed. But not today. "What do you mean by suicide clusters?"

Gregory startles at the unexpected response and then starts clasping and unclasping his hands. "It's when an unusual number of suicides happen around the same place and time." He swallows. "Thanks for listening."

"Thanks, Gregory." The group is well trained.

"Right, and can you say more about these clusters, Gregory? Maybe there's something we can figure out that will help you de-trigger."

"Uh, not really. It's not something we're supposed to talk about outside the business. People would get the wrong idea and it could cause even more problems, more deaths." Gregory rubs his palms on his thighs, looking sheepish, secretive. "Thanks for listening."

"Thanks, Gregory," the univoice chants reliably.

He knows something. Emma resolves to talk to him after the meeting. Although some of the group members see Emma for individual therapy, some, like Gregory, see Emma only at Mortal Wounds. So she needs to connect with him here.

"I'll go next." This from one of the newcomers. Steve is a twenty-eight-year-old financial analyst who contacted Emma two weeks ago to ask if she'd help him with his health anxiety (or hypochondria, as it used to be called and as Steve still refers to it). Emma agreed to take him on as a client, starting later this week, and recommended he also join Mortal Wounds. From the look of him, a healthy glow illuminating a tawny face that's as unlined as the stylish suit he's wearing, you'd never guess at the turmoil inside. Most people hide their pain as adeptly as they ride a bike. Emma can't help but think of the John Watson quote: *Be kind, for everyone you meet is fighting a hard battle.*

"Hi. I'm Steve, and I'm a hypochondriac."

Steve seems to be following Gregory's lead.

"I'm here because I'm afraid of getting sick. Especially

getting fatally ill. I'm going to work with Emma privately, too. I hope it helps." Steve gives a little nod to indicate he's done.

"'Fear is only as deep as the mind allows.'" Missy's tone is almost sing-song, like she's reciting a nursery rhyme.

"Please, Little Miss—" Emma catches herself before the rest of the epithet slips out. Her weariness and raw nerves are making her both less tolerant and less self-controlled.

"*What* did you call me? *Little Miss*?" Missy's big blue eyes are wide, her tone appalled. "Emma, that's really inappropriate. It's ageist, and—"

"I'm so sorry, Missy." Emma heads off what could become a major confrontation. "I was thinking about something unrelated, and I meant to say 'Missy,' and it came out wrong."

Perhaps it's time to hand this group over to another facilitator. Between the inconvenient content and the fact that Emma is clearly not up to par, keeping it could be professional suicide. Or worse.

Emma turns back to the group. "Who'd like to go next?"

Jenna raises her hand, as though she's in a classroom and Emma is the teacher. Emma nods her assent. "I'm Jenna, and I'm here because I lost my grandmother six weeks ago. And this is my husband, Alexander." She gestures to her left. "He's here so he can learn how to better support me in my grief."

Alexander is gazing out the window. The corners of his mouth are twitching and he looks like he's trying not to laugh at a private joke. After a long silence, he seems to realize that the group is waiting for him to say something. He focuses his eyes and straightens his posture until he's sitting bolt upright, and his expression becomes unnaturally serious, like he's overcompensating for his previous state. "Hi, I'm Alexander," he announces, as though he hadn't just been introduced.

Finally, the last newcomers introduce themselves. "Rasheda here, hi." Rasheda's stately composure and broad stature combine with her ornate gold bangles and soft head scarf draped below her shoulders to make her look like a UN dignitary. "I'm the executive director of an international NGO working to end global poverty, and my family is originally from Oman but we moved here thirty years ago, when I was six." She pauses, seeming to ponder what to say next. "I'm here with my partner, Jared. We have, um, different views on death."

The clean-cut, auburn-haired man wearing fitted jeans and orange Vans who Rasheda just referred to is, for some reason, sitting across the circle from her. He nods. "Hi everyone. It'd be great if this group can help me and Rasheda sort out our differences." He doesn't look at his partner, and his disregard seems strategic.

Hopefully, this couple isn't simply looking for a jury and judge to officiate in their own personal courtroom.

"Oh, and I'm Jared, and I'm a geologist. I work at MIT next door, in Cambridge, but I travel a lot." Jared cedes the floor back to Rasheda.

"I don't want children, and Jared does. I'm 'anti-natalist.' Meaning, I don't believe people should procreate unless they're able to make a fully informed decision, which means being aware of all other options and all the consequences of creating more human life. You also have to be aware of how you've been conditioned to believe that procreating is a given, something everyone is supposed to do and is inevitably going to do, so you can break out of that mindset." Rasheda has laid out her opening arguments.

Emma's hopes were in vain.

"And," an animated Jared counters, "I object to that position." He looks pointedly from one member to the next. "I think Rasheda turns conversations about having children into philosophical arguments as a way for her to justify her own selfish, unethical behavior." He rests his gaze on Emma.

"I may not be the brightest bulb on the porch," Arthur interjects, thankfully interrupting what's becoming a heated debate. "But it seems to me like the difference of opinion you two have is about life, not death."

"Life and death are two sides of the same coin." Rasheda's voice is authoritative. "You can't have an opinion about one without having an opinion about the other. And how can you possibly make an informed decision about whether it's better to live or die if you haven't examined your existence bias, your belief that existing is more important than not existing?"

It's as though SOS has commissioned Rasheda as its hired gun.

"Existence *what*?" Arthur tries to insert himself but the defendants aren't yet ready to engage the jury.

Seemingly aware that public opinion is on Rasheda's side, Jared plays what is apparently his trump card. "I think the good people in this room deserve to be treated like they aren't stupid, Rasheda. You think they can't see through your holier-than-thou posturing? That they don't know you're just trying to hide your own ethical misconduct, and rationalize taking an innocent life?"

The group members have been swinging their heads from side to side, in unison, transfixed as each speaker presents their case. They face Rasheda expectantly.

Rasheda's courtly demeanor has vanished and her light brown skin has turned a deathly white. "How did you know?" she whispers, her voice trembling.

"I may not run an international charity like you do, but I'm no fool," Jared spits out. "For the past three months since I got back from my *six-week* expedition, you've stopped drinking alcohol, you're nauseous all the time, and your boobs are like hot air balloons. When were you planning to tell me? After you'd murdered the baby?"

Emma groans inwardly. She *cannot* handle a blow-out today.

Fortunately, she doesn't have to. Her phone alarm vibrates. "Okay, everyone. We're out of time. Rasheda and Jared, let's talk briefly before you two head off." Turning to Gregory, Emma adds, "And before I talk to them, I need to quickly ask you something, okay?" Gregory's expression is unrevealing, but he appears to give a slight nod.

As the group is disbanding, Emma collects her coat and bag, taking care not to put stress on her injuries. She looks around the room for Gregory, but the coffin maker has disappeared. As she hurries toward the exit, she catches sight of him scurrying across the parking lot to his car. She doesn't have the strength to chase after him, but all her instincts tell her that he knows something. She can always tell when someone is keeping a secret.

As soon as she's home, Emma checks her email. There's a message from Amir, her radiologist friend.

Good news. There was an MRI cancellation tomorrow at 8 a.m. Let's see what's going on inside that head of yours! ;)

12

TEDMED

Day 11: Tuesday

"Seventy degrees and sunny! When just two days ago it was flurrying. That's New England for ya, right? Like they say, 'if you don't like the weather, wait a minute!'" The thick-bodied, fifty-something receptionist sporting a stiff feathered bob sits on the nineteenth floor of Massachusetts General Hospital and barks out a laugh that quickly devolves into a coughing fit. Somehow even her whooping has a Boston accent to it.

Emma's nose itches from the stale smoke emanating from the woman's clothes, and she tries not to think about the fact that so many healthcare workers are unhealthy. She needs to have faith in the system, especially today.

"Dr. Morelli's the fourth door down the hall on the left," the receptionist wheezes.

Dr. Morelli? What happened to Amir?

Emma walks tentatively down the wide corridor, which is somehow both alarmingly bright and depressingly dull.

Dr. Morelli's office is larger than the first apartment Emma had when she moved to Boston for graduate school. Framed on two sides by floor-to-ceiling windows with a spectacular view of the Boston Harbor, the 900-square-foot space looks more like a penthouse than a meeting room, with its wall-to-wall carpeting and ebony sofa–loveseat set encircling a glass coffee table. The main attraction, though, is a glossy teak behemoth that serves as a desk, where the doctor is sitting. At Dr. Morelli's gesture, Emma takes the seat opposite her.

"Nice to meet you, Ms. Parkland."

Actually, it's *Dr.* Parkland. The PhD designation is something MDs routinely and conveniently overlook. Emma lets out a breath and relaxes her posture. She wouldn't care about such superficiality if she weren't a suicidal wreck, and if the nauseating reek of new carpet weren't so overpowering.

Dr. Morelli's charcoal hair is cropped short, accentuating her narrow face with its tight features and amplifying her formidable height. "Dr. Traboulsi isn't on duty today, but he's briefed me on your situation. I hear you've been having headaches?" The doctor either doesn't notice or doesn't care about Emma's other, more obvious physical ailments.

"Um, yes." Emma raises her voice to bridge the vast wooden gulf between them. When will doctors learn to create an atmosphere that's connecting rather than intimidating? "They started about a week ago. So Amir—Dr. Traboulsi—arranged for an MRI."

"Right." Dr. Morelli looks at her Rolex, probably to make sure the appointment doesn't run over the allotted fifteen minutes. "We'll get you into the coffin—" She lets out a loud snort of laughter, which is especially disconcerting given how incongruous it is with the rest of her demeanor. "Sorry, that's medical gallows humor that just slipped out! We'll get you into the *tube* in a few minutes. First, here's what we'll be looking for."

Dr. Morelli shoves back her lofty chair and stands up, looming over Emma. In one large stride, she's in front of two darkened screens on the wall next to the desk. She picks up a small black device and clicks it to light up the first screen. It's a brain scan.

Taking a presentation pointer out of the pocket of her white lab coat, Dr. Morelli aims the laser beam at the image. "This," she says in the tone of someone about to deliver a TED talk, "is a normal brain. Healthy."

Emma's stomach does a backflip when she realizes what's coming next.

"But what if I told you that brains don't always look like this? What if I told you that you might have a brain that looks more like"—she pauses for effect—"*this*." With an exaggerated snap of her wrist, she clicks to illuminate the next image. It's of a brain peppered with horrid white spots.

Emma feels the blood rushing from her head and her vision starts to blur. Yes, she's suicidal. But she doesn't want to die this way.

"So if you take away one thing from this appointment, it should be this: with a little luck, your brain will look like the one on the left." The doctor pauses, her back straight and chin high. "Thank you for your attention."

Emma automatically starts to clap, before hurrying out of the office.

<hr>

By the time she's seated in the narrow hallway that serves as a waiting area outside the MRI room, Emma feels like fire ants are running through her veins. Why are medical professionals so out of touch with the relational needs of the people they serve? Skilled communication is always important, but it's especially so when people are at their most vulnerable, their most insecure and frightened.

Today could have been so different. Emma was almost looking forward to it, thinking—naively, she now realizes—that a brain tumor might be an easy out.

A plump technician who looks to be in her late thirties approaches. She has dark brown skin, a waist-length mane of beaded braids pulled back with a bright scrunchie, and a kind expression in her round eyes. "Emma Parkland?"

Emma manages a nod.

"Hi, I'm Yvonne, the MRI technician here." The woman's wide smile showcases her perfect white teeth, and she smells like a tropical flower. "I'll be getting you prepped and taking care of you during your scan."

The cortisol spike from Emma's encounter with Dr. Morelli starts to subside. It really takes so little to help someone feel more secure. Simply relating to someone as though they're a being rather than an object changes everything.

Yvonne leads Emma to a bulky, padded chair in an alcove further down the hallway and has her extend her arm to have her vitals taken. The phone on the narrow, stainless steel table next to the chair lights up, showing a photo of Yvonne on a white sand beach hugging a tan, scruffy little dog whose tongue lolls happily over the side of his or her mouth.

Yvonne glances solemnly at her phone and turns it off, the screen once again black.

Ever the shrink, Emma can't help but investigate what she senses is an emotional pain point. "Cute dog. Is she yours?"

Yvonne's mouth tightens. "Was. And he's a he. *Was* a he. He died last month."

"Oh, I'm sorry." Emma tries not to think of Annie dying. Or of herself dying on Annie.

"Thanks. It's okay. I can do death. I mean, I don't have a problem with death, you know? It's gonna happen to all of us. It's just a matter of time."

In which case, why not shave off a few decades? Emma squeezes her eyes closed to shut out the suicidal voice inside her.

"The problem is my family. We're Polynesian, and they don't get the whole pet thing. They don't get that I loved Zeus and he loved me. Nobody, not my boyfriend, my parents... nobody in my community understands what I'm going through. They keep telling me I'm over-reacting, and my boyfriend, he keeps saying I just need to get a new dog. Imagine saying that to someone who lost their kid!" Yvonne's eyes redden. Her stethoscope and pink scrubs are probably the only things stopping her from crying, keeping her safely contained in her profes-sional role. "And the worst part is, I feel embarrassed, like maybe I really *am* just too emotional."

If Emma had a dollar for every person who piled shame on top of pain because they believed they shouldn't be suffering in the first place, she'd be able to single-hand-edly fund the Candy Crush All Stars tournament. Feelings aren't wrong or right; they just are. Not judging your feelings, giving yourself permission to experience whatever is naturally arising, is one of the most healing things anyone can do.

"I'm really sorry. You clearly loved Zeus. And the sadness you feel, that's grief. That's a normal, healthy emotional response to losing someone you love, whether they were a human or a pet."

Yvonne's clouded eyes suddenly become clear. She's not smiling, but neither is she grimacing. "You a shrink or something?" She shakes her head slightly and lets out a soft laugh. "'Cause you sure sound like one. Thanks. Thanks for that. I dunno what you just did, but I feel a whole lot lighter."

All Emma did was to compassionately witness the woman, to listen to her without judgment and validate her. The practice is as simple as it is powerful, yet it's so lacking in the world that people are starved for it. Sometimes they binge on it when they finally get a taste of it, downloading their traumas to strangers on buses or in bars. Other times they pay professionals for it, which is probably the main reason psychologists like Emma stay in business.

YVONNE'S COMFORTING MANNER AND SWEET FRAGRANCE helped settle Emma's nervous system a bit. As did the foam ball she told Emma to squeeze "for any reason" to call her over during the procedure.

Still, Emma's heart is racing as she lies on her back in the claustrophobic tube, her neck brace digging painfully into the back of her head. The blaring and convulsing of the machine don't help her anxiety. Nor does the photo of a scenic mountain range affixed to the ceiling two inches above her nose, its decrepit, peeling corners making it dispiriting rather than relaxing.

The procedure takes about forty-five minutes, and by the time it's over and Emma has been slid out of the tube, she's drenched in sweat, woozy and shaky. She sits up and perches on the edge of the machine. The room swerves and she leans forward, breathing deeply to avoid passing out. Glancing up through the square window that opens to the adjoining control room, she sees Dr. Morelli standing next to Yvonne, looking intently at what are most likely Emma's scans.

The doctor leaves the room and seconds later saunters over to Emma, seeming not to notice that her patient is on the verge of collapsing.

"Ms. Parkland, I have to review the images fully, so I can't tell you anything conclusive just yet. But I wanted to let you know that, at first glance, your scan looks good."

Emma exhales audibly.

"There's only one suspicious spot, but hopefully it's nothing to worry about."

"Wait. What? There's a spot on my—"

Emma again feels herself starting to faint, and she forces herself to do the deep, diaphragmatic breathing exercises she learned in her trauma training, to keep herself conscious. She opens her mouth to speak, but nothing comes out.

"Unfortunately I've got a massive backlog of scans so I really don't know when I'll be able to get to yours, but I'll be in touch as soon as I am." And with that, Dr. Morelli and her triggering bedside manner exit the room.

THANKFULLY, EMMA HAS ALMOST AN HOUR TO PULL HERSELF together before her first Tuesday morning client shows up. As she sits at her office desk sipping green tea—drinking coffee after her nerve-wracking encounter with Morelli would surely trigger a panic attack—she opens her laptop. Seeing an email from Charité, her eyes widen and she impatiently opens it.

From: Steinermd@charitéhospital.de

Subject: RE: Trying to contact Dr. Hans Müller, Medical Director of Traumatic Injury Unit

Dear Mrs. Parkland,

I receive your message looking for Dr. Müller. I worked with Dr. Müller here in the Charité. But unfortunately he is not here since 10 years. But that you know. All what I can tell you is, he said he will go to India.

Viel Glück,

Prof. Dr. Friedrich Steiner, Traumatologie

Finally Emma's luck seems to be turning. How many Dr. Hans Müllers can there be in India?

After a full half hour of searching, Emma has her answer: zero. According to Google and ChatGPT, there is no Dr. Hans Müller to be found in India or even in neighboring Nepal, Pakistan, or Sri Lanka.

Emma decides to take the advice the bot gave her after it was unable to locate Müller, and she does a quick search for private investigators. She clicks on the first credible-looking firm that pops up, Busted.

It takes her all of five minutes to write up the required one-paragraph request and to pay the exorbitant fee for services. And in just two minutes, she receives a reply.

From: Buster49@Busted.com

Subject: Emma Parkland searching for Dr. Hans Müller

Dear Ms. Parkland,

Your request has been received and your order has been processed. One of our investigators will contact you as soon as we have information on Dr. Müller's whereabouts.

Why don't people take the extra thirty seconds to communicate clearly? Especially when they know a situation is dire? "As soon as" could be hours or days. Or months.

Emma isn't sure how much longer she can hold on.

13

"Something's wrong with me."

Day 13: Thursday

"**I** wasn't always like this." Less reserved than he'd been at Mortal Wounds two days ago, Steve sits with uncrossed arms and legs on the sofa opposite Emma, speaking in his unadulterated Midwestern accent. His light brown eyes are framed by lashes so lush it seems unjust, and his tightly coiled, jet black hair is buzzed short enough that his scalp shines in the afternoon sunlight slanting through the window.

"I used to be normal," he continues. "I could go to dinner with my friends and not freak out about their double-dipping and unwashed hands grabbing at the bread basket. I could read the news without being on high alert for a triggering headline about a scary illness or malpractice suit. Hell, going for a medical exam was no different than going for a haircut. Now I start getting panic attacks at least a week before a doctor's appointment."

He looks down, his fringe of eyelashes like a Japanese fan gracefully covering his angst.

"Something's wrong with me."

Maybe Steve's just had one too many encounters with the Dr. Morellis of the world. Emma's stomach knots at the thought that she'll again have to face the doctor with her sinister images of brain tumors—if the doctor finds time to review her scans before she's killed herself. Morelli should include trigger warnings in her presentations.

"Can you tell me about the time when you were, as you put it, 'normal'?" Emma tries to avoid using pathologizing language like "normal" and "abnormal." She doesn't want to add fuel to the collective fire of widespread shame around mental health issues. Or any issues.

Steve lets out a half-laugh. "Maybe I was never really *normal*. I was always kind of anxious, and definitely more sensitive to these things—to a lot of things—than everyone else. Like, I was the kid who worried about getting the flu when the other kids *wanted* to get sick so they could stay home from school. And I didn't like to play with guns or watch action movies because the violence made me queasy, it repelled me. When other kids pulled the wings off butterflies, they laughed and I cried."

Steve rolls his eyes. "Hearing myself say this, it's like, dude, get *over* yourself! I mean, it's not like I'm living in a freaking war zone or anything. But I *feel* like I am. Every day feels like an assault I've got to try to survive."

Be kind, for everyone you meet is fighting a hard battle. Emma recalls this quote at least twenty times a week.

Steve looks the epitome of wellness. He's in the prime of his life, fit, well-dressed—wearing creased khaki chinos and a pressed white polo shirt—affluent, and on the cusp of a promising career. And yet, in his inner world he's in the trenches of a war.

If everyone's inner reality were as visible as their outer one, how much kinder would the world be?

"So it sounds like you've always been sensitive."

"Yeah. Yeah, I guess you could say that. Things like loud noises, bright lights, they really bother me. Also just bad things happening to people, school shootings and famines, all that, it really gets to me. I feel like there's so much upsetting stuff going on. So if that makes me sensitive, then yeah, that's right."

Steve looks at his large hands, which he's folded on his lap. He contemplates, perhaps for the first time, what it means to be a sensitive person in an insensitive world. To have the gift, and the curse, of feeling deeply.

"When did the health anxiety start?"

"It started maybe two years before Covid. I was at my girlfriend's family's place for Thanksgiving. I was talking to her uncle, who started telling me this story about how he'd been in perfect health, and then he started getting these headaches, and it turned out he had this rare kind of brain tumor." Steve shudders.

So does Emma. She strains to hear Steve's words over the thundering of her heart.

"He told me all the details, from the first aches in his temple that he thought were nothing, to the blurry vision, to all the exams and scans and the final diagnosis. And then—" Steve swallows, his eyes haunted and unfocused as he stares back into the traumatic memory. "He went on and on about his treatments and deterioration. The surgery, the tremors and convulsions, waking up covered in his own urine—" Steve stops abruptly, his eyes wide.

Emma has been leaning forward, listening intently, and

holds her position, assuming he'll continue. But he doesn't. He just looks at her quizzically, his mouth hanging slightly open as though he wants to say something but can't.

Feeling a drop of water land on her thumb, she looks down at her hands in her lap. They're clasped so tightly that her knuckles are white. More drops fall, as though a little storm cloud is hovering right over her thighs. Horrified, she realizes that the drops are coming from her face, which is streaming with sweat. And that her soft linen shirt is clinging to her chest and armpits.

"Emma… Emma? God, Emma, are you all right? Do you need help?"

No, and yes.

Emma forces out a laugh that's louder than she'd intended. It sounds inhuman, and frightening even to her own ears. "Oh! Ha! Yes, I'm fine. Hormones!" Because she's in perimenopause, she's not actually telling a lie.

At the sight of Steve's still-dismayed face, Emma produces another laugh, this time softer and more feminine, as if to say *haha, wink wink, you caught me having a hot flash, lol.*

Steve's posture relaxes and he lets out a little whistle as he exhales. He looks so relieved that Emma wonders what kind of psychological harm her bizarre episode may have caused him.

She wipes her face with a tissue and hastily brings her professional self back online. "So your girlfriend's uncle basically downloaded a major traumatic experience to you, without your consent, and you got triggered by it."

"Yeah, right. But he didn't mean anything by it. He was just telling me his story. Anyway, after that conversation, I started doing crazy stuff. Like, I kept thinking my vision was blurry, so I'd be rubbing my eyes, closing one eye and then the other to test my sight, and using all kinds of eye drops. I remember this one day on the subway—" He pauses and shakes his head in disbelief at his own absurdity. "This huge, like six-foot-three, clown was sitting across from me. Probably on his way home from a gig. And he kept winking and blowing kisses at me over his outstretched hand, and giving me these coy smiles. I was totally creeped out. Then I realized he thought *I'd* been winking at *him*!"

Still reeling from Steve's brain tumor story and her own unseemly reaction, Emma is so disturbed by the image of a towering, sexually inappropriate clown that she momentarily dissociates. She feels like she's floating outside her body.

"So I started googling to figure out what was going on with my vision. And that's when my fear of a brain tumor turned into a fear of everything health-related."

Emma cautions all her clients to avoid symptom surfing, which almost never ends well.

"Even when I stopped the searching and tried to block out scary information, I couldn't. It was everywhere. Pop-up ads selling remedies to health problems I'd never even heard of, news headlines about deadly misdiagnoses and genetic mutations that you can't test for but might kill you. Facebook posts about salmonella outbreaks in foods you can't avoid. Colleagues telling you the details of their brother-in-law's out-of-the-blue stroke during a coffee break!"

Steve's right. The Internet has created a communication free-for-all, everyone indiscriminately spewing traumatizing materials all over the shared landscape of human consciousness. Most people at least know better than to launch into a graphic description of certain traumas, like rape, without giving warnings and getting consent. But triggering communication is everywhere, much of it creating what Emma thinks of as "microtraumas," which, over time, build up and take people down.

"Then came Covid," Steve continues. "My roommate refused to wear a mask, or to wash his hands regularly, and he was always touching food we shared. Even when he got infected, he'd leave his mask hanging below his nose and sneeze away. I felt like there was nowhere I could go that was safe. And the worst part of all was that he kept saying the problem was me. He said I had OCD—and the more he didn't do the basic hygiene stuff, the more squeamish I got until I really did start feeling obsessive."

Emma had counseled many couples during the Covid years, and their problem was almost always the same. One partner was more "disgust prone," in that they had a stronger reaction to being exposed to disgusting things like germs and other contaminants. And the other was treating that sensitivity as though it were a choice. Someone who is disgust prone can't just turn off their disgust any more than someone who has autism can just stop being autistic. Plus, hygiene needs are safety needs, and in relationships, safety needs are generally non-negotiable. Disinfect or divorce.

"So that's my story. My descent into madness." Steve leans back on the sofa and crosses a long leg over his knee. Waiting for Emma to fix him.

"Steve, imagine that someone you care about tells

you that they think there's something wrong with them because they don't take pleasure pulling the wings off an insect or watching people brutalize each other on TV. Or because they get anxious when they're exposed to the gruesome details of a fatal illness, or they find it unhygienic to eat food that's been handled by someone who doesn't believe in washing their hands. What would you think of them?"

"What would I think of them? Um, I'd think it made sense that they were bothered by those things." Steve's smooth forehead furrows slightly. "So you're saying that maybe the reason there's something wrong with me is because there's something wrong with the world?"

"What do *you* think?"

"Well, I see your point. But still. Other people live in this same world and they're not basket cases like I am. And even if they were, I can't go on living this way."

"These issues aren't mutually exclusive. It's hard enough to get through the day when you're not particularly sensitive; stressors are everywhere. Given the reality we live in, it makes sense that you're struggling with health anxiety. At the same time, we need to work on ways to mitigate the anxiety, and build your psychological resilience so you can feel safer moving through the world."

Steve's posture relaxes as he takes in Emma's words. He gives her a sideways grin. "You know, when I think about it, I'm actually not afraid of death. I'm afraid of dying." He lets out an ironic laugh. "So maybe the solution is just to kill myself."

His laughter does nothing to dispel the lump in Emma's throat.

"COME!" SHANA LIKES TO PRETEND SHE'S CAPTAIN PICARD on the Enterprise and her office is like his ready room. Emma walks through the door as naturally as possible, hoping she doesn't look like someone whose head and chest and hand and neck are throbbing wildly. Or like someone on the verge of suicidal madness.

Shana is sitting at her stately desk, flipping through a file. Her wall-to-wall bookshelves boast an impressive array of titles, including her own, *Black, Female, and Tween: From Psychopharmacological Intervention to Social Empowerment,* which has a cover photo of her wearing a flowing burnt orange kimono cardigan and chunky beaded necklaces and earrings. The room smells of her essential oil blend, an infusion of sandalwood and smoky jasmine, at once earthy and sweet.

Shana looks up and peers over the top of her reading glasses, one of her chin-length, blonde-streaked cornrows falling forward, and her mouth drops. "What the flippin' flip happened to you?!" An imposing, full-bodied figure with a powerful frame, she has a loud voice even when she's not emotional, and now she sounds like she's yelling.

Emma has prepared for this. Smiling broadly and wiping back the hair she just realized is still clinging to her damp cheek, she laughs. "I know, right? I had a fender bender and it's been a helluva few days trying to get back on track. I definitely need to get better about taking my multivitamins."

Shana's eyes narrow. There's no way the astute psychiatrist doesn't sense something is off. "Em, you gonna tell me what's going on?"

Should she?

Shana is a renowned thought leader. No matter what challenge she takes on, whether it's uncovering covert racism in pediatric psychological diagnoses or resolving treatment-resistant mental health issues, she consistently solves the problem. Plus, her academic affiliations and status as a bestselling author have given her direct access to leading doctors, psychologists, and researchers. Surely, she would be a powerful ally for Emma to have by her side.

But no. Shana has a full load of clients and Emma doesn't need to add her own convoluted case to it.

"It's just been a hard few days, what with having the flu and then the accident. And because I haven't been feeling well, I haven't been sleeping well so it's adding up. And I have a client I'm concerned about, who just left my office, which is what I wanted to talk to you about."

Shana's eyes are still narrowed and she holds Emma's gaze just long enough to let Emma know she'll be watching her. "All right. For now. Shoot."

Emma summarizes her session with Steve. "So, cutting to the chase, I was hoping to refer him to you. Especially since you've had so much success with difficult-to-treat clients, including those who've been suicidal."

A smile spreads across Shana's broad face. "Ha. Thanks for the vote of confidence." With a sly expression she adds, "I wish I could take all the credit."

Emma waits for Shana to explain what she means, but the psychiatrist has moved on.

"As luck would have it, the Harris family just hit the

pause button on therapy so I have a slot available. So sure, send him over."

Now Emma just has to figure out how to eliminate the other potential causes of her suicidality.

14

The View from the Inside

Day 17: Monday

His Oxford shirt is buttoned up a bit too high and his fine sandy hair, parted on the side, is combed a bit too neatly. It's as though Alexander, who's in the hot seat today, is preparing to give a class presentation. Despite his efforts to look the part, he seems to have forgotten to iron his pants, which are as wrinkled as ever.

Sitting straight-backed in his usual spot next to Jenna on the thick sofa amid a handful of soft throw pillows, Alexander appears more alert than Emma has ever seen him.

"How've you two been?" Emma last saw the couple at Mortal Wounds last week. Which thankfully had to be canceled today due to a plumbing issue in the YMCA where the meeting takes place.

Jenna is unusually silent, and simply looks at Alexander, her fractured ankle in its shapeless black bootie stretched out before her. Perhaps she remembers that when their last session left off, they'd agreed that Alexander would have the floor today.

But Alexander just looks back at his wife and gives her a warm smile, seeming to think that's what she's after. Jenna returns the smile, albeit hesitantly.

"We've been okay. I mean, *I've* been okay. I can't speak for Alexander." Jenna again turns to her husband, waiting for him to step up and step in.

Alexander smiles at Jenna again, and takes one of his hands out of his pockets to rest it on her knee, which he squeezes affectionately.

This time Jenna doesn't smile back.

Emma wonders how long to let this dance of communicative misses continue before intervening. She normally gives clients ample time to identify and work out their own problems. But over the weekend, her headache had worsened and the wound in her chest had bled through her bandages, sending her back to the hospital. The attending ER nurse was the same one who'd been on duty the night of the stabbing, and they noted that the wound looked almost as fresh as it had when she was first admitted. Apparently, Emma's body isn't healing itself. Maybe it's not only her psyche that's trying to kill her.

Although it's only Monday morning, Emma's patience is already wearing thin. Even her flowing linen pants and creamy cotton top feel irritating. Still, she wants to hold the space for the couple a little longer.

Jenna sits still, too still, like she's exercising her Fifth Amendment rights. Perhaps in an attempt to remain optimistic, Alexander continues to smile, though it's now just a half grin, and he's biting his lip and looking at the curtain rod over the window.

Click! Click! Click!

Emma jumps at what sounds like a stapler, noting that her startle response is way out of whack. Another indication that she's been chronically dysregulated. Her nervous system is stuck on high alert.

Click! Click! Click! Click! Click! Click!

How could she possibly hear Shana's stapler across a hall and through two closed doors?

Click! Click! Click! Click! Click! Click! Click! Click! Click! Click! Click! Click!

Emma has held the space long enough. She raises her voice to be heard over the stapler. "Alexander, we were planning to pick up today where we left off last week. I'd asked you what you thought about what Jenna had shared. She said she feels like some of the problems you two have, like the messes and inattention, get better but then revert back almost to where they had been before. Two steps forward, 1.99 steps back, I think she said."

Jenna nods assent.

Click! Click! Click! Click! Click! Click!

"And Jenna worries that this cycle will make her burn out on your relationship. She also said that she feels like she doesn't matter to you, because you keep doing things that you know cause her a lot of pain."

Click! Click! Click! Click! Click! Click!

"You said that you can understand Jenna's perspective, but that 'the view from the inside' was very different. Could you share your thoughts with us?"

Click!

"Of course. I've written them down. I was waiting for you to say it was time for me to talk." Alexander takes his hand out of his pocket, and deposits a little yellow plastic and metal bauble on the sofa cushion beside him. His fidget. The click-toy he uses to keep himself from disrupting conversations and which is meant to be clicked sparingly. Apparently Emma's comment last week about his humming being bothersome got through to him. Or not.

He pulls out a miniature red Moleskine from his back pocket and starts flipping through it, and then holds it open above his lap. Emma sees the heading of a section, which says *You matter to me more than anything in the world. I love you so much! I'm sorry*. Beneath that are bullet points where Alexander's chicken scratch is too small to read.

Jenna has also peered over at the notebook. Her face has softened and she looks at Alexander expectantly.

"You matter to me more than anything in the world. I love you so much! I'm sorry," Alexander reads out. Then he takes a pen out of his shirt pocket and writes something down. "I'm sorry and I really want to make you happy."

Jenna's eyes are moist, and she's holding her breath as she stares at her husband.

"I know the messes—and other things—are real problems," Alexander continues, still looking at the notebook but sounding less like he's reciting. "And I'll keep working on those things. But I don't do things that upset you because I don't care about you. A lot of times it's actually the opposite."

Alexander makes what looks like a little checkmark in his book.

"Like the pile you tripped over the night you hurt your foot…"

"*Fractured my ankle*," Jenna corrects, tight-lipped.

"Fractured your ankle," Alexander repeats, unfazed,

as he looks up from his notebook. "The reason there was even a pile in the hallway was because I'd promised you I wouldn't just stuff things in a drawer. That I'd sort everything and make sure things got put back where they belonged. And that I'd keep our home clean. I'd been cleaning, and I'd separated all the things I needed to put away into different piles and then I put the piles closest to where the items had to go. I got through three piles but by the time I started on the fourth one, the one next to the linen closet outside the bathroom, it was getting late and I knew you wanted to go to bed before ten. Looking back, I get it that leaving a pile with a roller skate outside the bathroom door probably wasn't a great idea." He starts to grin, but thinks better of it. "But it wasn't because I don't care about you."

Emma recalls the time Annie emerged from the basement, a tragic, blood-soaked dead mouse in his mouth. He trotted over to the living room to drop it in front of Emma's feet on the brand-new plush carpet. His golden, squinting eyes oozed cat love as he sat looking up at her from behind his hard-won gift. How many gifts of love get lost in translation?

Alexander turns the page, to a heading that says *I always want to listen to you. It's not easy for me. I'm not like you. Please know I'm trying. I love you!*

Clearing his throat, seemingly in an attempt to hide the fact that he's teared up, Alexander continues. "I always want to listen to you. It's not easy for me. I'm not like you. Please know I'm trying. I love you!"

Emma and Jenna exchange meaningful glances, a shared understanding of the specialness of this man.

It's impossible not to root for Alexander, not to be touched by his earnestness and openness. And it's impossible for Emma not to root for the couple. Apart from their differences in regard to neurodivergence, they're a great match. When Alexander isn't under stress and puts in the effort, he can actually relate in a pretty sophisticated way.

After crossing out something lower down the page, Alexander looks up and turns to Jenna.

"When we were talking about the roller skate—about your fractured ankle—and I turned around to lay down in bed—"

"Turned your back on me, to face *away* from me," Jenna corrects, miffed.

"I didn't turn my back on you. I was trying to pay attention to you. You were really upset. And I knew if I didn't stay focused you'd get even more upset. You know that when we're having an emotional conversation I have trouble following—'tracking,' as you call it. I've told you this before, but you forget. Looking out a window helps me focus. And my stomach against the mattress calms me down. I was trying to give you what you always say you need."

Jenna removes the throw pillow between her and Alexander and slides a little closer to him.

Teary-eyed, she takes his hand in hers, and places her other one on top of it. "Alexander, thank you. Thank you for this explanation. It helps, it really helps to know what's going on for you. And I'm sorry if—*that*—I don't always see how hard you're trying. I really appreciate how much you stretch for me, for us."

Alexander leans over and kisses Jenna sweetly on the

side of her head, and Jenna closes her eyes. The moment is so tender, Emma feels like she should look away.

Jenna shifts her body so she's sitting more upright. "Can you just help me understand," she asks tentatively, seeming to not want to spoil the moment but also wanting to avoid leaving a relational loose end, "why you didn't just explain what you were doing? If you'd just told me why you were turning around, I would have been totally fine with it."

"Sometimes, in the moment, *I* don't even understand why I do what I do." Alexander's introspection often takes Emma by surprise. He's far more insightful than he seems. It's usually just a matter of him seeing clearly, of him having decluttered the inside of his head.

"Plus," he adds, foolishly, "you seemed really invested in venting at me."

Emma winces. When Alexander's not seeing clearly, he can really miss the mark.

Jenna snatches her hand from Alexander's and wheels around to face him squarely. *"What?!* *What* did you just say?!"

Turning back to Emma, Jenna hisses, "*See?!* Do you *see* what I mean?! One minute we're having a breakthrough and then—bam!—we're right back where we started!"

And just like that Jenna has slid back into despair. Zero to a hundred.

One hallmark of relationship burnout is that it only takes a spark to ignite a conflagration. Emma always explains to her clients that, contrary to popular belief, most relationships don't die from a single, deadly blow. They die the death of a thousand cuts, the thousands of little infractions—the failures to be tuned in and responsive to the other person's needs—that chip away at one (or both) partner's ability to feel connected with the other. And, as Jenna has been experiencing, the more disconnected someone becomes, the more dysregulated they become, making them easily irritated. Jenna didn't start out this way. But now, after years of ongoing dysregulation, things that wouldn't normally irritate her do, little irritants feel big, and big irritants feel overwhelming. Her irritation, in turn, is making her feel even more disconnected from Alexander, in a painful feedback loop. Emma's professor, Dr. Xi, used to say that relationship burnout often results from being chronically dysregulated, and from feeling hopeless that things will ever change.

Could it be that Emma is burned out on her relationship with herself? Like everyone, she's always relating to herself through things like her self-talk and the choices she makes that impact her future self, her self of five minutes or months or years in the future. Everyone's primary relationship is with themselves. Could Emma's dysregulation and irritability be driving her suicidality, rather than the other way around?

"I can't do this," Jenna cries.

Jenna's exclamation snaps Emma back to her senses.

"He has *no idea*. No idea how much I struggle. Every. Single. Day. To keep my chin up as I stop what I'm doing to pick his dirty socks off the floor when I'm already running late to work. To strategically ask him the right questions in the right way so he doesn't tune me out—"

Jenna's crying has devolved into fat, sloppy sobs. The sound of a woman choking on her own breaking heart.

Alexander looks like a deer in headlights, clearly not having anticipated this. He looks down at his little Moleskine that's still open in his lap as though searching for a magic line to make it all go away.

"And you know what? I hate myself for it. I hate that I feel like a nag."

Why is it that when a man openly expresses his needs he's called progressive, but when a woman expresses her needs—repeatedly because they weren't listened to the first times—she's called a nag?

"I feel like a shrieking shrew. A nitpicker." Tears are coursing down Jenna's face. "I hate who I've become. I feel like I have to make a horrible choice. The worst possible choice." Jenna lets out a teary cough. "I have to choose between Alexander and my sanity. And I can't live without my sanity."

Alexander sits like a statue. Pale, frozen, and unblinking.

"Listen, Jenna. I hear you. And I'm so sorry it's been so hard for you." Emma turns to Alexander. "For both of you."

"Just hear me out," she continues, in damage-control mode. "You're really triggered right now. This isn't the time to be making any major decisions. I've been working with you two for half a year now, and I know how challenging your relationship can be. I also know how rewarding it can be. And how far you've both come, even though it doesn't seem that way right now. So let's pick this conversation back up next week, when emotions aren't running so high. Until then, I'd like the two of you to avoid any hot topics. Okay?"

"Okay." Jenna's whisper is hoarse.

Emma stands by the door as the pair exit, listening to the fading *click click click* as the fidget disappears down the hallway.

PLACING THE BOWL OF OATMEAL SHE BROUGHT IN FOR BREAK-fast on the desk next to her, Emma opens her laptop to check her email. There's a message from Busted.

From: Buster49@Busted.com

Subject: Report for Emma Parkland re Dr. Hans Müller

Dear Ms. Parkland,

I've located Dr. Hans Müller and can confirm that he is the individual you're seeking. Dr. Müller is the founder and Medical Director of Touch and Go Healing Center, a medical clinic outside of Matheran and whose exact address is not available. Matheran is a town in the state of Maharashtra in India. The clinic does not have a website but they do list their phone number, which I've pasted below. I tried phoning them multiple times but the line was busy and my fee got used up. So you'll have to try reaching him yourself. Good luck.

Sincerely,

Buster49

According to Google, it's 6:40 p.m. in Matheran, nine and a half hours later than it is in Massachusetts. Knowing the chances of getting through to someone are impossibly low, Emma affords herself a large spoonful of oatmeal as she dials the number.

"Hello, Touch and Go Healing. How can I help you?"

Before she can swallow, Emma's heart leaps into her throat.

15

The Wounded Healer

Day 18: Tuesday

During Emma's childhood, whenever Nick was mad at her he would rip the head off her favorite doll—the porcelain one, with curly blonde hair and big round blue eyes—and throw it in the toilet. After a drowning, reaffixing the head, with its drenched hair and dull eyes stuck at half-mast, was always a disturbing and repulsive experience. Emma tries to keep this memory at bay as she sits across from the resuscitated doll's spitting image.

Missy has been chugging her Starbucks venti like a parched marathon runner gulping Gatorade since arriving at Emma's office five minutes ago for her 10:00 a.m. appointment. The intern has had some sort of crisis, and asked to see Emma today rather than wait for her usual Friday appointment. She seems to be hoping that once her caffeine level is high enough, she'll have the nerve to finally respond to Emma's question about what happened.

Missy's preoccupation with her coffee gives Emma space to think back on yesterday's conversation with the receptionist at Touch and Go. The man on the phone had explained, in a thick Indian accent, that Dr. Müller is in "very, very high demand!" and he only sees select patients who meet strict criteria. Reaching him—finding his number and getting through to the clinic, which has only one phone line—is the first criterion. Next, the "candidate" must submit an application for treatment, describing their condition and why they believe they should be chosen. They must also submit their full medical history, as well as their astrological chart. Emma's heart skipped a beat upon hearing this last point, since she'd already feared that Dr. Müller might be some sort of a charlatan, but she knew he was still her best hope of survival. Finally, international "contestants" need to send a copy of their passport so the clinic can arrange their travel.

"So, Miss Parkland, you send application to contestant@touchandgo.com and the doctor, he review it, and if he think he can help you we give you appointment within timeframe that is in keeping with your problem. Urgent cases get priority. What this mean is, if doctor agree, then you are winner. If he no agree to see you, you no hear from us. Bye!"

Missy sniffs and sets her cup on the glossy end table beside the sofa. The calming aromas of fresh coffee and dried lavender that suffuse the office seem to have had no effect on her mood. "'Failure at some point in your life is inevitable, but giving up is unforgivable.'"

Whatever has happened hasn't made Little Miss Meme any less trite.

"I'm an unforgivable failure. I've failed, *and* I'm giving

up." Missy's tone is defiant. "So I'm a double failure." She gazes out the square window on the side of the room, her eyes bloodshot and swollen, her bottom lip protruding.

Perhaps if Emma speaks the intern's own language she'll have a better chance of getting through to her. "'You simply haven't lived until you learn to let go.'"

Emma realizes her mistake too late. Missy has burst into tears.

"You don't understand! I *failed*. I failed the Merriweathers, and I'm a failure as a therapist. I'm a danger to the profession." Missy raises her hands to cover her face, sniffling behind her palms.

Emma should have known better. The first, most important step in any conversation—let alone a sensitive one—is expressing empathic concern and validation, compassionate witnessing. Without that, nothing else matters. And sometimes, nothing else is needed.

"Missy, I'm so sorry." Emma's voice is soft. "I can see how much you're hurting. I know how much it means to you to feel like you're helping your clients, and I can only imagine how you must be feeling right now."

Missy takes her hands away from her face and looks at Emma. Locks of blonde hair are sticking to her forehead and cheeks at random angles, and her large blue eyes are hooded. Her cream shirt with its rounded, lace-trimmed collar and three-quarter-length puffed sleeves has wet stains where coffee must have dripped on it. *Deadby*. That's what Nick used to call Emma's doll, Debby, after he'd tried to drown it.

Emma's limbs go cold and the floor feels like it's shifting beneath her feet.

Collecting herself, she asks, "So, Missy, what happened that's caused you to feel this way?"

To Emma's dismay, Missy doesn't bother to smooth her hair back. "It backfired. It… blew up. My intervention." Missy is now speaking slowly, almost robotically, as though she hasn't just downed over four hundred milligrams of caffeine. "Weeks of researching… weeks of planning… Everything… everything just fell apart."

Emma waits for Missy to elaborate. But the intern just sits there, her pale face impassive and unmoving except for her eyes, which blink lethargically. Sweat has soaked through the front of her thin blouse that's now clinging to her skin.

The sight of the sodden, doll-faced intern is too much. Emma's vision closes in and the taste of metal floods her mouth. Realizing she's starting to have a panic attack, she pulls out every psychological hack she knows—breathing into her belly, pressing her feet on the floor to ground herself, and averting her eyes from the ghastly figure sitting before her.

"The Merriweathers are worse off now than they were before they ever met me. And they'll probably sue me for damages." Missy is finally ready to tell her story.

As it turned out, Missy hadn't heeded Emma's request that she not move forward with the intervention she'd concocted before discussing it in this week's supervision meeting. And the intern's attempt to "cure" Janie Merriweather, the girl suffering from triskaidekaphobia—the fear of the number thirteen—and whose thirteenth birthday is a couple of weeks away, ended up being less of an intervention and more of an assault. Hence the potential lawsuit.

After doing a deep dive into the literature on treatments for phobias, which included consulting Missy's favorite reference, TikTok, the intern had come up with a plan to use something called Group Intervention Flooding Therapy, or GIFT.

Missy had first learned of the controversial method in her *History of Clinical Psychological Interventions* textbook. GIFT was created by a nineteenth-century Swiss psychoanalyst and has had a recent resurgence of popularity on social media, even though it's never been endorsed by the American Psychological Association. Emma remembers from her college language studies that *Gift* is the German word for "poison" and wonders if the choice of name for the intervention had been a Freudian slip.

The premise of GIFT is that phobias are cured when the patient—as practitioners refer to those being treated—is simultaneously flooded by triggering and calming stimuli. A patient is tied down and forcibly exposed to as many forms of the trigger as possible, while their senses are inundated with calming elements, such as soothing music, earthy incense, deep massages, dim candles, and so on.

When Missy first proposed the approach to Janie's parents, they had refused, thinking it was too risky. But after she shared GIFT success stories—most of which were from Swiss psychoanalysts' personal, handwritten journals from the early 1800s and from TikTok influencers—the desperate parents relented. Together with Missy, they constructed an elaborate plan to cure Janie's phobia.

On the day of the assault, Missy was hiding behind the oversized sectional sofa in the Merriweathers' living room, where she was crouched down and could watch the scene unfold. The lights were dim, frankincense was burning, and "The Girl from Ipanema" was playing through the ceiling speakers. Janie was sitting in her favorite La-Z-Boy chair reading a picture book that the thirteenth page had been torn out of.

The girl's parents entered the room from opposite doorways to block Janie from both sides in case she tried to escape before they could tie her down. They quickly pulled out a giant roll of plastic wrap, which they stretched around her arms and torso and outstretched calves, binding her to the chair, all the while saying how much they loved her and what a wonderful daughter she was. At the same time, Janie's two siblings, a brother, aged ten, and sister, aged sixteen, inserted an eye speculum to keep the girl's eyes open and a gag to stop her screams.

Once Janie was secured in place, the parents turned on the huge, flatscreen television Janie was facing, which featured the movie *Thirteen*. They then turned on an audio loop of James Earl Jones saying "thirteen," and Janie's siblings grabbed picket signs with "13" and "thirteen" scrawled all over and marched back and forth chanting the word, pausing occasionally to put moisturizing drops in her eyes. Missy came out from hiding and joined the fray, scribbling the number in permanent marker all over Janie's exposed skin—on her wrists, hands, face, ankles, and feet. The parents, meanwhile, massaged Janie wherever they could, crying and professing their undying love for, and commitment to protecting, the girl.

Needless to say, GIFT had not yielded the intended results. Janie had to be taken by ambulance to Beth Israel Hospital and is still in the psychiatry ward, undergoing intensive care.

By the time Missy has finished what turned into a horror story, Emma is so dumbstruck that all she can do is eke out a meme. "'So many words to say and no way to say them.'"

"I can't believe what I did." Missy's voice is thin. "I'm a failure as a therapist." Mercifully, the intern covers her wan face with her hands.

"Missy," Emma ventures, "if one of your clients hadn't succeeded at something they tried to do, would you consider them a failure?"

"Of course not. 'When we give ourselves permission to fail, we give ourselves permission to excel.'"

"So why do you consider yourself a failure, just because your assau—um, intervention—didn't succeed?"

And perhaps caused irreversible psychological damage. But still.

"Because. I'm supposed to be a therapist. I'm supposed to heal people, not make them sicker. I shouldn't be treating people. I've told my advisor I'm dropping out of the program, and I won't be coming back for supervision after today." Missy's features have hardened, making her colorless face look almost ceramic.

Emma instinctively squeezes her eyes closed, to prevent what feels like the onset of a hallucination.

"I'm sorry, Emma. I know I'm a disappointment to you, too."

Emma looks at Missy. "That's not what I'm trying to communicate. I've just got a headache." Emma rubs her temples to drive home her point. And because they're throbbing.

There's no question that Missy shouldn't be treating clients. But the young woman isn't a psychologist yet. She's an intern. With more training, she just might become the therapist she aspires to be.

"Missy, I understand why you'd want to leave the profession. I can imagine how disillusioned you must feel. Internships are hard, people make mistakes, and—"

"Emma, it's really nice of you to try to make me feel better, but I've made up my mind."

"I'm not trying to get you to change your mind, just not to make an important decision while you're so dysregulated."

Even first-year psychology students know that dysregulation distorts perceptions and emotions, making it difficult, if not impossible, to think clearly and act rationally. People who make decisions while in a dysregulated state often end up regretful, which is why Emma always counsels her clients to hold off on decision-making until they're regulated, whenever possible. Unfortunately, being dysregulated also compels people to take action, and it's in such a state that a lot of people decide to end their relationship or career. Or their life.

"I get your point, Emma. But I hate myself for not taking care of the people who trusted me. There's nothing left for me in this profession. There's nothing left for me anywhere. What good am I if I can't fix people's problems?"

With a sad smile, Missy adds, "Am I the poster child for the wounded healer, or what?"

As Emma looks at the empty Starbucks cup that Missy left behind, its snowy plastic lid smeared with light pink lipstick, her throat tightens. It's not Missy who failed. It was Emma's job to guide and protect the intern, and if she'd done it right, she could have prevented the young woman's professional suicide, and the collateral damage that came with it.

Fortunately, Emma has a few minutes before her next session to clear her mind of the disturbing conversation with Missy. She decides to check her voicemail. There's a message from Morelli's office—the doctor has reviewed her brain scan and would like her to call back to schedule an appointment as soon as possible.

As soon as possible? Emma's temples throb even more intensely—either from the stress or a brain tumor.

She taps the doctor's number.

"Dr. Morelli's office."

"Hello? Hi, this is Emma Parkland, returning your call about making an appointment to see Dr. Morelli."

"Hi Ms. Parkland. The doctor would like to see you at the soonest possible date."

Sweat beads on Emma's forehead and under her arms, and her heart feels like it's going to jump out of her chest.

"Um, I can come in any time. Any time at all." Her voice is shaking. "I can get there in an hour. Or after that, in the afternoon?"

"I'm afraid that won't be possible. Dr. Morelli has a very busy schedule. The soonest she can fit you in is next month. How's May 22, at 9:45 a.m.?"

"I thought you said I should come in as soon as possible?"

"You most definitely should, Ms. Parkland. Which is why the doctor will see you on May 22, her first available slot. We'll email your confirmation. Enjoy the rest of your day!"

Emma drops her face into her hands and lets out a desperate groan. The roller coaster she's been on for the past couple of weeks has just thrown her for another loop.

16

Dirty Scans and Virginia Woolf

Day 19: Wednesday

"**I** *magine*." The speaker pauses for effect.

"Imagine a world where everyone, all people—big and small, short and tall; old and young, smart and dumb—can move freely. Think clearly. Live, fully." Another poignant pause, as stock photo after stock photo of diverse people laughing, gardening, hugging, hiking, and clinking glasses in a merry toast appear and fade out on the flat screen that's suspended on the wide, white wall.

Dr. Morelli stands poised, her posture erect so that she reaches her full height of six feet. Emma has been the doctor's captive audience for the past ten minutes, since arriving at Massachusetts General Hospital at 3:30 to discuss her MRI results. When she got the call from the doctor's office earlier in the day saying there had been a last-minute cancellation and the doctor could see her in a few hours, she'd jumped on the opportunity. Just yesterday, she'd been told she'd have to wait nearly a month for this appointment.

Thus far, Emma has learned about the lifesaving accomplishments of the **MRI**, the importance of using contrast in brain scans, and the need to practice good "brain hygiene" to help prevent degeneration and disease. But she hasn't learned anything about the status of her own head.

She can't help but feel unstable sitting in this high-end, high-backed swivel chair with its glossy vinyl seat. The chair rolls too easily over the plastic mat that separates it from the smelly new carpet, and it tilts too quickly and sharply. Plus, her linen pants keep sliding on the slippery material, like a toboggan on an icy slope. She rests her hands on the desk in front of her to steady herself.

"And what if I told you that if you don't take your brain health seriously, your brain could end up like *this*." Now the screen shows a video collage with footage spanning the 1930s to today, of doctors in scrubs performing autopsies on brains. Brains with growths, deformities, and discolorations.

Emma gasps. She can't avert her eyes because Dr. Morelli is looking right at her, making sure that her patient is taking everything in.

"But there's good news." The doctor's smile is wide. "This doesn't have to be you."

Thankfully, Emma's fifteen-minute appointment is going to be over soon. Dr. Morelli seems to realize this as well, as she glances down at her Rolex and quickly delivers her ending statement about brain health protocol, her voice shrill, sounding more like a pixie than a giant, like in infomercials where they speed up the final lines about how certain restrictions may apply.

The doctor clicks off the flat screen monitor and flips on the office lights. "So, Ms. Parkland, we're going to need to wrap up since we're just about out of time." Seating herself at her grandiose desk opposite Emma, she picks up a file and flips it open. "I've looked over your scan results."

The moment of truth has finally arrived. An ambulance siren wails in the street below, as paramedics race off to another emergency. Emma's ears start ringing, and she can't tell whether the fading siren is in the distance or in her head.

"I saw a suspicious spot on your left central occipital cerebral carpal lobe along the medulla oblongata."

If Emma lives through this nightmare, she's going to create a communication course for medical professionals.

"But it turns out that was a spot on the film, not on the brain." Dr. Morelli laughs softly. "In the biz, we call this a 'dirty scan.' Happens all the time. Probably ninety-five percent of the spots that show up are the result of dirty scans." The doctor smiles and shakes her head, as though she's talking about a naughty child's prank.

"So your scan is clean. You don't have a brain tumor. *Yet*." Dr. Morelli wags a cautionary finger.

Emma is numb. The news is so unexpected that her enervated body and debilitated psyche don't know how to respond. She gets up to leave, mumbling her thanks to the doctor for her time.

"But remember!" Morelli calls after her, as Emma heads through the door. "Brain hygiene. Otherwise, you're basically a ticking time bomb."

If the doctor only knew.

———

EMMA'S RELIEF THAT SHE DOESN'T HAVE A BRAIN TUMOR—
"yet"—is overshadowed by her intensifying urge to kill
herself. She feels a pang of nostalgia remembering her
life before SOS, when she was oblivious to the agony the
condition causes. Perhaps it's because of her job, in which
she has a front row seat to trauma and tragedy, or perhaps
it's because she knows of the horrors that so many less
fortunate individuals in the world have to contend with,
but Emma has always had an acute awareness of the pre-
ciousness of life, and the privilege of her own.

Still nauseated and clammy from being confronted
with the video of dissected, sickly brains, and shaken up
from the ordeal of getting her scan results, Emma decides
to stop at the hospital cafeteria to get a cup of tea before
heading to the parking lot. Hopefully, the hot beverage
will calm her nerves before she has to drive back through
the busy streets of Boston to her office in Arlington.

The cafeteria is bustling, and Emma stands in a long
line waiting to order. The food here isn't much healthier
than the KitKats and Doritos and Cokes and other addic-
tive toxins displayed in the vending machines stationed
throughout the campus. Emma grimaces as the doctor in
front of her helps himself to a glob of viscous mystery
meat, followed by a wad of runny scalloped potatoes and
a jiggling bowl of lumpy rice pudding that's reminiscent
of Dr. Morelli's autopsied brains.

Perhaps the health-anxious Steves of the world have
got it right. Does it really make sense to trust an institution
that actively encourages the opposite behaviors of those

its own research has deemed necessary to offset illness and premature death?

She pays for her tea and scans for an open table, to no avail. Spotting a two-top with only one occupant, she approaches it and pulls out the empty chair. The metal feet drag along the floor and add to the din of discordant voices, clinking cutlery, and intercom announcements paging medical staff.

Sitting in the chair across from her is a full-bodied girl who looks to be about seventeen, with an unassuming nose, run-of-the-mill freckles, and a strawberry blonde ponytail pulled through a Red Sox baseball cap. She looks up from the book she's been reading as Emma takes her seat. "Sorry," the girl says, for no apparent reason. Then she slides her banana peel and empty bagel wrapper closer to her side of the table.

If Emma could strike one word from every girl and woman's vocabulary, it would be "sorry." Especially when the apology is for occupying a little slice of space in the world.

"There's no need to be sorry that your food was half an inch over my side of the table—a table you hadn't even been sharing with anyone when you put it there." Emma smiles to take any hint of rebuke out of her statement.

"Um, yeah. Okay. You're right. Sorry." The girl flushes. "I mean, thanks."

Emma resists the urge to say there's nothing to thank her for.

Noticing the somber look on the girl's face, Emma slips into therapist mode. "Are you reading anything interesting?"

The girl flips over the paperback and looks at the cover, which is an ornate, colorful drawing of dragons and swords. "Not really. It's fantasy. Just to take my mind off things."

It turns out the girl, Mandy, is at the hospital for her weekly family therapy session. Today, the psychologist said he wanted to use the last thirty minutes to talk to her parents privately, so Mandy came to the cafeteria to read.

The family started therapy six months ago, after Mandy's twenty-two-year-old brother, Sean, loaded his pockets with rocks and wandered into the Hudson River and drowned, Virginia Woolf style. The family had been visiting friends in Tarrytown, a few miles north of Manhattan.

"I'm so sorry, Mandy. What a tragedy you and your parents are dealing with." Unlike Sean, Emma's suicidality is the cause, rather than the result, of her feelings of depression. She cringes at the thought of how much pain someone must be in when they take their own life.

"Thanks. I'm okay. It's my parents I'm worried about. They can't handle what happened. They're blaming themselves and each other and… they're just a mess." Mandy lowers her eyes, and looks blankly at the book lying on the table.

Emma feels a twinge of guilt, envisioning Nick's grimace as he identifies her bloated, waterlogged body at the morgue. And then his horror at having to call their father, for the first time in over five years, to explain that Emma's decomposing corpse has just been found under the George Washington Bridge. But she wouldn't put them through that. She'd never drown herself in the filthy

Hudson River. Most likely, she'd do it in the comfort of her own bathtub. Listening to "Bohemian Rhapsody." Or in her gold Toyota, parked in her little garage. Burning citrus incense to offset the stench of exhaust, and—

With a shudder, she pulls herself back to the suicidal content at hand.

"I'm sad because I miss Sean. And because my parents are so messed up." Mandy's young eyes seem older than their years. There's a solemnity to them, a seriousness. A depth. "But… I know this is what Sean wanted, so I don't really feel bad that he did it. I just wish people weren't so judgmental. They judge Sean for making a 'selfish choice' and they judge my parents for raising a screwed up kid and not being able to protect him from himself. They say things like 'If I were Sean, I wouldn't have given up so easily.' Well, if they were born and raised and lived as Sean they would have done exactly what he did, because they would have been him. People have no idea what other people really need, or what they can cope with." Mandy shakes her head. "Anyway, like I said, I'm doing okay."

"Can you tell me a little more about why your brother's suicide hasn't hit you as hard as it's hit your parents?" Emma's inner therapist is at full throttle. But her motivation isn't purely altruistic.

"I knew Sean a lot better than they did. So I wasn't hugely surprised that he did it. He always said that he didn't feel 'attached' to life the way other people do. He never understood why people in really bad situations didn't just end their lives. He joked about it, but it wasn't really a joke. He wasn't a fan of life."

Mandy's words echo what Rasheda said at Mortal Wounds. *How can you make an informed decision about whether it's better to live or die if you haven't examined your existence bias?*

If not for our hardwired drive to survive at all costs, would we all just kill ourselves?

"Sean used to say that the survival instinct is like the instinct to procreate. Some people are born without it. Or with a much weaker version of it."

Of course, a lot of factors can lead to suicidality, like childhood trauma, mood disorders, and so on. But what if some people just have—or *also* have—less of a drive to survive? And what if SOS somehow targets this drive? Like a virus that infects the part of the brain responsible for making you want to stay alive despite the fact that life is hard, even for the most privileged of people?

But Emma has always felt that life is a gift. She recalls the meme that popped up on her Instagram feed last month: *When the voice in your mind has quieted so you can hear the silent music of existence, you get a taste of how fortunate you are to be alive.* A sob builds in the back of her throat at the thought of her precious life being stolen from her, and by none other than herself.

Swallowing, she brings her attention back to Mandy and wraps up the conversation with the girl the way she ends a therapy session. She thanks Mandy for her openness, and shares recommendations to help her along her journey.

EMMA DROVE HERSELF TO THE HOSPITAL TODAY AGAINST HER better judgment. Just last night she'd tripped at the top of her staircase and almost went down headfirst, and this morning the tip of her shoe was run over by a bicycle she'd stepped in front of on her way to pick up a sandwich for lunch. But when she got the call from Dr. Morelli's office, she didn't want to wait for an Uber. She'd promised herself she'd drive carefully and climbed into her Toyota.

She makes her way toward the exit to the parking lot, through the impossibly large hospital complex with its glass-encased skywalks and multiple elevator banks and wide, winding corridors. Never great with directions, she has to stop frequently to check the maps affixed to the walls every few yards. Perhaps the best indication of the magnitude of a building complex is its need for "you are here" signs.

By the time she reaches the revolving door to leave the building, she realizes she must have taken a wrong turn somewhere. She's ended up at the ER entrance.

Preferring to walk outside rather than stay trapped in the labyrinth of the hospital searching for the right exit, she quickly slips through the narrow opening of the automatic revolving door before she misses her window of opportunity.

Outside, the cool breeze smells like ocean, a refreshing change from the stale air within the building, with its pervasive stench of disinfectant, construction materials, and, worst of all, sickness. Most people are wearing street clothes rather than scrubs, and the sounds of the city—horns, squeaky bus brakes, Bostonians in the grip of road rage dropping their "Rs" as they yell out car windows—replace the blaring intercoms and beeps and whirring transport carts inside the hospital. The normality of it all helps Emma's nervous system start to settle, and the memories of Dr. Morelli with her harrowing presentation and Mandy with her unsettling suicide story start to fade.

Her relief at surviving the harrowing morning finally starting to kick in, Emma steps into the wide access drive in front of the ER entrance. As she's crossing to the other side, she hears a siren—and then a blaring horn. She startles, and freezes in place. Turning in the direction of the vehicle, she sees the flashing lights of an ambulance careening directly toward her. But by the time she tries to jump out of the way, it's too late.

17

The Buttery Nipple and the
Curious Case of Anan O.

Day 20: Thursday

Hey. how ru? any chance you could meet for dinner tonight? I need to talk to you. it's important.

To Emma's relief, three dots appear on the screen of her phone. Today is not a day she can tolerate waiting for anything, let alone a response to an urgent request. Sharp pains erupt in and around her torso, as though she's wearing a girdle of barbed wire, and her head feels like it's going to burst. Plus, her suicidality seems to have jumped from an eight to a nine out of ten. A couple of hours ago, before stepping into the chilly morning with its foreboding dark clouds to take an Uber to her office, she'd spent forty-five minutes googling "least painful ways to die." When she realized what she was doing, she slammed her laptop shut.

The dots have disappeared.

Normally, Emma wouldn't assume that the writer behind the dots has also disappeared. But she knows Nick's attention span rarely lasts longer than twenty seconds, which have already passed.

Can u lmk asap? it's urgent. if u can't meet for dinner i can come to u. whenever. She tries to keep her tone as even as possible, masking both her irritation and rising anxiety.

Emma's training has taught her to avoid using hyperbole. So when she says something is urgent, she doesn't mean it's a strong preference, as in "I have to pee urgently or my bladder's gonna burst!" Of course, to do her job effectively, she also has to speak the language of her clients, which means that she has to use Modern American. She learned this the hard way, when she told Little Miss Meme that the intern had done a "very good job" developing a treatment protocol for a client with bipolar disorder, and the young woman had burst into tears. Realizing her mistake, Emma had quickly shifted gears to restore the intern's self-esteem. "Really, Missy, the protocol was *AMAZING*."

Meeting with Nick *is* urgent. Yesterday at the hospital was the closest brush with death Emma has had since developing SOS. She walked right in front of an oncoming ambulance, and froze when she realized what was happening. The driver, understandably assuming she'd get out of the way, didn't course correct until the last moment. His quick reflexes prevented her from being mowed down and killed. She was just sideswiped and ended up with severely bruised ribs.

As luck would have it, the attending ER nurse was the same one who'd treated her for both the stabbing and recent redressing of the festering wound. This time, though, the concern behind their amber contact lenses was tinged with suspicion. "Is there anything you'd like to tell me?" The nurse's eyes were narrowed and their thin lips a straight line as they wrapped thick bandages around Emma's sensitive lower torso, yanking them tightly at the end of each revolution.

"Um, that's kind of tight," Emma gasped. As she struggled to breathe, the glaring fluorescent lights above the stainless steel medical cart holding the roll of bandages seemed to dim. Feeling increasingly lightheaded, she feared she'd topple off the gurney.

"I know it isn't comfortable, but if the bandages aren't tight enough you risk causing serious damage to yourself."

And we certainly wouldn't want that.

"Is there anything else you'd like to tell me? Like how you've been feeling lately? Or if there are any particularly stressful things going on in your life?"

Oh, god. Emma felt the heat rush to her face. They were thinking she's got some sort of mental illness, like a factitious disorder where someone keeps injuring themselves for attention.

She mustered a little laugh, which felt like it cracked her ribs. "I'm not mentally ill, if that's what you're getting at." It wasn't a lie, since SOS isn't classified as a mental illness in the DSM-5-TR, the current edition of the *Diagnostic and Statistical Manual of Mental Disorders*. Not yet, anyway.

The last time she was being treated, Emma had told the nurse what her profession was, making small talk. Maybe they forgot. "I'm a psychologist."

"Exactly." The nurse was looking intently at their handiwork, deftly wrapping more and more gauze around Emma's fragile torso.

"Excuse me?"

"You people aren't exactly the epitome of mental

health."

Thankfully, Emma was able to reassure the nurse that she wasn't in "imminent danger" of hurting herself. Which could be true, depending on how you defined "imminent."

The three dots have returned. Emma is cautiously optimistic.

hey

Exasperated, Emma picks up the phone and dials Nick. "Hey, I've been trying to pin down a plan for us to meet later."

One of the most confounding things about relating to people with ADHD is that it can feel like you're dealing with a moving target. You never know when you'll get an immediate reply, a late reply, or any reply at all. You can never tell whether they're coming or going. Emma isn't surprised that Nick's wife, who'd originally had a slightly higher than average preference for order and control, eventually turned into the embodiment of an organizational drill sergeant. Over a decade of marriage to Nick has radicalized her.

"Sorry, it's a bit chaotic here." Nick is speaking at full volume to be heard over the usual clamor of shouting kids and wife, barking dog, a television, and video game explosions. "Yeah, I can do dinner. Six?"

"That's perfect." Emma states this with a finality, to prevent Nick from perseverating. "See you in a bit!"

As soon as she hangs up, she books an Uber to get her to the restaurant by 6:10 so she'll only have to wait for Nick for ten minutes.

IT'S 6:30, AND NICK IS JUST WALKING THROUGH THE DOOR of The Buttery Nipple, Emma and Nick's usual meeting spot in Concord, which is about halfway between his home in Westford and hers in Arlington. The restaurant is named after one of the cocktails it serves, and it's known for its unusual drinks menu. The dim lights, dark wood paneling, and smell of freshly baked bread give the place a pub-like feel, as do the photos lining the walls—pictures of celebrities raising glasses of vibrant mixed drinks. The bartender, who knows Emma and Nick as regular patrons, often sends over a complimentary cocktail at the end of their meal.

"Hey, sorry," Nick says absentmindedly, making the last quick strides to the table through the crowded room. "Traffic was terrible."

No more terrible than it always is at this time of day, but whatever.

He takes off his navy blue track jacket, which is damp and beaded from the drizzle preceding an impending storm, and hangs it on the back of his chair. Seating himself across from Emma, he picks up the drinks menu and scans it. "I think I'll go for a Red-Headed Slut. I haven't had one of those in a while. What're you having?"

As Nick looks up at Emma, his grin fades. "Holy *shit*, Em. What the *hell* is going on with you? Last time I saw you, you already looked pretty rough around the edges. But now—" He seems at a loss for words as his eyes search Emma's face and body, taking in her deathly pallor, unwashed hair—it's been impossible to shower properly with all the aches and wrappings—neck brace, and bandages. Not to mention her unnatural posture, as she leans slightly askew to avoid pinching a rib. She must look like the walking dead. Which she essentially is.

Emma doesn't waste any time. "Nick, I need you to do something. For me. Not for Dad, not for the family, but for me." She leans forward, to the best of her ability, looking at her brother intently.

"Yeah, all right. Are you going to tell me what's going on?"

The server appears, a twenty-something hipster with low-rise skinny jeans, a black studded belt, and a neck tattoo that says "straight edge." With his too-perfect posture and self-satisfied sneer, his preferred drink would surely be the virgin Furious Nun. His fitted black T-shirt sports the motto of the restaurant, *We'll drown your sorrows!*, over a cartoon of a giant martini glass with a patron's head being forcibly held under the liquid, bubbles erupting from his screaming mouth. Emma has never found the image funny, and she's especially put off by it now.

"What can I get you?" he asks, looking down his nose at Emma and Nick. It's odd how mere strangers can make you feel less-than, with nothing more than a tilt of their chin. So much of Emma's work is helping people recognize their inherent worth so they're not so affected by the shaming stories others tell them about themselves. Stories that are always ultimately about the storyteller anyway.

Nick orders his Red-Headed Slut. Emma has stopped drinking alcohol since developing SOS, not wanting to risk having impaired impulse control. "I'll have a virgin Wet Fart."

As soon as the server leaves, Emma cuts to the chase. "I need you to talk to Dad, and to reconcile with him." She puts her hand up, palm facing out, as her brother opens his mouth to object. "I'm well aware of how you feel about this. But I'm asking you, again. For me. *Please.*"

"What in the hell is going on, Em? You show up looking like you've been in a plane crash, and you don't explain why. Then, after a GAZILLION times of me telling you that reconciling with Dad is a THOUSAND percent non-negotiable, you come back with it!"

Nick has an impressive command of Modern American.

"Nick, time is running out. If you don't—"

"I know, I get it, Dad's going to die, and—"

"Dad's not the only one who's going to die," she cuts in.

It just came out. Emma is mute, stunned.

Nick's jaw has dropped and he's looking at his sister like her face is a jigsaw puzzle he's trying to piece together. "What are you trying to say?"

Not wanting to lie, but not ready to speak the truth, Emma remains silent. She's suddenly aware of the ambient hum of clinking dinnerware, the jazz piano soundtrack, and the buzz of conversational voices occasionally punctuated by a loud laugh.

"Are you sick, Em?"

Emma's eyes burn, and tears spill over.

"Oh my god. What is it? Is it cancer?"

Emma has been trying to protect Nick from the stress of knowing about her condition. Now that she's come out with the truth, though, she realizes she's also been trying to protect herself. Somehow, not sharing a painful reality makes it feel less real.

Wiping her eyes, she takes a deep breath. "Look, Nick. What I'm about to tell you is probably going to sound… pretty far-fetched. So please just suspend disbelief, at least till I'm done. And it goes without saying, but this stays between us."

For the next hour, over the course of dinner and another round of drinks, Emma walks Nick through all the events of the past three weeks. She doesn't leave out a single detail. Nick has listened as though he's doubled down on his Ritalin, and he looks at her in concern, but with a hint of incredulity.

"So you're saying that this condition, this SOS, is going to make you kill yourself if I don't reconcile with Dad?"

Put that way, the SOS does sound a bit too convenient.

"Um, yeah. Well, not exactly. I mean, I don't know if it'll work. All I know is what I told you, and what you read yourself in the CouchGPT discussion I just showed you. That unresolved relationship issues are listed as the top potential cause of SOS."

"Look, Em. I know I don't have to tell you that this is bonkers. It makes no sense. You're the shrink. You of all people should know that."

"You think I *don't?*" Emma's mini-outburst tugs at her ribs and she inhales sharply, then takes loud, deep breaths to cope with the pain.

Nick's face softens at the sight of her. "Okay. All right. I'll do it. I mean, this really is nuts. But that doesn't mean it's not true. And even if there's just a five percent chance this gets you out of whatever hole it is you slid down, then of course I'll do it."

The rush of gratitude and love that fills Emma's heart as she looks at her younger brother almost washes away her misery.

"But why didn't you tell me this before? It's pretty unreasonable to keep the fact that you're at high risk of killing yourself a secret. Especially from me."

Emma had never questioned her decision to hide her deadly secret from Nick, or from anyone else who could help her. It just felt like the right thing to do, to not burden them. Maybe she needs to start making more of an effort to practice what she preaches.

"I'm sorry. I'll be more open with you moving forward. I promise." Emma gives Nick the answer he needs, rather than the one he asked for.

Nick nods. "There's just one thing. You showed me the AI discussion on SOS and the one on Dr. Müller. Were there any others?"

"No, it was just those two."

"So that hyperlink about fatalities didn't open up a different one?"

Hyperlink?

"Um, what link?" Emma's stomach flutters. She unlocks her phone to pull up the discussion and hands it to her brother.

After a few seconds of scrolling, Nick leans across the table to show her. "Here."

Because the rate of known <u>fatalities</u> from SOS is 94%, it's not possible to determine whether increasing suicidal impulsivity or madness is to blame for most deaths.

"I must have missed it," Emma says meekly.

Nick sits back in his chair and taps the link. "It goes to an obscure page on the Medizinische Universität Wien website. Looks like it hasn't been updated in forever. Hang on, lemme do translate." He taps the screen a few times. "'Kay. Got it. So it's an article written by that doctor, Müller, called 'The Curious Case of Anan O.'"

Nick reads aloud: "Of the 197 individuals known to have died as a result of SOS, the longest recorded duration before the person took their life was fifty-three days. However, the individual in question, to whom I'll refer as Anan O., would likely have died sooner had he and his family not undertaken heroic efforts to keep him alive. He was confined to his room while a cure was sought. The room, which was locked from the outside, had padded walls and was devoid of furniture, except for a bare mattress on the floor, and the windows were barred. Food, served on paper plates and without utensils, was delivered through a slat in the door, as were sponges with which he bathed. Anan O. remained naked, to prevent him from hanging himself with his clothing, and a bucket was used to collect his excrement, to prevent him from accessing running water and drowning himself. The only hard object allowed in his room was a rounded white noise machine, to help distract him from the voice of his abusive dead uncle, which had started looping in his head about two weeks after the development of his condition."

Can unresolved relationship issues involve people who are deceased?

"Anan O. nevertheless managed to kill himself. Fifty-three days after developing SOS, he pressed his face against a thickly padded wall and held it there until he suffocated to death. All other known SOS fatalities occurred within thirty-seven days of the onset of the condition. It is thus logical to assume that the average SOS sufferer will die within five weeks."

Nick looks up from his phone and locks eyes with Emma. They're both thinking the same thing. Emma has seventeen days to find a cure.

Nick's face is pale. "Let's do this."

Emma pulls out her phone to let her father know that Nick will be over shortly, but pauses as the purse-lipped server approaches with the bill and two drinks. "One Shit on the Grass, and one virgin Brain Hemorrhage, on the house." Emma grimaces.

As soon as the server is out of earshot, she dials Warmer Planet. Nick looks at her expectantly.

"Hi, Amala. It's Emma Parkland. Can you put me through to—" Emma pauses as the nurse cuts in, the woman's usually mellow voice shrill.

Her mouth agape and eyes bulging, Emma lets her phone drop to the floor before Amala has finished talking.

"Em? What is it?" Nick's voice is tight.

"It's Dad," Emma whispers hoarsely. "He's in a coma."

18

Earworm

Day 20: Thursday

"**D**ad's in a *coma*? When did it happen? What does this mean?" Nick is tapping his glass straw impatiently on the table, as Emma stares catatonically into the space behind him. "What exactly did the nurse say?"

Emma feels like she's left her body and is floating above it, looking through a muddied piece of film, the edges of her vision oddly bent, like a convex mirror. Despite Nick's agitation, his words seem slowed and his voice sounds muffled, as though he's speaking into an empty toilet paper tube whose other end is covered. It's like she and Nick are wrapped in a timeless, soundless bubble.

"Another round of Blood Clots, on me!" Howls of laughter and applause from the table next to them break through Emma's dissociative trance.

"It happened this evening. Warmer Planet had been trying to reach me, but my phone's been off." Emma's voice is robotic as she continues to stare past Nick.

"Oh, shit. *Shit*. Poor Dad." Nick doesn't sound like

someone who cut his father out of his life five years ago. "And what about you? What are we going to do about you?"

We. Even in her daze, Emma is moved by Nick's use of the first-person plural. She feels less alone than she has since this whole mess started. What's wrong with her that she didn't reach out to him sooner?

"Apparently it happens sometimes in cases like Dad's." Returning to her senses, Emma shifts her gaze to look at her brother. "Amala, the nurse, said that there's no saying whether he'll come out of it, or when. It could be days or weeks. Or, if the cancer progresses quickly—which she said often happens once someone's in a coma—he could die without ever regaining consciousness."

"Shit, Em." Nick seems at a loss for anything else to say. Then: "Wait. I remember this documentary, about a team of doctors who were experimenting with unconventional methods for treating people in comas. They took these patients who were supposedly in a permanent vegetative state and treated them with things like playing their favorite music and giving them daily infusions of some mix of medications and nutrients… I don't remember all of it, but a lot of the patients woke up. I'll do some research."

Even the odds of Müller curing her seem higher.

"And anyway," Nick continues, "Müller's thirty-seven-day life expectancy estimate is just an estimate. It's possible that a lot of the unreported victims lasted longer than that before killing themselves."

Seeing Emma's expression, Nick realizes his slipup. "Um, and obviously a lot more people must have gotten cured and just never realized that they'd had SOS."

"Right." Emma's voice is flat. Her situation is getting more hopeless by the minute. "But Müller's the leading authority on SOS so it wouldn't be very smart of us not to take his thirty-seven-day calculation seriously."

Nick's face falls. "Yeah, okay. You're right. All the more reason to find a way to wake Dad up. I know it seems like a long shot, but I'm on it. I think me reconciling with him has a way better chance of curing you than Müller, who seems like he's some sort of quack."

It's all too much to take in. Suddenly bone-tired, Emma lets Nick know she has to get going and calls an Uber. Nick waits with her for her ride to arrive, and then he bids her goodbye, giving her an unusually long hug and making her promise to call him "before doing anything stupid."

The Uber is an inexcusably large black SUV, which smells like a fast food joint, no doubt due to the half-eaten, partially rewrapped Sausage McMuffin and empty hash browns wrapper on the passenger seat. After a brief exchange with the driver about practicalities, Emma leans back against the headrest. Judging from his accent, the driver is from Eastern Europe, for which Emma is grateful. He'll probably be comfortable in shared silence and not feel the need to fill the space with idle chatter.

Emma is about to ask the driver to turn the radio off when she realizes that the annoying song she wants to end is actually playing inside her head.

Oh, I'd love to be an Oscar Mayer Wiener, that is what I'd truly like to be-ee-ee…

The maniacal jingle fills Emma's auditory space as though it's a concert hall.

'Cause if I were an Oscar Mayer Wiener, everyone would be in love with me!

With a start, Emma becomes aware that the insidious tune has been looping in her skull off and on for days, since an ad for a cooking video on how to bake an Easter ham popped up after she'd typed in a search for "how to kill yourself by sticking your head in the oven." Never one to fall prey to earworms, Emma has always appreciated having what seems like a special immunity to an irksome and potentially debilitating condition. Clearly, things have changed.

She once had a client with a ruinous earworm, a middle-aged man who was a dead ringer for Wallace Shawn, who played the Grand Nagus in *Star Trek: Deep Space Nine* and Dr. John Sturgis in *Young Sheldon*. The opening notes of Beethoven's Fifth Symphony—*da da da DA, da da da DA*—had been stuck in his head for eight years. But the worst part was that the music—which always gave him a fright—would get triggered by random experiences, like opening a wedding invitation or entering a conference room for a board meeting or being handed the bill at the end of a dinner date. Those two musical phrases became the soundtrack to his life, turning it into a veritable horror movie.

And what did Nick read from the CouchGPT link, about the abusive dead uncle's voice looping in Anan O.'s mind? Could this hideous jingle be Emma's version of what happened to him?

Emma leans her forehead against the rain-streaked window and looks out into the cold, starless spring night. Her heart is heavy with grief, knowing she may never speak with her father again. The last time she saw him, two weeks ago, he'd been weepy from the aching loneliness from having lost all connection with his only son and grandchildren. He was ravaged by sorrow, repentant but with nobody who could offer him the forgiveness he needed. He's grown so much, relationally and emotionally, that him dying in such a desperate state seems like an injustice.

She wishes, for the umpteenth time, that Nick would see the difference between Dad 2.0 and the capricious man who raised them. Even when their father's unfortunate behaviors traumatized Nick and his family five years ago, those actions had been a far cry from the kinds of things he used to do when she and Nick were growing up. In fact, it's likely that the more recent trauma brought to the surface Nick's deeper anger over his childhood traumas at his father's hands. If their father wakes up, Nick's going to need to process this older anger in order to truly reconcile with him.

Emma can understand Nick's anger at their father's unskilled parenting. Anger is the normal emotional response to witnessing injustice, unfair treatment, toward yourself or others. She'd be angry, too, in his circumstances. The only reason she hasn't had much anger of her own is because her focus on protecting her little brother detached her, to some degree, from her own personal feelings of distress.

Hopefully, Nick will one day accept that their father, like everyone, did the best he could, given who he is. Nobody can be different than who and how they are, because each individual is nothing more nor less than the hardwiring and biology they're born with plus every experience they've had.

But how many times has she had the same, frustrating conversation with Nick about this topic? Just a couple of months ago, they had a fraught exchange over dinner at her house, where Nick essentially accused her of condoning violence.

"So according to your logic, Dad isn't responsible for all the selfish, narcissistic crap he pulled. Like the drinking and reckless driving that could've killed us, and other people. You're basically excusing abuse."

"Nick, of course I'm not saying that. This is an explanation, not an excuse. Dad *was* selfish and narcissistic. I'm just saying that these egotistical tendencies were all part of the same personality constellation he inherited from his body, mind, and environment. He—"

"Remember Brad? From Little League? His father grew up in foster care, dirt poor. He worked his butt off and ended up with a successful business and was twice the father Dad could ever hope to be. Why do you always give Dad a free pass to shirk responsibility?"

"I'm not saying Dad isn't responsible for his actions. But your comparison doesn't make sense. Maybe Brad's father didn't have the same psychological vulnerabilities as Dad. Or maybe he had a positive role model that Dad didn't. There are literally countless factors that influence people so that their lives go in one direction or another."

"So you're saying it's not Dad's fault he did what he did. Hell, why not just throw open the doors to all the prisons, while you're at it?"

"What I'm saying is that we can hold people accountable for their harmful behaviors while honoring their dignity, staying connected to our compassion. And understanding *why* people do the harmful things they do is what enables us to do this."

As she gazes out the window of the SUV, the streaks of rain intermittently illuminated by passing streetlights, Emma is transported back to 1986, when Nick was just nine and she was eleven.

The children were in the bed of the family's blue-paneled Ford pickup truck, on the way home after visiting Dell's Vineyard, which was a forty-minute drive away. Her father used to go to Dell's every few months to pick up his supply of wholesale wine to resell at their orchard. He'd also spend a couple of hours sampling the wines and catching up with the owner, Joe Dell.

It was a crisp autumn day, the cloudless sky an intense cobalt blue. The New England foliage was at its peak, a natural display so spectacular as to attract tourists from all over the world. The two-lane, tree-lined Route 2 was like a tunnel through arches of gold, crimson, pink, and fiery orange. Emma closed her eyes to savor the sweet scent of decaying leaves, mingled with the salty ocean breeze and the tang of gasoline.

Once they reached a section of the road that didn't have much traffic, their father sped up and intentionally zigzagged, sending the children into fits of laughter as they slid from side to side across the bed of the truck. Watching them in the rearview mirror, he shared their humor.

Soon, though, he was laughing even harder than they were, and rounding turns so fast that the children were flung against the sides of the truck. One such turn sent Emma hurtling across the bed into Nick, her weight adding to the pressure that slammed him into the sideboard. Nick screamed as his ribs hit the side and his shoulder twisted from trying to brace himself against the impact. Emma's heart clenched, and her throat tightened as she reached out to grab him.

"Stop!" Emma shouted as loud as she could to cut through the whipping wind. But it was to no avail. Her father had turned the radio to full volume, and he was singing along with it, drumming his hands on the steering wheel, driving faster and faster.

Emma gripped the side of the truck with her arms protectively around Nick, to shield him from more hits. He was crying, hysterically begging her to make their father stop. But all she could do was try to make sure her little brother—and she, herself—didn't get hurled against a sideboard, hit by a wine crate, or tossed out of the truck.

When they finally pulled into their driveway, Emma's father purposely speeding up to its end and then slamming the brake so the children would lunge forward, Emma and Nick were unmoving except for their trembling limbs and dripping tears. Their father turned off the music and hopped out of the truck, striding around to the back to collect the wine crates.

Flipping down the tailgate, he caught his breath at the sight of his whimpering, quivering children. "Heyyyyyyy, kiddos." His voice was softer than usual. He looked at them intently, as though trying to figure out how to respond to their disheveled and distressed state. "What's going on here?"

The children didn't answer.

"You guys nauseous?" He chuckled, apparently finding the idea that they might be ill funny. "Your tummies get a little topsy-turvy?"

Emma glared at her father, who seemed to finally start to realize that the children weren't simply queasy. A realization that lasted as long as his attention span, which was about fifteen seconds.

"Look, kiddos." He frowned in mock seriousness. "I know *just* the thing to cheer you up, warm you up, and"—he paused for effect, making a drum roll in the air—"fatten you up! Pizza! Your favorite!" Laughing, he leaned into the truck and started pinching the children on their cheeks and legs. "Gotta put some meat on those bones!"

Nick and Emma eventually gave in to his charm, which was impossible to resist for very long, and their father reached into the truck to heave them up and plop them down on the ground like he always did, starting with Emma. As she was lifted in the air, Emma caught wind of his breath and the recent ordeal suddenly made sense. Alcohol. Her father wasn't drunk, but neither was he sober.

As he reached for Nick, the boy scurried back to cower in the far corner of the truck and started bawling. Cradling his left arm in his right one, Nick refused to let their father touch him. Several minutes passed, and when their father finally got close enough to inspect the limp arm, he assured Nick it would be better in the morning. It wasn't. And by the time Nick was taken to the hospital, almost a week later, his broken shoulder and humerus were permanently misaligned.

After dinner that night, Emma headed to the barn, where she flipped on the light to see Blossom lying on his side in the thick hay. The pig raised his large head and made happy grunting sounds, his thin tail swishing across the ground. Emma entered the pen and knelt down next to him, unfolding the napkin in which she'd smuggled two slices of pizza. Blossom hefted his huge body upright and immediately began devouring the food, his tail flailing ever faster.

Nothing made Emma's heart sing more than seeing her beloved companion so happy. It was a sign of true friendship, the ability to share in another's joy. She stayed kneeling, smiling next to the pig as he enthusiastically gobbled down the final piece of crust.

As soon as he'd finished, Blossom turned his head to face her. His tail stopped wagging, and he made the special little grunts that signaled he was trying to comfort her. He sat down and pressed his nose into her chest, still grunting, nudging her softly.

Somehow, Blossom was always able to sense Emma's feelings. He seemed to know when she needed a nuzzle, a murmur, the warm, solid body of a friend. Blossom was the only individual in her life who truly understood her, who didn't project onto her what he thought she should feel, or what he wanted her to feel. He didn't judge her for her sadness or fear or confusion. He saw her, and accepted her, for who she was. He loved her.

THE UBER SLOWS TO A STOP IN FRONT OF EMMA'S HOUSE. Pulling her keys from her bag, Emma thanks the driver. He gives her a nod as he picks up his leftover sandwich and takes an enormous bite.

Oh, I wish I were an Oscar Mayer Wiener, that is what I'd truly like to be-ee-ee. 'Cause if I were an Oscar Mayer Wiener, everyone would be in love with me!

19

Making the Connection

"You were right." With his clean-shaven face, square jaw, and chiseled features, Ricardo looks as statuesque as ever this morning. "Volunteering—especially doing something hands-on— was definitely a powerful experience." He's leaning back on the sofa, his long arms extended across its back, while he crosses and uncrosses his legs. His upper and lower body seem to be telling different stories.

Emma takes a sip of coffee and stifles a yawn, doing her best to stay focused on her client. Her eyes are sandy and her brain fog feels more like brain clog. After the shocking news yesterday evening about her father's coma, squashing her hopes of curing her SOS, she spent most of the night lying awake, her thoughts jumping between trying to figure out how to save herself and devising a plan to kill herself.

"I wasn't going to do it. I mean, I was open to the idea when you brought it up, but then later I was like, I want no part of the activism world again, full of hypocrites who say they're all about integrity but then turn on their own colleagues." A shadow passes over Ricardo's face as he remembers the betrayal of his boss, Kaleem, that catapulted him into his depression. "Fuck that."

The expletive breaks through Emma's mind-wandering. "Um, so, you feel conflicted about doing the volunteering. I get it. What about giving it a try anyway?"

Ricardo looks pointedly at Emma, his dark eyes squinting. "I *did* give it a try. That's what I've been telling you." His tone isn't quite peeved, but neither is it not.

He scans Emma from head to toe, and then back up again. Suddenly self-conscious under the scrutiny of this well-groomed man, Emma instinctively raises her hand to straighten the hair clip she's started using to manage her unwashed hair, and smooths her wrinkled linen pants. There's not much she can do about the rest of her battered appearance.

"Right, right. I heard that, sorry. I'm just a little under the weather today." Emma gives Ricardo what she hopes is a reassuring smile, and takes a gulp of coffee out of the giant thermos she's started lugging around with her. Her face heats up as she feels a stream of the liquid make its way down her chin and into her neck brace, where it pools uncomfortably against her sticky skin before continuing down, to stain the top of her white linen blouse.

Ricardo makes a point of not looking at her as she wipes her face and shirt, and this small act of pity only embarrasses her further.

"The only place I found where I could volunteer right away was an animal shelter, in Dorchester. Mostly for dogs, but they had some cats. I went on Saturday, the day after our last session."

Ricardo recrosses his legs.

"Anyway, all they needed help with was walking the dogs. But it was really rewarding. To see the direct effects of my helping… I haven't felt that way in a long time. Those dogs were so desperate for any kind of attention, and so grateful to be out of those damn crates they spend their lives in. I wanted to take them all home with me." Ricardo no longer looks like the depressed, defeated misanthrope he'd seemed just two weeks ago.

"Ricardo, I'm thrilled to hear this, and I hope you're proud of yourself. This is a pretty big step for you to take." Emma has become more animated, naturally calibrating her mannerisms to match Ricardo's. Hopefully he feels like she's paying closer attention to him, which she's trying her best to do.

Ricardo continues as though he hasn't heard her. "You were also right about my need to be around like-minded people. I had no idea how much I'd been missing that."

Suddenly, there's a loud bang outside the window behind Ricardo, and Emma jumps and lets out a scream.

Ricardo's eyes bulge and he swings around to see if there's a shooter or bomb behind him.

A rusty silver Honda pulls out of a parking spot in front of the office and sputters down the street, lurching forward and backfiring as it crawls away.

Ricardo turns back around. "Emma? Are you okay?" Both client and therapist know that Emma's reaction was not appropriate.

"Yes, yes, sorry. Maybe it's time to cut back." Emma

chuckles and taps her bloated, one-gallon thermos, which seems to make Ricardo feel even more disturbed.

"Anyway," Ricardo continues, "I met this woman, another volunteer. Freya. She was so… driven. Committed. Caring. She's also a lawyer, like me, if you can believe it. And she used to work for Oxfam, too, but before I worked there. Now she's working for an animal rights organization that campaigns against factory farming."

Oh, I'd love to be an Oscar Mayer Wiener…

Oh. No.

That is what I'd truly like to be-ee-ee.

No. No no no no no no no…

Aghast, Emma pushes out of her mind the image of Wallace Shawn, his arms waving wildly over his head like a conductor directing an orchestra as he belts out the *da da da DA!* of Beethoven's Fifth.

What if Emma's earworm becomes Wallace-esque, triggered by random events and becoming the soundtrack to *her* life, like it had for her client, turning it into a twisted parody?

"… and over dinner at the Hungry Herbivore she told me why she thinks her work on factory farming is critical for human and environmental rights, not just animal rights."

Emma hopes that whatever she's just missed isn't essential for therapy today. The political nature of the conversation is adding a layer of complexity that her brain can't handle at the moment.

"So how are you feeling now that you have this new connection with Freda?"

"*Freya.*" Ricardo frowns and wrinkles his nose. He looks

at the stain on Emma's shirt and then at the jug of coffee.

"Freya. Right. Sorry."

"How do I feel? I feel like a selfish, ignorant asshole. I don't think I've ever felt so bad about myself in my entire life."

What? Emma definitely didn't see this coming.

"I thought you were feeling reinspired?"

"I was, at first. When I was blissfully ignorant and I thought I was some kind of hero, walking homeless dogs. I had no clue what a shitshow this world is for animals—a shitshow I directly participated in my whole life because I somehow never made the connection between my taquitos and animals' lives. Do you have any *idea* what they do to farm animals? They're basically tortured from the moment they're born. About 130 *billion* of them a year, if you include fish. And why? Not because we *need* to eat them. But just so we can have our hamburgers and hot dogs."

'Cause if I were an Oscar Mayer Wiener…

Stop!

"That's what I said, when Freya first started telling me about all this. I know it's hard to hear, Emma."

Oh, no. Emma hadn't realized she'd vocalized her reaction to the earworm. "I can imagine how distressing it must be to learn about these things. It sounds, though, like maybe you've found a new cause. Something you can really get behind."

Slumping forward, Ricardo lets out a sigh. "I… don't know. It was bad enough thinking about all the poverty and wars and climate disasters. But this"—his eyes are moist—"this is beyond anything I've ever seen. The extent of the suffering of these an—" Ricardo chokes on the word and lowers his head.

Emma waits, giving him space to feel and express his sadness. Tears that are held back tend to find their way out at some point. And the longer they're kept in, the harder it usually is to connect them with, and heal, the original trigger.

"It was almost better to feel disconnected, like I was before, when I was totally shut down. I mean, I *still* feel disconnected in a lot of ways. But now I also feel like I'm too connected. Too open. Raw."

Her heart full, Emma's tone is soft. "I know it's hard. The fact that you've been able to feel motivated and engaged with like-minded people and a cause is a good sign. The key, and the challenge, is finding the sweet spot. It's being able to, as the psychotherapist Terrence Real says, have boundaries that allow you to be both connected *and* protected."

Ricardo looks toward the ceiling, seeming to consider Emma's words, before continuing. "Did you know that cows form lifelong relationships with other cows, and also with people? And that pigs are more intelligent than dogs?"

Oh, I'm glad I'm not an Oscar Mayer Wiener. That is what I'd never want to be-ee-ee…

The earworm is too much. Emma starts to cry.

"I didn't think you'd be so sensitive about this issue, Emma. It's actually comforting to know you care so much about animals, too."

"I have a cat," Emma manages, sounding ridiculous even to herself.

Ricardo is unfazed. "I'm such a jerk. I used to tease

my vegan cousin, just for being vegan. And worse, I'm a hypocrite. I, of all people, should have known better. How is it that I never made the connection? All my years of talking about how 'every' life matters. Do animals not have lives that matter? And when I think about all the time I spent trying to get people to understand the danger of thinking in moral categories—some people we bomb, some we save… What about the fact that some animals we eat, some we love? The exact same mentality that makes us exploit humans makes us exploit animals. How did I not see what was right in front of me?"

Before Emma can respond, Ricardo has cocked his head and is facing the wall. He holds up a finger, as though listening for something.

"Jeez, I must be losing it," he says slowly. "I could've sworn I heard the Oscar Mayer Wiener jingle."

***

Sitting at her desk after Ricardo has left, Emma writes a note to herself to assess him for suicidality during their next session. If she's still alive.

A knock on the door interrupts her descent down the morbid slippery slope she's started on. "Hey, you!" Shana pokes her head in, her reading glasses hanging from an amber-beaded chain that matches her gold cardigan and slacks. The fragrance of her essential oil blend follows her into the office as she steps through the door. "I just wanted to pop by and say 'hey,' and see if I could borrow a stapler."

"Hey. Sure." Emma lets out a little yelp of pain as

she leans forward to open the drawer where she keeps the device.

"Whoa, someone is *not* looking so good. You doing all right, Em? I thought it was just a fender bender you'd had, and you just needed to catch up on some sleep."

"It was, but you know how it is. Especially when you're pushing fifty. Things don't heal the way they used to." Emma gives Shana what she hopes looks like the knowing grin of a middle-aged woman.

"Oh, I *do* get that!" Shana chuckles. Thankfully, she's bought Emma's story. Which is, technically, true. "Still." Shana's smile has faded. "You gotta start taking care of yourself like you tell all your clients to do. I mean it. I'm starting to worry about you."

"Yes, doctor. I promise." Emma puts as much enthusiasm into her voice as she can muster.

Appeased for now, Shana shifts gears. "By the way, I wanted to let you know that Steve, your health anxiety guy? He's in good hands, and he's gonna be just fine."

Emma looks at Shana quizzically. After just eight days, how could the psychiatrist possibly know that?

Shana laughs. "See, I got this little secret. The secret ingredient in my special therapeutic sauce." Her tone is conspiratorial. "I send my tough cases to the Program. It's not well known and it's pretty, um, alternative. But it works. They can cure *anything*. Anorexia, rosacea, alien hand syndrome, baldness, chronic suicidal ideation, you name it."

Suicidal ideation?

"How on earth… I mean, what's the catch?"

"There is no catch. As long as you can pay—it's not

cheap, lemme tell you—and as long as you're over eighteen, you can enroll. Hell, I even did it myself. And I've got a one hundred percent success rate with the clients I've sent."

"Um, wow. I, uh, know someone who might be a good candidate. What's the name of the program?"

"The Program. That's the name. Here." Shana grabs a pad of paper and pen off Emma's desk and scribbles down the website. "Tell your client they won't be disappointed."

Consider it done.

20

Compassion-Forward

Day 24: Monday

"**S***hhhh*! People can hear you!"

Silence reigns for a few seconds before the hysterical giggles resume. Emma opens her office door, to let the couple in the waiting room know it's time for their session. Their heads are together and they're speaking in loud whispers, punctuated by snorts of laughter, like children sharing a private joke.

"Oh, hi, Emma." Jenna's eyes are bright and she seems like she'd forgotten where she was. "We didn't realize what time it was." She looks like she's about to burst into laughter as she hoists herself up with her crutches. Alexander remains seated, looking at his bare feet, which are next to his unlaced sneakers and balled up socks. A crooked smile on his face, he pokes the top of a foot and wiggles his toes, snickering. He doesn't seem to realize that playtime has ended.

Emma walks back into the office with Jenna in tow. The women make casual conversation as they wait for Alexander to put his shoes back on and come join them for their Monday morning session.

Listening to Jenna's chitchat, Emma can't tell if there's subtext that could be useful for their work today, and she doesn't have the energy to try. One of the most upsetting side effects of SOS is her waning ability to hone in on her clients' inner experiences. Usually, her relational superpower enables her to dig deeply and focus sharply. Now, it feels impossible to pay attention in any conversation that's not critically important. Maybe this is what life is always like for people with ADHD.

As Jenna details the trials and tribulations of giving a bath to her two-year-old niece, who she and Alexander babysat over the weekend, Emma's wandering mind returns to Friday, when she'd pulled up theprogramwillsaveyou.com as soon as Shana had left her office.

The Program's methodology is based on a simple formula, the Four Rs: Recovery = Release + Reconfigure + Receive. This method uses the age-old practice of homeopathy, but with unique modifications. The Program guides clients through a series of customized exercises and movements that open their minds and reconfigure their fascia. So the custom-made homeopathic tincture, when finally ingested, resonates with the new molecular configuration of the client's body. Essentially, the Program prepares the client's body to receive a healing tincture that it normally would not recognize as healing. Rather than reject the tincture as a foreign agent that the body needs to protect itself against, it welcomes it and allows it to work its magic.

Emma had immediately called the Program to enroll, and was told she could start the next day, even though it was Saturday. Apparently, when the symptoms have been present for only a short time—twenty days, in her case—the Program takes about a week. Given that the average life expectancy of an SOS sufferer is thirty-seven days, the Program should cure her with ten days to spare. This was especially good to hear, since Nick had just told her that the claims of being able to wake people from comas turned out to be fabricated, leaving little hope for a reconciliation.

The consultant she spoke with told her that the first day involves a physical examination, including a full blood workup, and a psychological evaluation. The client is then assigned a variety of exercises that are to be done on site for three hours every day, between 6:00 and 9:00 a.m. Five days later, more blood is drawn, and the custom tincture, sometimes referred to as an "elixir," is created. The client takes the tincture, which can take up to three days to have an effect, while continuing to do their daily exercises.

Jenna's sneeze snaps Emma out of her reverie. The woman has been talking for five minutes, and there's still no sign of Alexander except for stray whispers and chuckles coming from outside the office. Emma is about to get up and see what's going on when Jenna calls out. "Alexander! We're waiting for you!" She looks at Emma apologetically, like a parent whose child has made an adorable mess eating blueberry pie.

Alexander traipses into the office, barefoot and with empty shoes in hand. He's apparently left his crumpled socks on the floor of the waiting room—his signature mess, according to his wife. Unlike last week, he doesn't look like he's trying to dress to impress. He's back in his usual getup of mismatched wrinkled clothes, a cluster of his fine hair standing impossibly upright and askew on top of his head. He takes his usual spot on the sofa.

Emma's temples suddenly throb and she takes a sip of coffee, hoping the warm liquid will distract her from the pain and soothe her rapidly fraying nerves. She tries to ignore Alexander's bare feet rubbing against her carpet, toes clenching and unclenching the thick plush material.

Clearly things have changed since Alexander and Jenna's last session, when Jenna said she was burned out and possibly going to leave him. The two of them are sitting side by side on the sage green sofa, their elbows and knees touching. Jenna's dark, almond eyes are twinkling and Alexander looks like a boy who's about to discuss his exceptional report card.

"From the looks of it, things have changed since we last talked. Alexander, why don't we start with you. How are you?"

Alexander looks at Jenna questioningly. Like many men, especially those with neurodivergent brains, Alexander has outsourced his self-awareness to his wife.

"We've had a really good week," Jenna answers. "We had a breakthrough."

"That's wonderful to hear." Emma turns back to Alexander. "Alexander, do you want to tell me what happened?"

Alexander looks at Jenna again. This time, Jenna doesn't return his gaze and knows better than to answer for him.

"Um, okay." Alexander is hesitant, blinking, as though he's trying to remember disparate details of an event that took place years ago. He directs his answer to the middle of the room, the space between the people occupying it, rather than to the people themselves. "Latesha's girlfriend was going on and on and on about her belly button lint collection. I was really bored and after I was in the bathroom and Jenna freaked out, we learned about Arby."

How badly has Emma's brain degenerated in the past three weeks?

"Um, Latesha? Who's Latesha?"

"Camille's girlfriend." Alexander states this as though it should be obvious.

"And Camille is…?"

"*Latesha's* girlfriend." Alexander says this in a sing-song voice, and looks disgustedly at Emma, like he can't comprehend her ineptitude.

"Latesha's my best friend from college," Jenna offers. "We'd made plans months ago to meet her and Camille when they're in town. So we had dinner with them last week."

Alexander gives Emma a "There. *See?*" look, as if Jenna just had to spell something out for a three-year-old.

"So what happened at dinner, Alexander?"

"I told you. She was really mad, and they were wondering what happened for the forty minutes and that's why we had the fight."

"'She' being Jenna?"

"Yeah, Jenna. Jenna was really mad."

"C'mon, Middle Man," Jenna cuts in genially. Turning to Emma she adds, "I call him 'Middle Man' when he pieces the middle of multiple sentences together. There's no beginning or end, and it can get really confusing."

She chuckles. Her relational gallows humor is one of her most important coping mechanisms.

"I can't really remember everything that happened." Alexander addresses Jenna now. "You know I have a bad memory for these things." These things, Emma knows from prior conversations, are social interactions and emotional conversations. Both of which apparently took place.

"So, shortly into dinner, Alexander got up from his seat, without saying a word, and walked off. He came back forty minutes later and sat back down, as if nothing had happened." Everyone seems to be in agreement that Jenna's going to have to do the explaining. "I was furious. I was really embarrassed, and worried that my friends were offended. When we got back home, we had a huge fight."

Alexander's little toes have gone into overdrive.

"Alexander told me he'd been bored and had hidden in the bathroom where he played on his phone. I couldn't believe he'd be so rude. But then"—Jenna's eyes redden—"then he showed me the puncture wounds on his thigh, where he'd been stabbing himself under the table with his fork so he could tolerate the boredom of having to listen to Camille's story about her six-year hobby of collecting lint from her navel. And that changed everything for us."

Startled by the admission that Alexander had harmed himself, Emma wonders if he might be suicidal. But she quickly dismisses the idea, because people who engage in self-harming behaviors are usually doing so in order to cope with life, not end it.

"Anyway, it turns out that Alexander doesn't feel boredom like I do."

"I'd rather be dead than bored," Alexander interjects.

At the thought of Alexander fanatically jabbing himself to death with a fork, his odd tuft of upright hair undulating softly, Emma looks away, feeling like she's about to have another hallucination.

"I googled it. And did you know there are *five* different types of boredom?" Jenna is in her element: learning, teaching, and healing. She could have been a therapist. "One type, called reactive boredom, is so painful it's almost intolerable, and it's what people with ADHD often have."

"Arby!" Alexander laughs impishly.

Her brows raised and eyes uncomprehending, Emma looks at Jenna.

"RB is for reactive boredom. We decided to name this part of Alexander's personality 'Arby.' So whenever he's bored, or at risk of getting bored, we have a way to talk about it."

Emma feels pride in and for this couple, who always seem to find their way back to each other, through all the muddy quagmires they've had to traverse. They really do put their therapy learnings into practice. It was only a month ago that Emma introduced them to Internal Family Systems, a psychotherapeutic approach that views individuals as composed of a variety of sub-personalities, or "parts." Every part, she told them, is motivated to protect us, even when it acts in a way that's counterproductive. Like the part of Jenna that made her feel disconnected from Alexander to avoid disappointment when their painful pattern played out again. Emma explained to the couple that listening to your own and your partner's parts with compassion, to understand what a part fears and is trying to achieve, can be deeply healing.

Maybe Emma should try listening to her suicidal part. Or not.

"This whole conversation made me realize just how different Alexander's world is, and how I have to stop making assumptions about him not caring about me, or my friends, or whatever. I have to be more accepting—and appreciative—of the ways that he's different from me."

Alexander smiles lovingly at his wife, stroking her back. Emma has long admired how, whether Jenna is infuriated or despairing or fearful, Alexander always reaches out to her. It helps that he has a limited ability to read micro-expressions—and sometimes even macro-expressions—and that he isn't terribly emotional. He's not very reactive to Jenna's heightened feeling states.

"So we had a really nice week. I think the combination of Alexander being extra careful not to make messes and tune me out—because of our session last week—and me not making up stories about him not caring about how he affects me and other people, shifted something. It's like we've taken a big step forward."

"Right. And it's important for both of you to remember that your progress isn't going to come completely undone when you encounter a challenge." Emma builds on Jenna's insights. "It's just that when you're feeling worn down, when you're chronically dysregulated, it's like your psychological and emotional immune system is low. You have less resistance to stressors, and are more easily dysregulated by them."

"*Exactly.*" Jenna nods emphatically. "And all these little things, they matter, and they add up."

It's what Emma's colleague, Mykhailo Adamovich, calls the Unpleasantness Factor. In a relationship, unpleasant behaviors—anything from poor hygiene to listening to loud music to teasing someone who isn't laughing—tend to fly under the radar. These things seem benign, but they're dysregulating. And enough dysregulation can destroy any relationship.

"I think maybe I didn't really understand how hard some things are for Jenna." Alexander turns to Jenna. "I didn't get that my messiness isn't something that 'just bothers' you. I mean, I should have. You told me enough times. But, I don't know… I just didn't. Now I get that it's—like you said—dysregulating. Intolerable. Like boredom is for Arby." Surprisingly, Alexander remains serious. "I can definitely do better. I promise."

Emma regards the couple appreciatively. Jenna and Alexander are ordinary people struggling under extraordinary circumstances. They're managing their challenges by taking what Emma describes as a compassion-forward approach: leading with compassion when making assumptions and choosing actions.

"It's like what you always say about grace," Jenna chimes in, directing her commentary to Emma. "How it's one of the most important qualities in a relationship. I feel like now that I understand Arby, I'm less defensive and more compassionate, so I can—how do you always say it?—practice grace." Jenna smiles, her chin high, proud of putting all her relational hard work into action.

Emma's heart swells. This is really the crux of her

work with couples. Relationships, like people, are messy and complicated and stunningly imperfect. As Dr. Xi used to say, allowing others, and ourselves, room to be the beautiful mess we all are enables love and affection to thrive, and it's one of the greatest gifts anyone can give.

DURING HER LUNCH BREAK, EMMA LIMPS TO CVS TO PICK up dry shampoo and aerosol deodorant—necessities, now that she's too banged up to bathe. She can no longer walk normally because, thanks to the intensive activities of the Program, she now has muscle soreness to contend with on top of her other aches and pains.

She'd spent her entire Saturday on site at the Program. She was poked and prodded and then interrogated about everything from what position she sleeps in to what her favorite childhood toy was. She was then given a list of the exercises—like water ballet, bobbing for apples, and tantric stretching—which would be part of her treatment protocol. Finally, she was instructed on how to do the exercises, including how to modify two of them to accommodate her physical limitations.

One of the exercises she had to modify was jumping laughter yoga, which was a group activity. While the others in the group bounced up and down on a trampoline, forcing out howls of fake laughter, Emma had to do the exercise on the floor beside them, bending and unbending her knees and taking inelegant little steps while eking out giggles, like a toddler stamping to a rap song. The other modified exercise involved riding a tricycle with a four-foot-high seat, a tiny front wheel, and giant back ones. The cycle had a sidecar of a similar height that contained a ventriloquist-style puppet of herself, with which she was supposed to discuss and "process" her symptoms. Because Emma couldn't pedal normally, she'd been provided with an electric version of the bike.

Despite the fact that she's sore and drained and rattled from all the activity, she's cautiously optimistic. As she hobbles down Main Street on this bright spring day, she feels, for the first time since coming down with SOS, a glimmer of hope. Maybe it's all the smoothies and exercise the Program has foisted on her—or maybe it's that the Program is starting to work its magic.

21

Existence Bias and Suicide Clusters

Day 24: Monday

Emma hurries across what feels like an Olympic-sized gymnasium rather than a stuffy, repurposed YMCA fitness studio. She's trying, unsuccessfully, to move as quickly as possible without limping or wincing. She'd ordered an Uber, which ended up taking longer than expected to arrive and then got stuck in Monday evening traffic, so she's late for her Mortal Wounds meeting, for the first time.

The group members have already taken their usual seats in the circle, full mugs in hands. Jackets are draped over the backs of their metal chairs, bags squatting at their feet, and the scents of freshly brewed coffee and Olivia's trendy rhubarb-vanilla perfume mingle with the funk of the yoga mats piled along the wall. The members are chatting amiably, but at the sight of Emma, the conversations grind to a halt. Nine spectators—ten if you include Karry-on Karl—are fixated on her performance as she hobbles, hops, and strides like an unskilled acrobat to take her empty seat in the circle.

"Hi everyone! So sorry I'm late." Emma musters her brightest voice as she sits down, swallowing a scream of pain. "I had to take an Uber because I'm having car problems." She is, after all, having problems with her car. She can't drive it safely.

"Yeah, fender benders are like the gift that keeps on giving!" Arthur laughs, thankfully breaking the spell that's fallen over the room.

"Haha, right." Emma breathes a sigh of relief as she tries to ignore the shooting pains throughout her body that her sprinting brought on.

"Before we start with check-ins, I wanted to let you know that a couple of people won't be joining us anymore." Emma's comment elicits a collective groan, and more than a few pairs of eyes tear up. Loss of any kind triggers this group. "There's nothing to worry about. Steve has found another… service that's a better fit for his needs. And Missy is, um, taking some time for herself." Quitting therapy is, technically, an opportunity to use your time to pursue personal interests.

Silence hangs in the air. The two empty chairs in the circle suddenly seem bleak.

"You were a good kid, Missy. Always wanting to help." A moist-eyed Arthur is addressing the bare metal seat to Emma's right. "But you shouldn't've told me about your client with that—what's that problem? Dacryphilia, getting turned on when someone cries. The client who fakes problems to get into support groups, just so they can get aroused." A collective gasp fills the room. Members exchange furtive glances and then quickly look away, nobody wanting to look like they're suspicious of others or guilty themselves. "And you *stunk*, little lady. Your perfume was really—"

"Ahem, Arthur." Emma finally finds the wherewithal to intervene. "What are you doing?"

"Gestalt therapy," Arthur answers, his chin raised. Arthur knows enough about therapy to speak the language of the profession, but not enough to avoid misusing his knowledge. "You know, where you process your feelings about someone by imagining them sitting in an empty chair."

"Foul old man."

As always, the German accent jolts Emma and the other members.

"*Me?*" Arthur counters, talking to the suitcase, rather than to the woman who voiced the statement. "*I'm* not the one—"

"How about we hit the brakes on this conversation so we can stay on topic, okay?" Emma tries to sound both calm and confident, neither of which she feels.

"Ja, *you* probably *are* the one who has the dacryph—"

"ZIP it, Karl!" Arthur shouts.

Olivia gasps. "How *dare* you, you *bigot!*"

It's five minutes before Emma can restore order to the group. They're unusually wound up tonight, no doubt due to the loss of two members as well as to her disturbing appearance and unusual behavior. She needs to get everyone back on track. "Why don't we hear from Liz and Bock next, since they weren't at our last meeting." Emma addresses the pair she just mentioned. "In fact, why don't the two of you also introduce yourselves for Rasheda and Jared, who just started last week."

Liz gives an acquiescent nod.

"Hi. I'm Liz, and this is my son, Bock." The blonde woman's squinted hazel eyes and downturned mouth betray the worry that seems to have been erased from the rest of her face, probably by Botox. Next to her, fifteen-year-old Bock sports a messy shock of mousy hair that shoots out of his hoodie. He slouches heavily and stares at the wall, the consummate adolescent.

Liz, a single mother, started bringing Bock to Mortal Wounds "preemptively," after a distant uncle died and Bock, then twelve, had cried at the funeral. She wanted to prepare the boy for future deaths he'd encounter. To protect him, as it were, from death. And, therefore, from life. Like Gregory, Liz and Bock don't see Emma for individual therapy, just at Mortal Wounds.

Emma has been trying to help Liz understand the difference between being protective and being restrictive, so Bock can be free to live his life and learn his lessons. And so Liz can be free of the shackles of fear and shame that bind you when you make yourself responsible for someone else's existence.

"We're really glad to be a part of this group." Liz swallows, her unmoving brow somehow seeming to furrow. "Especially now."

Bock's foot starts twitching, but he remains otherwise motionless in his slump.

"Bock found a lump on his neck on Wednesday." Liz pauses, giving the group a moment to gawk or gasp or tisk. "We went straight to the clinic, and they immediately did a biopsy. The doctor said they can't tell us anything definitive until the results come back, but she said by the look of it, it's more likely malignant than not." Liz squeezes her creaseless eyes closed and rubs her temples. "I… I'd actually like to leave it at that."

"Thanks for the update, Liz." Emma tries to sound reassuring. "I'm so sorry to hear about this development."

Rasheda clears her throat, jostling her soft headscarf and large earrings. "We can go next," she offers.

"Speak for yourself." Jared, again sitting on the opposite side of the circle, has positioned himself as his partner's adversary. His auburn hair is perfectly tousled, making him look shabby chic, like a retro plant stand.

"Okay, *I'll* go next," Rasheda retorts. "First of all, thanks to all of you who bore witness to our challenging conversation last week. As you may recall, I don't want children and Jared does. We have different beliefs about life and death—procreation and abortion, to name just a couple of—"

"Who the hell is the father?!" Karl barks out the question nobody else dares to ask. Emma is starting to see the value of having a sociopathic mouthpiece.

Rasheda remains on script. "Last week, Jared said he'd noticed that I'd been acting pregnant for the past three months, following his six-week expedition." She seems aware that juries need reminding of prior events. "He was right, I am pregnant." The group looks at Jared as though he's a jilted lover on a reality television show.

"But I'm *not* three months pregnant. Just five weeks. The baby is Jared's." The audience "oohs" as the case takes yet another unexpected turn.

"Soon to be *no* weeks pregnant," Jared snorts.

Liz, the paragon of maternal virtue, tears up, but

quickly wipes her eyes, probably remembering Arthur's unfortunate disclosure.

Rasheda is undeterred. "The world doesn't need more people. *Twenty-five thousand* people die every day from hunger. Every single child that's born in the US adds thousands of tons of carbon dioxide to a planet that's already burning. There are 140 million orphans who need a home. And—"

Jared cuts Rasheda off before she can finish what's starting to seem like a winning argument. "I don't disagree that these are real problems. But I do contend that"—he lifts a finger, a courtly gesture to alert the jury that he's about to say something of note—"it's not up to us to play god. The minute we appoint ourselves the arbiters of others' lives and deaths, we're crossing a dangerous ethical line." He gives a self-satisfied nod, letting the group know he's done making his case.

"And we're *not* the arbiters of others' lives when we're deciding to bring them into existence in the first place? Or to keep them existing, like you wanted to do with Slo-Mo?"

"Slo-Mo," Jared interjects, addressing the audience, "was our dog who had cancer and who *she*"—he tilts his chin derisively in Rasheda's direction—"insisted on euthanizing."

"Tell me, Jared, why is it that we're only 'playing god' when we're talking about *ending* life, rather than beginning or sustaining it? Why is living poorly considered so much better than dying well?" Rasheda addresses the group. "I'll tell you why. Because we have an existence bias. We believe that it's better *to* exist than *not* to exist—without any data whatsoever to support this belief. With no knowledge of nonexistence, how can we possibly argue that it's worse than existence?"

Emma is trying to block out Rasheda's words, humming to herself under her breath like she does when she plugs her ears in order to avoid a disturbing scene in a movie.

Not listening, not listening, not listening…

"By your account, we should all just kill ourselves." Gregory, the coffin maker, lets out a strange little laugh, like he's trying to make it look like he's joking when he's actually serious.

Not listening, not listening, not listening…

"No, by my account we should all just be a little more humble and not assume that we have all the answers. Obviously there's no one-size-fits-all to suicide. And obviously, when someone takes their own life, they take others' lives as well."

Who would take care of Annie? Visit Walter? And what other therapist would let Alexander zealously toe-stim their carpet?

Emma has to stop this runaway train before it takes the couple—and herself—down. "Rasheda, Jared, listen. You two clearly care a lot about ethics, about what it means to be a good person. And you want the person you spend your life with to understand and respect your values." For once, both partners seem to be listening, rather than waiting for an opening to make their next argument. "You're navigating heavy, complex issues that have no easy answers. In some ways, what matters most is not what your differences are, but how you *relate* to those differences. When you can discuss, rather than debate, your differences, you'll be able to approach these big life issues as allies rather than opponents. I want to give others the opportunity to share before we're out of time today, but I'll send you some communication resources and we can pick this conversation back up next week, okay?"

Chastened, both partners give a little nod. Court is adjourned.

Gregory raises a hand. "Hi everyone."

"Hi, Gregory," the group chants.

"I've got something I'd like to get off my chest today." Gregory's long, lined face is taut, his soft Haitian accent somehow sounding harsh. "It hasn't been an easy week. There's been a huge demand for coffins, like nothing I've ever seen."

The hair on Emma's arms stands up, and a tingle travels up her spine. Suicide clusters.

"But that's not what I'm here to talk about."

"Why not?" The words are out of Emma's mouth before she realizes she's said them. Her interjection is so out of character that the room falls silent. The group looks at her in shock and, to her horror, pity.

"Because my trauma, my thanatophobia, it's really kicked up and that's much more of a problem for me than the stress of having to meet the demand of a suicide cluster."

So it *is* a suicide cluster. This time Emma manages to keep her mouth shut. She'll talk to Gregory after the meeting.

"We got an order. From this rich guy. Jack Jones was his name. The order was actually from his kids, because

Jack died. Jack was some sort of joker, and he wrote in his will that he wanted a special coffin for his funeral. A custom coffin, which is why the family came to us." Gregory pauses, his eyes haunted.

"So this Jack Jones, he thought it would be funny to have a jack-in-the-box coffin. Sort of a mix between a music box and a casket. At the start of the funeral, the coffin would be closed. But 'Pop Goes the Weasel' would be playing, over and over and over. Then, when everyone is seated and the eulogy is about to start, the casket would flip open, and Jack would pop up."

Gregory swallows, looking at his hands. All the members' expressions are deadly serious. Except for smiley Alexander, who seems to find the story comical and keeps whispering to Jenna, who shushes him.

"I wasn't going to do it. But they offered me a pretty penny. And besides, I didn't want to compromise the values Out of the Box is founded on. Refusing would have been off brand."

A stifled chortle emanates from Alexander as he dashes off to the bathroom, his hand over his mouth and nose. Jenna looks after him reproachfully.

Gregory forges on. "Of course, if I'm going to do something, I'm going to do it right. Which meant I had to create a prototype and test it until I was sure the coffin would perform to Out of the Box standards. I had to rig an old coffin and use a human dummy to try out the contraption. And the tester dummy we have in the storeroom is of a Black female with an afro."

Jenna lets out a little shout, a few members clasp their hands over their mouths, and a hushed murmur breaks out. Only Jared and Rasheda don't react, since they don't know that Gregory's thanatophobia was caused by seeing his mother pop out of a coffin while secretly having sex with his father.

"I've had that damn image and the 'Pop Goes the Weasel' song stuck in my head for days." Gregory shakes his head despondently. "Anyway, thanks for listening."

"Thanks, Gregory," the group replies in univoice.

Olivia is waving her hand in the air like an eager student who knows the answer to a question. "I know we're almost out of time, so I just want to let everyone know that Karl and I won't be here next week."

Her announcement is met with a few nods, a seemingly disappointing response. Olivia often relates to the group like she's a social media influencer vying for likes.

"We're going away," she adds enthusiastically, as though this is the best news a group of people trying to navigate death and dying could ask for. "To Cancun, where we started our relationship." She sits back and crosses her arms, gloating.

Olivia went to Cancun a couple of years ago after a devastating breakup with her then-fiancée. While she was drinking margaritas on the balcony of her hotel room, she mistakenly swallowed the worm from the bottom of the tequila bottle. Terrified that she'd start hallucinating, she tried to make herself vomit, but couldn't.

Within minutes, a handsome German stranger in a blue suit, who called himself Karl, was sitting beside her. The two struck up a conversation that lasted into the night, and by dawn Olivia was desperately in love. "I knew he was my soulmate," she'd told Emma. "It was like he could read my mind."

Once Olivia had sobered up—Emma knew that mezcal worms were not hallucinogens and that the woman had just been drunk—she worried that she'd hallucinated the whole experience. But to her delight she hadn't. Her new love did, in fact, exist. The only thing that she'd imagined was that Karl had been human.

"Congratulations, that's great, Olivia!" Emma gives Olivia the attention the woman has been craving, so she can finally wrap up the meeting. "Okay, everyone. It looks like we're at time. Well done today. Have a good week and I'll see you next Monday."

As the members stand up, Emma rushes over to Gregory before he can sneak away. He's starting toward the door while hurriedly pulling on his jacket. "Gregory, hi. I was hoping we could speak for a minute?"

Gregory turns toward Emma and looks like the cat who swallowed the canary. So he *was* planning to slip out again. "It'll just take a moment," Emma tries to reassure him. "I just wanted to ask you about the suicide cluster."

"Gee, Emma, I'd like to help you, but it's really not a good time. I'm not in a great place psychologically. We can catch up next week, okay?" He turns away and walks toward the exit so quickly he may as well be running.

Not this time.

Emma limps after him. "Gregory, wait. Please. I think you might know something that can help someone in need."

Gregory stops and looks back at Emma. "Look, Emma. I can't talk about this. Nothing good ever comes out of these conversations. They just lead to more death."

And with that, he turns on his heel and dashes out the door, running away from Emma and taking his secret with him.

22

Champagne Suicide
and a Patented Formula

Day 25: Tuesday

"**I**s it all right if I come in?"

Emma jumps at the unexpected voice at her office door, which she's left ajar as she often does during her lunch break. It's Shana, who Emma realizes has been knocking for what seems like several minutes.

"Sure!" Emma scrambles to come up with an explanation for her oblivion.

"You on Ritalin or something? I've been knocking away!" Shana says this with a smile, but her dark eyes are narrowed as she searches Emma's face, looking more like Emma's attending psychiatrist than a colleague or friend.

"Oh, ha. I was actually just giving my brain a break between clients. Playing Candy Crush." Emma grins sheepishly.

With the sound turned off, to avoid the obscene jingle getting lodged in my brain.

Shana rolls her eyes and shakes her head in mock consternation, her blonde-streaked cornrows swaying like wheat stalks in a breeze.

Today is the first time since developing SOS that Emma has been able to play the silly video game without fantasizing about being crushed herself and evaporating in little multicolored explosions. Plus, she hasn't had a headache all day and she even made it through Mortal Wounds last night without so much as a twinge. The Program just might be working.

"And you're not usually in on Tuesdays, so I wasn't expecting anyone to come by," Emma adds.

"I had to pick up some mail, and I wanted to talk to you. I figured I'd swing over during your break. Do you have a minute?" Shana is looking at Emma a bit too intently, and her usually relaxed mouth is tight.

"Of course." Emma gets up from her desk and walks over to the cushioned chair she sits in across from clients. Shana takes a seat on the sofa opposite her, her sweet, earthy scent wafting through the room. Emma tries to keep her voice, and mood, light. "What's up?"

A high extravert, Shana is uncharacteristically silent. She looks at her hands, which are folded in her generous lap, her sturdy thumbs twiddling. "Uh, Emma. I don't know how to say this, so I'm just gonna come right out with it."

A chill creeps up Emma's spine and she shivers despite the mild spring day, instinctively pulling her fringed shawl more tightly around her.

"It's Steve." Shana's deep voice is grave. "He's all right—he's going to be okay," she interjects quickly. "But… there's been an incident."

"An incident? What kind of incident?" Emma's throat is tight.

"A suicide attempt." Shana lets Emma absorb this statement before continuing. "Involving slit wrists and a champagne bubble bath. Yesterday."

Emma's thoughts are racing, and she can't find her words. None of this makes sense. Steve was in the Program. Shana has a one hundred percent success rate with her referrals. How could this have happened?

"So he's alive?" Those three words are all that Emma can muster. Did the Program fail if Steve didn't actually die?

"Yeah, but only because his roommate came home from vacation early and found him before it was too late. The paramedics said if the roommate had come thirty minutes later, Steve would've been dead. So the suicide attempt wasn't just a gesture. Plus, he'd emptied his bank account to pay for the champagne. Dom Pérignon. He didn't seem like someone who planned on staying alive."

Emma's hands are trembling and her linen shirt clings to her damp skin. Holding back tears, she replies weakly, "Um, wow. That's, that's really… a shock."

Maybe SOS makes you progressively inarticulate.

"I know, and I am so sorry. I can see how much you care about him. This is what makes you such a great shrink. You feel so much for your clients."

Emma used to, anyway. Before she got saddled with a dysfunctional, high-maintenance, treatment-resistant new client: herself.

"It gets me every time." Usually upbeat and always bold, Shana looks as though she's folding in on herself. "Suicide. I mean, I get it—people kill themselves when they feel they don't have the resources to cope with whatever it is they're trying to cope with. When their pain is greater than their capacity to cope with the pain. It's just, so many suicides could have been prevented. It really kills me. No pun. People have to learn basic survival skills, like how to swim, but almost nobody is taught basic *psychological* survival skills—and so they don't have the tools they need to keep their head above water till help comes, or the tide changes, or they find the strength to swim to the shore. Or to prevent themselves from getting stranded in the water in the first place. It's a real shame."

Hear, hear. And sadly, even lifeguards sometimes drown.

"And because people are so emotionally myopic, so honed in on whatever their current emotional experience is, they assume their feelings are never gonna change, even though feelings are always changing." Shana shakes her head slowly.

"Uh, Shana, what do you make of what happened with Steve? I thought you'd had a one hundred percent success rate with the clients you sent to the Program?"

"Yeah, that's right. I do. *Did*. This is the first time since I started sending folks there that something's gone wrong. I dunno. Maybe Steve didn't follow the protocol or something. Or maybe if he'd held on till taking his tincture, he'd have been okay. But…" Shana trails off, seeming to be running some kind of mental calculation.

"But what?" Emma has started sweating profusely.

"Come to think of it, he *had* taken the tincture. Yeah, right. He told me about it when he said he had to cancel our last appointment because of some sort of scheduling conflict. The Program was a short stint for him, because he'd only just started thinking about suicide. And he was actually feeling really optimistic about his prognosis."

Emma's own optimism of just a few minutes ago has vanished like a crushed piece of digital candy.

"But you know, I wouldn't give up on the Program just yet. Or at all. If you still wanna send that client you mentioned, I think you should. So now the success rate is 99.9 percent. By my calculations, that's still pretty damn good. Better than any psychopharmaceutical I know of!"

Maybe Shana's right. Maybe what happened with Steve was a fluke. Emma *has* been feeling better since she enrolled—which is especially promising since she's arguably in late-stage SOS. She'll see for herself, soon enough, whether the Program works. Her elixir is supposed to be delivered today, and if all goes according to plan, she'll be cured in a few days.

"Hey, why don't you come by for dinner tonight?" Shana's voice is upbeat, perhaps in an attempt to cheer Emma up. "It's Tuesday. Pizza night. Theresa's making her famous Pepperoni Pandemonium, and we'd love to have you."

'Cause if I were an Oscar Mayer Wiener, there would soon be nothing left of me!

Emma feels a rush of hysterical laughter well up in her throat, but she manages to stifle it and politely declines.

EMMA'S LAST CLIENT OF THE DAY HAS JUST LEFT AND SHE'S grateful that she'll soon be heading home and not to pizza night. There was no way she was going to accept Shana's invitation. Not only is she barely able to keep her eyes open past 7:00 these days, thanks to doing three hours of strenuous Program activities every morning at the crack of dawn, but the last thing she needs is to make chitchat with psychologically sophisticated people who would see right through her facade of mental health. Then again, maybe that's exactly what she needs. But not now. She'll see what happens with the elixir first and if it doesn't work, she'll consider opening up to the psychiatrist.

Sorting through her mail, Emma spots a padded yellow envelope. It's from the Program. Tearing it open, she finds a tiny vial inside, with a rolled up piece of parchment paper tied with a red ribbon, like an ancient scroll. She unrolls the paper to see a message written in calligraphy.

Dear Ms. Emma Parkland,

Enclosed is your unique, custom elixir, meant to cure your inexplicable urge to kill yourself. This formula is a mix of herbal extracts, refurbished serum from your own blood, and other things that we are not at liberty to disclose in order to protect our special, secret patent. The elixir is sweetened with NutraSweet, so it won't cause cavities.

Put four drops under your tongue before bed tonight. Do not eat, drink, or brush your teeth afterward. The following day, take three drops under your tongue a minimum of two hours before eating or drinking or putting anything in your mouth, including things like pencils you might like to chew on.

It is extremely important that you avoid anything touching the underside of your tongue while you are taking the elixir. You must therefore use a straw for your consumption of food and beverages, placing it as far back in your throat as possible. You can eat whatever you want, as long as it is sufficiently blended so as to be easily sucked through the tube. The tincture is extremely delicate. Do NOT brush or floss your teeth during this period. Doing so will compromise the cure.

Emma blinks. Could this be another hallucination?

She pinches herself over her arms and legs. Her pain receptors seem to be working normally. She walks back and forth across the office, looking at it from different angles. Nothing seems distorted.

As if dirty hair and wrinkled clothing weren't embarrassing and unprofessional enough, now she'll have to deal with bad breath?

You should begin to feel the effects of the elixir within 24 hours, but it can take 72 hours before you're cured. If you don't feel better at that point, repeat the dropping procedure on the third night and fourth morning, and give it another 72 hours.

You must continue all your Program exercises while taking the elixir. Please respect other patrons and be sure to wear a mask while doing any exercises where you have to exhale deeply, as you will stink.

If you are not cured by the time you've taken the maximum dosage of your elixir, you must have done something wrong. Or there is simply no cure for you.

Please note there are no refunds.

Her heart racing with both anticipation and trepidation, Emma quickly packs up her items so she can get home and take the first dose. As challenging as the next few days may be, there's no time to lose.

As she's pulling on her coat, her phone rings.

Unknown caller.

"Um, hello?"

"Emma, hi." The voice is familiar but Emma can't quite place it.

"Gregory here. Look, Emma. I wanted to say I'm sorry I ran out on you last night."

It's Gregory from Mortal Wounds!

"I got spooked, is all. But it wasn't right, and I want to apologize."

"Oh, uh, Gregory, thank you. And it's no problem."

"Well, if what's going on with that person you want to support is what I think it is, then it *is* a problem. A big one."

"Um, so, you know what's going on?"

"These days, pretty much anyone in the death business knows what's going on. At least, anyone who knows how to use AI to dig for information. We've got to be careful talking about it, though. Almost everyone is at risk, and it's not the kind of thing you can get vaccinated against, if you know what I mean."

"Um, I think so?"

"We need to talk in person. Not on the phone, and definitely not by email or text. It's not safe."

"So, um, Gregory, just to be sure… you know what's causing the suicide clusters—and what kind of problems the clusters might be causing?"

"I'll tell you everything after Mortal Wounds next week, when we can talk in person. I think I can tell you what you need to know to help this friend of yours. Bye!"

Next week?

"Uh, Gregory—" But Gregory has hung up.

Emma starts to text him. He's got to understand that

this is urgent. As she's writing, she sees three dots from his number, and then a text.

SOS.

Emma's breath catches. With shaking thumbs she bangs out a message in response, and hits send.

Message not delivered.

Gregory has blocked her number.

23

"Emergency!"

Day 28: Friday

The cold, wet nose and tickly whiskers brushing Emma's cheek feel oddly incongruent with her scratchy throat. Annie has been rubbing his face against her ever since he stopped hiding from the deafening whir of the blender.

Emma is sitting at her round, oak kitchen table where she always eats breakfast, and she's been in a coughing fit since a lump of unblended oatmeal that somehow made it through the straw got stuck in her windpipe. Because shopping has become more taxing than facilitating Mortal Wounds on the Day of the Dead, she's been avoiding buying groceries, living largely on takeout. Since she used up her smoothie ingredients the first two days of her elixir regimen, all she had left for breakfast today was oatmeal and some dried berries and nuts, which she cooked up and threw in a blender.

Emma wipes her eyes as the coughing subsides. She strokes Annie's silky head, letting him know she's okay. Suddenly, he freezes. His head cocked, eyes wide, and ears

233

flat, he stares into an empty corner of the room—and bolts off to chase after some imaginary prey. Emma will never understand the berserk behavior of cats.

At the sight of the half-empty bowl of lumpy oatmeal with the fat straw, sticky and sodden around the rim she's been sucking on, Emma's stomach lurches. She pushes the food away and tries to ignore the mossy slime coating her mouth. Although she felt queasy wearing a mask during her strenuous exercises at the Program, her foul breath trapped and recirculating like pollution in a tunnel during rush hour, she can understand this requirement. Less understandable is the requirement that her dummy doppelganger in the sidecar of her electric tricycle also wear one.

So far, she hasn't felt any effect from the elixir, but the potion can take up to twelve doses to work and she only just took the sixth one before heading to the Program this morning. She decided to come home before going to the office so she could give herself a sponge bath in an attempt to maintain some semblance of hygiene. Her visible deterioration has been disquieting enough for her clients.

While she was cleaning herself, squatting in the tub, she noticed that the puncture where her blood was drawn by the phlebotomist at the Program—who, to Emma's consternation, had also been the sales rep who'd signed her up—was as fresh as it had been a week ago. And the mottled, crimson-purple bruise around it was spreading up and down her arm.

At precisely 10:35, the doorbell rings. Walter, who was supposed to pick her up at 10:45 to give her a ride to work, is, predictably, ten minutes early. Walter is one of those people who always shows up before he's expected, saying he's happy to wait and assuming that others are happy to have him wait.

Walter offered to drive Emma the ten minutes to her office when he saw her climbing into yet another Uber the other day, which she'd informed him she had to do until she recovered from her fender bender. Normally Emma wouldn't want to put Walter out, but opening up to Nick has got her thinking about the importance of letting people give to you. To her. Giving helps people practice their integrity, because it helps them put their values into action. It also helps people feel competent and needed. It's important for people to be able to give, a concept Emma frequently explains to her clients but rarely applies to herself.

Walter lets himself in, the cool April morning fog clinging to him as he walks across the creaky hardwood floor of the foyer. "Emma! Your chariot awaits!" The lanky septuagenarian sports his usual wide grin.

"Hi, Walter. Thanks so much. I'll be right there. I just need a couple of minutes to finish getting ready."

"Not a problem! I'm at your service." Walter bows dramatically and remains standing in the foyer as Emma rushes to collect her items and pull on her coat, feeling an irrational pressure not to keep him waiting.

Walter's miniature three-wheel, two-passenger covered moped is waiting at the curb, adorable in an undefinable way. If motor vehicles had babies, they would probably look like this. Walking to the passenger door, Emma catches sight of a chicken in the seat she'll soon be occupying, pecking on the side window. Charles. Walter brings him everywhere, since the chicken enjoys both the travel and hanging out in the vehicle as Walter runs his errands.

"Don't worry about Charles. He'll be happy as a lark on your lap!" At his play on bird words, Walter giggles like a schoolgirl, which is oddly unnerving. "It's true," he continues. "Charles is a lap chicken."

Looking down at her dark linen pants, one of the only clean pairs she has left, Emma stifles a groan.

Once everyone is seated in the tiny compartment, Charles cooing contentedly like the well-loved pet he is, the silly vehicle pulls into the street and zips off toward Emma's office.

The trio rides in companionable silence for a few minutes. Then: "Um, Walter, do you mind if we open the vents?" Emma keeps her voice casual. "I'm a little warm in this winter coat." This is true. As is the fact that, when Charles put his head under his wing, Emma realized that her breath had already permeated the stuffy little cabin.

"Sure, Emma. Whatever you want. We're a full-service service!" Walter cracks up. And then cracks his window and raises his nose to the fresh air.

Fortunately, the ten-minute ride is over before Emma's gotten too much of a chill. Thanking Walter, she opens her door and gently lifts Charles—who keeps his head turned away from her—off her lap and deposits him onto the seat. She waves at the pair before turning to head up the path through the front lawn to the gray Victorian.

Once settled at her desk, Emma checks her voicemail. There's a message from Warmer Planet.

Hi, Emma, Amala here. I've got good news. Your father's come out of his coma and he's fully conscious. I'm sure he'll be calling you once the doctors are done seeing him, but I wanted to let you know right away.

Her pulse quickening, Emma replays the message to make sure she didn't misunderstand. Or hallucinate. She heard right. Not only does she have her father back, if only for a few months, but now there's hope that the unresolved relationship issue will get fixed! She immediately dials Nick.

"Em! How're you doing? You okay?" Ever since she told Nick about her condition, on top of checking in on her regularly, he's been answering all her calls and responding to all her texts. It's like her SOS has cured his ADHD.

"Yes, I'm fine." Considering. "I'm calling about Dad. He's out of the coma and he's coherent." Emma can't keep the excitement—or is it desperation?—out of her voice.

"Holy cow. That's crazy! I mean, that's *great*—I just wasn't expecting it. I'll head to Warmer Planet in a few minutes to talk with him."

"Um, yeah, okay. But don't you think I should be there? I mean, to help facilitate what I'm sure is not going to be an easy conversation? My last client leaves at five so I can come right after that."

"Well, yeah, it'd be great if you wanted to come. But we need to do this *now*. Who knows how long Dad's going to stay conscious. And you're at risk of something happening to you every minute."

He has a point. But today's clients are especially needy and Emma can't cancel on them last-minute.

"Nick, are you *sure* you're okay to do this without me?"

"Honestly, once I agreed to do it, I almost started

wanting to. I guess a part of me has been waiting for an excuse to talk to Dad again." Emma's heart warms at Nick's growing self-awareness and his newfound compassion for his father. "Plus, it's time I stopped always acting like a little brother and relying on you to fix my life."

To Emma's surprise, she agrees.

"Thanks, Nick. And please, text me as soon as you're done."

And with that, Nick is off to try to fix his big sister's life.

No matter how Nick and her father's conversation affects her suicidality, Emma is grateful that the two men are finally reconnecting after that horrible incident five years ago.

It had been an especially busy time for Nick's family. He and Marina had to go out of town overnight on separate work trips and were in a bind. Emma, who usually babysat, already had plans to visit a housebound client with agoraphobia who lived in New Hampshire. Unable to find another babysitter to stay overnight with their eight-year-old twins, Sofia and Kai, the couple reluctantly turned to Emma's father, who they knew was like a glorified child himself but who lived in Acton, just twenty minutes away.

Early in the evening of the sleepover, Kai said he wasn't feeling well. He had a headache and stomach-ache and was dizzy. Emma's father laid the boy down on the sofa, covered him in blankets, and put on *Evil Dead II*, since "laughter is the best medicine"—no matter that the horror comedy was rated R. Her father then stepped out to meet a friend who lived nearby and who'd called about borrowing a power tool that was in the back of her father's truck. Four hours and twice as many drinks later, he returned, having "ducked into the local bar," assuming the kids had fallen asleep in front of the television.

But the children hadn't fallen asleep. Kai, who it turned out had drunk Drano after seeing an ad online and wanted to find out "how much poo it would push out," was on the floor having a seizure, while Sofia was screaming hysterically by his side. Apparently Sofia, whose cell phone was automatically locked after 5:00 p.m., had gone to the two closest neighbors for help but nobody was home, and she was afraid to wander further and leave Kai alone. Emma's father arrived just in time to call an ambulance and flip Kai on his side before the boy suffocated on his own saliva.

Nick never forgave his father, or himself, for not protecting his children. It didn't help that Nick had a history of neglect at his father's hands, and a lifetime of built-up resentment. Thankfully, Kai didn't suffer permanent damage. Not physically, anyway; the trauma from the poisoning, and from watching *Evil Dead II*, has remained with him.

For Emma's father, the incident was sobering, literally and figuratively. It was the rock-bottom moment that caused him to stop drinking and start taking his responsibilities seriously. The recovery work he's been doing since then, from twelve-step programs to short-term therapy, combined with his cancer diagnosis, has made him a changed man. Perhaps now Nick will finally see that.

EMMA'S LAST CLIENT OF THE DAY HAS JUST LEFT, AFTER MAK-ing the unfortunate decision to engage in what therapists refer to as "doorknob therapy." The client's figurative hand was on the door handle to leave when he dropped a bomb that couldn't be ignored. So Emma spent another thirty minutes trying to help him stop hyperventilating and self-regulate, and now that he's finally gone she's got a splitting headache.

Impatient for news from Nick and her father, Emma grabs her phone. There's a text from each of them. Nick's was sent three hours ago, a selfie of him leaning in toward their father, who's sitting up in bed. Their faces are close together, both of them smiling into the camera and giving the thumbs up. Her father sent a nearly identical photo a few minutes later, and followed up with a text.

Thanks honey. Now I can rest in peace. lol. [two winking icons] *come visit soon sweetie love, dad*

Emma gives herself a moment to take this in. Five long years of heartache and estrangement have finally ended. And it took just one conversation for the seem-ingly irreparable rift to be repaired. Of course, healing a relationship is in some ways like healing a body; if you try to rush the process, you can end up causing further harm. And looking back, Emma can appreciate that Nick needed time to get to the point where he felt ready to address and resolve the issue.

But her relief is short-lived, and she freezes when the reality hits her. The unresolved relationship issue. The most likely cause of SOS. It's now no longer a potential causal factor, but her suicidality is no better.

The reconciliation didn't work.

A sharp pain across her temples alerts her that her headache has worsened. Her *headache*. She'd stopped having headaches two days after starting the Program. She clasps a hand over her mouth. What if the elixir doesn't work?

Another stabbing pain in her head cuts her thoughts short. She lifts her purse off the floor, plops it onto her lap, and sees, to her horror, white splotches of chicken poop and tufts of down covering the brown pants she's been wearing all day. She grabs a bottle of ibuprofen out of her bag and shakes four into her hand, knowing it will take at least that many to relieve the pain.

Forty minutes later, after sending off the last of her emails and ordering an Uber, Emma heads out of the office. But when she tries to lock the door behind her, she can't seem to get the key into the hole. For some reason, it doesn't fit.

Has someone changed the locks?

After several minutes of trying to shove what seems like an oversized key into a miniature opening, she's overcome with exhaustion and leans against the door to hold herself up. With clumsy, limp fingers, she gives the key one more try and manages to slide it in.

But now she can't seem to stand upright again. Her body feels leaden. And the floor beneath her is moving, tilting. In slow motion.

The pills.

Still leaning against the door, Emma digs clumsily in her purse and pulls out the pill bottle. *Xanax*. She hasn't used the medication in months and only keeps it on her in case of emergency, when she needs to calm down quickly—in which case she takes a quarter of a tablet. And she's just taken four full ones. On an empty stomach.

Mustering all her strength, Emma drags herself outside to the waiting Uber and clambers into the back seat like a rapidly deflating balloon. She can barely feel her body, and doesn't even flinch when she pulls her foot free from where it got wedged between the side of the pushed-back passenger seat and the back seat, and hears her ankle snap.

The last thing she remembers is staring into the back of the driver's seat and croaking, "Emergency!"

24

Clusterf**k

Day 31: Monday

All the members of the Monday evening Mortal Wounds group are excitedly focused on something within the little cluster they've formed. So they don't notice Emma limping through the door on crutches and stumbling past the folding table with its coffee and tea dispensers and mismatched mugs. Thankfully, whatever it is that's captured the group's attention gives Emma a few more seconds to figure out how to explain her most recent injury without having to lie, which won't be easy this time.

Emma woke up Friday evening after having swallowed the Xanax, hazy and discombobulated, an intravenous tube in her arm and her foot bandaged and raised. A familiar face was leaning over her. It was the testy ER nurse who'd treated her for all her previous mishaps.

"Welcome back."

Emma couldn't tell if the nurse was trying to be comforting or sarcastic.

"You're lucky your Uber driver got you here when he

did, or your suicide attempt wouldn't have been just an attempt."

Suicide attempt?

"Um…" Emma tried to croak out an explanation, but her throat felt dry and scratched from what must have been an intubation tube. She felt more like a prisoner than a patient, under the garish fluorescent lights in the bleak, windowless room.

"When the driver realized you'd overdosed, he brought you here instead of taking you home. Just in time."

"No." Emma managed a hoarse whisper. "It wasn't a suicide attempt…"

Was it?

"We pumped your stomach, set your broken ankle, and redressed the knife wounds in your chest and palm, which opened up again." The nurse stated this like they were telling a child it was time for no more monkey games.

The nurse's utter lack of empathy somehow made Emma desperately sad. And lonely. If someone *were* consciously harming themselves, would that make them any less deserving of kindness and support? Perhaps it should make them even more so.

"We'll need to keep you overnight for observation, but if there are no complications you'll be discharged in the morning." The nurse was perfunctory, seeming in a hurry to stop wasting their time on a patient who was wasting taxpayers' money. "My colleague will be in to see you shortly."

An hour later, the attending psychiatrist was sitting in a chair next to Emma's bed asking her a battery of questions. The doctor was assessing her not only for suicidality, but also for a variety of psychological disorders.

"I'm a psychologist," Emma reassured her.

"Right." The doctor snorted. "If I could tell you how many times I've heard that from people lying right where you are."

Emma was discharged the following morning, but only with the provision that she return in a week for a follow-up psych evaluation.

———

A LIGHT FLASHES FROM THE CENTER OF THE GROUP HUDDLE across the room, followed by laughter and clapping.

"*Nein!*" The German interjection sounds guttural even without any "R" sounds.

More laughing and applause. Emma hobbles toward the group to see what in the world is going on.

At the sight of their facilitator approaching, the members expand the circle to make an opening for her. There in the center is Karl, his handle pulled up high and proud, with Arthur squatting by his side. Arthur's gray hair is jutting out in all directions, as though he's moussed it and fluffed it up without knowing what the outcome should be. He's bending forward and leaning slightly sideways like a rapper, one hand gripping Karl's handle and the other making an L with his pointer and thumb, while Olivia's phone camera flashes away like the paparazzi.

"Um, hi everyone." Emma's concern that she'll have to explain her crutches has vanished. "We should probably get started."

"Oh, NO! Mom, I didn't get a chance to take a picture with him!" Bock has broken the unspoken teenager rule to never look like you care.

Liz turns to Emma. "It'll only be a minute. Bock's been talking about seeing Karl all weekend and he promised his friends he'd get a selfie."

Unable to hide her gloating, Olivia grabs Bock by the elbow and positions him next to Karl, bending one of the boy's knees toward the shiny wooden floor. Kneeling, Bock raises both hands over his head, each in the L configuration, with his thumbs pointing toward each other. He looks like he's celebrating a winning soccer team.

"Sieg Heil!" Karl yells, shocking the group into silence. "I mean, *ja*, victory!"

It turns out that on Friday evening, while Emma was in the hospital having her stomach pumped, Karl and Olivia were thrust into the public spotlight thanks to what the couple realized in retrospect was a happy accident. They were at the gate of the airport, headed for their romantic Cancun getaway, when Olivia was told that there was no more room for carry-on luggage, so she would have to check her bag. After an increasingly heated back-and-forth between Olivia and the gate agents, Karl had a meltdown.

A German man's crass voice coming out of a slight, elegant woman grabbed the attention of the other passengers, and soon Karl and Olivia had drawn a crowd. Seizing the opportunity, Olivia shoved her phone at a tween and told the boy to stream the event on her Instagram.

Shouting and snarling like only a German speaker can, Karl denounced the airline for harming his dignity by treating him "like an object" and refusing to allow him to travel in the same class as his partner. His radical analysis, in which he assailed policymakers on both sides of the political spectrum and denounced institutional norms and backwards, bigoted traditions, lasted until airport security escorted Olivia off the premises. At which point throngs of observers had shared the incident on social media and Olivia's video had gone viral.

News anchors across the nation were talking about "Karry-on Khaos," and the incident unleashed an outpouring of support. People from all over the world shared their stories with Olivia on Instagram. Like the man who's kept his twenty-three-year marriage to a bowling ball a secret, and a woman who's been filling her husband, a vase, with fresh flowers to pretend that he's a centerpiece just so that he can be a part of holiday dinners.

By Sunday, vigils were being held around the globe, with demonstrators holding up placards of Karl and Olivia and singing "Love Is in the Air." And #LoveThingsLove is considered the next It movement, with people holding their hands in an L shape demanding respect for so-called "objects" of affection and the people who love them.

Emma finally understands why she feels more like she's at a red carpet event than a death support group.

Once everyone has settled into their regular seats in the ring of folding chairs, Emma does her usual check-in. There are only eight attendees tonight, counting Karl, because Alexander and Jenna are away on an impromptu trip to an ASMR convention, Crinkle Me This, that Alexander wanted to attend. As she scans the faces around her,

Emma catches Gregory's eye. The slim, weathered man is staring intently at her, and he gives an almost imperceptible nod, as if to acknowledge that they have a shared secret. She quickly looks away, not wanting to create an awkward dynamic for the others. "Who'd like to share first?"

Liz lifts a finger. "I'll start." She smiles softly, her hazel eyes twinkling. "We've got great news. Bock's biopsy came back negative."

Despite this revelation, Bock is slouching in his hoodie, refusing to emote, back to being a full-on teenager.

The group members let out little exclamations of relief and gratitude. A few of them even start clapping, probably because they got into the habit from cheering for Karl earlier.

"And there's other news," Liz adds, this time somber. "We won't be coming to Mortal Wounds after today."

Knowing the routine, Liz pauses to give the others time to well up over yet another loss. Mournful faces gaze at Liz and Bock, the mirrors on the far wall reflecting their solemn expressions and intensifying the aura of sadness permeating the room.

"I've realized that *we* don't need to learn how to deal with *death*," Liz continues. "*I* need to learn how to deal with *life*. I think that the fact that I wasn't able to save my younger sister from drowning when we were kids made me feel like it's my responsibility to protect everyone around me from getting hurt. Which, I'm finally seeing, is not only impossible, but is hurting *me*. I'm going to start my own therapy to work through this. I need to learn to take care of myself, to love myself the way Emma always describes loving. I need to honor my dignity, to see myself as having inherent worth and to treat myself with compassion and respect."

Liz has been in the group for long enough to have formed strong connections with many of the others. Their eyes are watery, and filled with pride for her Big Insight. Olivia raises her hands to start clapping but thinks better of it, and instead leans over to dab at Karl's zipper with a tissue.

Emma has been hoping that Liz would come to this point, and her heart is full. "We'll miss you two, but it's great to hear that you're taking these steps to really empower yourself and, ultimately, Bock as well."

Unable to help himself, Arthur ruins the moment. "One piece of advice for young people like you, Bock, is don't get old!" Arthur is, as usual, the only one laughing. "I mean it! Your life's gonna just be one fractured joint, one suspicious mole, one pair of adult diapers after another!" He guffaws at his joke. Which is actually not a joke.

"Would you cut it out, Arthur? That's really triggering." Olivia's got Arthur's number. "Older people are supposed to help us younger ones. Usher us into the future and all that. I mean, what are we supposed to do? We're already afraid of getting old and dying. You guys, you older people who have gone before us, you're supposed to be our *mentors*, help us come to terms with aging. Not tell us all the reasons we should be even more afraid of something we literally can't do anything about!" Apparently surprised at her own insightfulness, Olivia raises her well-defined chin and, her dark eyes flashing, adds, "I'm going to post about this."

Emma senses someone staring at her. It's Gregory.

Again. Reluctantly, she meets his eyes, and he raises an eyebrow and winks at her conspiratorially. She turns away and shivers.

Her ankle is throbbing and her head is aching, making it harder than ever to focus. She didn't want to take any painkillers today, fearing that they might kill more than just the pain. More distressing than all the physical discomfort, though, is that the elixir still hasn't kicked in. She took her twelfth and final dose this morning and in a couple of hours, it'll be the maximum time for it to have taken effect. Plus, in just six days, it will be day thirty-seven since the onset of her SOS. After that, she'll have exceeded the average life expectancy of a victim of the condition. If she makes it that far.

"I think we can go next." Rasheda looks questioningly at Jared, who, for once, is sitting next to, rather than across from, her.

With a nod from her partner, Rasheda continues, smoothing the top of her long, paisley skirt. "We actually had a really good week." Her courtly tone and posture have given way to a more relational and relatable manner. "We read those resources you sent us, Emma, and they really helped." She reaches over and clutches Jared's hand and cedes the floor to him.

"They did help." Jared rests a Converse high-top-clad ankle on his knee. "Especially the part about how the *content* of a conversation—what you're talking about—is less important than the *process*—how you're talking. And that when your process is healthy, you can talk about anything without arguing and when it's not, you can't talk about anything without arguing." Jared gives a little nod, apparently letting Rasheda know she can chime in.

"So, um, yeah. So we practiced using a healthy process. We made the goal of our communication not to win, or to be right, but mutual understanding. That alone helped; we shifted from debating issues to discussing them."

"We still need to figure out what to do about our life and death decisions," Jared adds. "But now that we're not thinking in terms of winners and losers, it's made talking so much easier."

The others nod politely, but they can't fully hide their disappointment at not getting front row seats to another riveting episode of Court TV.

Next up is Gregory, whose hand has been raised since before Jared and Rasheda were finished. "I wouldn't mind saying something. Hi, everyone."

"Hi, Gregory," the chorus chants obligingly.

Gregory is again staring right at Emma, and he addresses his comment to her rather than the group. "Actually, come to think of it, I'd rather just listen tonight. Thanks."

"Thanks, Gregory," the group replies in unison.

Still looking straight at Emma, Gregory mouths a silent and overly enunciated *Ess... Oh... Ess* and then gives her a little thumbs up.

This is too much. They're just about at time anyway, so Emma decides to wrap things up. "Okay everyone, good work tonight."

Rather than start in on goodbyes, though, the members look at Emma speechlessly.

She gives it another try. "So, I guess we can wrap things up here, if nobody else has anything to add?"

Silence.

Has Emma said something inappropriate that she isn't aware of?

"So, um, I'll look forward to reconvening in a week, and…" Seeing the ring of unblinking eyes and mouths hanging ajar, Emma lets her voice trail off.

"STIGMATA!!!" The thick German accent makes the scream even more unnerving.

Seven pairs of bulging eyes are fixated on the foot of Emma's chair. Emma follows their gaze and sees blood running down its leg and pooling on the floor beside her. It's dripping from the center of the white bandage wrapped around her hand, which hangs limply by her side.

GREGORY STANDS BY THE DOOR AS EMMA FINISHES WIPING the blood off the hardwood floor. Thankfully, she was able to calm everyone down and even made a few of them laugh with her silly story about how she'd been so preoccupied thinking about a client's perplexing symptoms that she'd grabbed a steak knife at the wrong end. She simply left out the fact that the client was herself. Once the floor is clean, Emma hobbles over to Gregory. Before she can say anything, though, he makes some sort of hand signal, which looks like a secret code.

"I don't really understand what you're trying to say, Gregory." She hopes she's kept the irritation and trepidation out of her voice.

The coffin maker waves her forward, gesticulating wildly and pointing to a long, shiny black vehicle in the parking lot. This time Emma understands the message. "You want to go to that car? Is that your car?"

Still mute, Gregory nods emphatically and strides off toward the hearse. Emma follows him apprehensively.

The inside of the hearse smells like mothballs and stale perfume, reminding Emma of when she used to visit her great-grandparents' house. There's a stillness in the air, a silence. Perhaps it's all the satin cushions dampening the sound. Or maybe it's the aura of death.

Gregory turns to Emma and whispers, "Let's talk about SOS."

"Uh, yeah, of course. But why are you whispering?" Emma's sense of foreboding has intensified, and her intuition is telling her to get the hell out of the car. But she needs answers.

"Because they're listening. They have ears everywhere." The whites of Gregory's dark eyes are showing and the hair on the back of Emma's neck stands up.

"They? Who are *they*? Gregory, what's going on?" The blood is flowing to Emma's arms and legs, readying her to flee.

"The anti-natalists. Like that Rasheda lady. The ones behind the homicide clusters."

"But what about the suicide clusters? The SOS?"

"*Suicide* is what the anti-natalists want us to think it is. But *we* know the truth. Our operatives determined that the people who have been dying in so-called suicide clusters have a higher-than-average number of offspring. You know what happens when you kill off people who procreate? You kill off *people*. Human extinction!"

"Your operatives?"

"That friend of yours who needs help? They have what—four, five, six kids? And now they're asking questions about why people in their community are killing themselves, right? They're next. The anti-natalists will do whatever it takes to keep them quiet." Gregory's whisper is shrill, and there's a fanatical gleam in his eye. "We're going to expose the anti-natalist global conspiracy for what it is. Soon everyone will know about Babygate. And the Rashedas of the world will get what they deserve!"

The incident involving Gregory's parents in the coffin apparently did more harm than Emma had realized.

"Gregory, uh, thanks for taking the time to talk with me. I'm, um, really not feeling well, though, and I think it's best I get an Uber home now."

"SOS!" Gregory roars, suddenly no longer whispering. "Save! Our! Species!" And he breaks out in maniacal laughter that follows Emma all the way across the parking lot as she does her best to run away, with her booted foot and clumsy crutches.

It's 8:05 p.m. Emma has been sitting at her white Ikea desk in her home office staring at the digital display on her laptop since 7:45, when she got home from her nightmarish encounter with the coffin maker. The maximum time for the elixir to take effect ended five minutes ago. She feels no change in her condition. At least, no change for the better.

She'd opened her computer to ask CouchGPT for tips on writing comforting suicide notes, and somehow got mesmerized by the time display. It's as though she's bearing witness to the final minutes of her life.

8:07. Emma clicks the icon to open the chatbot.

Just as the tab is loading, an email notification comes in. It's from Touch and Go, with the subject heading *Congratulations Winner*.

25

The Scream

Days 32–33: Tuesday–Wednesday

To: Ms Ema Parkland

From: contestant@touchandgo.com

Subject: Congratulations Winner

Dear Ms Parkland,

Congratulations, you are winner! You have appointment with venerable Dr. Hans Müller on Thursday 11:00 a.m., it will last fifteen minutes so don't be late, if you miss there will be no second chance. Someone will meet you at airport. You're flights, you're visa and hotel are arranged and costs are included in invoice, attached below. Visa documents and flight and travel information also attached. Doctor believes you probably have by now injuries, we made accommodations for you. Please transfer required funding to account number in invoice BEFORE your appointment.

C u in 3 days!

When she read the email a few hours ago, Emma felt like she'd stuck her finger into a socket. Or what she imagined she'd feel like if she did that. It was like an electric current was coursing through her veins. Flooded by a deluge of emotions that rarely coexist, her muscles twitched and her breath was fast and shallow. So she did what any emotionally intelligent psychologist who couldn't make sense of such contradictory feelings would do: Emma screamed.

The ungodly sound spewed forth from some deep, primal place within her. It was guttural and earsplitting, profoundly ugly. It was an embodiment of all the fear and confusion, the despairing and striving and hoping and daring that began a month ago. It was Emma's version of Edvard Munch's blood-curdling painting.

Seeing Annie's tail swiftly vanish around the corner as he sprinted out of the little home office to hide, Emma felt a pang of guilt. He'd been in her lap kneading her thighs through their favorite, well-worn fleece blanket and purring contentedly when the heinous sound emerged. Annie had never heard Emma howl like that. Neither had Emma.

Now, at 4:00 a.m., Emma's scream has long since been swallowed up by the stillness of the night. The world is cloaked in silence. At this hour, it's like the edges of reality are softened, the walls of the world padded. Emma feels like she should be listening for something, but she's not sure what.

The Uber is due to arrive in thirty minutes to take her to Logan Airport for her 7:05 a.m. flight. If all goes as planned, she'll arrive in Mumbai tomorrow at 11:25

a.m. On Thursday she'll travel to a mountain village whose name she can't pronounce to see the doctor, and then take a red-eye home that same night. And she'll be cured. Hopefully.

Emma had to cancel all her clients this week, last-minute, which was a first for her. But once she'd sent off the last of the emails explaining that she was sick and wouldn't be available for the rest of the week—not a lie—the guilt she'd expected to feel never came. Instead, she felt relief. And an inexplicable sense of freedom.

Now that she's been given the opportunity to see Dr. Müller, Emma has started feeling hopeful. Müller is the only person in the world who's worked on a cure for SOS. And he has a prestigious background, having trained at top medical institutions and achieved acclaim during his long career. None of the other potential remedies—the family reconciliation, the Program, Gregory's secret—had been based on actual research into SOS. Plus, Dr. Müller only sees patients he thinks he can cure, so that's got to count for something.

A ping on her phone alerts her that her Uber is out front. She grabs the handle of her compact maroon suitcase, slings her canvas laptop bag over her shoulder, and bends down to give Annie one more kiss and scratch under the chin. Since recovering from Emma's outburst, the cat has been meowing and rubbing against her ankles, sensing that his person is going away.

"It's okay, sweetheart," Emma coos. "Walter's going to be checking on you and I'll be home in just a couple of days."

Unless I trip and fall in front of a rickshaw in Mumbai.

Or fill my pockets with sandstone and walk into the Arabian Sea. Or …

Emma winces at the thought of never returning to Annie. Even though she knows he'll be taken care of—after the stabbing, the first one, in her chest, she told Walter that if anything should ever happen to her, she wanted Annie to be his charge, to which Walter gave a royal salute. She's hopeful that Annie would eventually warm to the kindly old man, and maybe even to Charles. But still, Emma would never want to put the cat through another devastating loss.

She climbs into the Uber, which is a dented-up Honda Civic that smells of new car and stale smoke, and pulls on a mask to block the stench. Thankfully, unlike last week, the mask is protecting *her* by keeping the stink *out*, rather than protecting others by keeping it in.

Gazing out the window, she's reminded of the last time she made the drive to Logan. It was four years ago, when she went to Argentina for a conference on working with trauma survivors. She gave a talk on the ways that post-traumatic stress can be expressed indirectly. Traumatologist Judith Herman had famously pointed out that people sometimes engage in behaviors that simultaneously conceal and reveal the origins of their trauma. A child who's been abused may play with dolls and seem to be having fun, while at the same time acting out the abuse by making the dolls fight. Emma built on Herman's points, explaining how repressed traumatic memories often trickle into conscious awareness over time, as the survivor becomes resilient enough to handle them. How Emma wishes that she were on her way to another inspiring professional gathering, rather than making a bizarre, last-ditch effort to save her life.

AFTER A HARROWING TREK THROUGH VARIOUS AIRPORT checkpoints, with their snaking lines and snapping agents and senseless protocol, Emma is finally boarding the plane. Air travel seems like a metaphor for so much that's wrong with the world—from gross ineptitude to gross wastes of time to just plain grossness, as evidenced by the bacteria-ridden security bins filled with bacteria-ridden shoes and bags. And her compromised condition has been no help at all. She declined a wheelchair, feeling like that would be overkill, especially since she no longer needs to use crutches. But then she was treated as though she was just as mobile as everyone else, even though she was hobbling along in a boot cast.

35B. Emma peers at the tiny seat she's been assigned. Have planes gotten smaller since she last flew? At least she's got an aisle seat. She hoists her suitcase up and slides it into the overhead compartment with the help of a fellow passenger who saw her struggling, and then tosses her purse on top of it.

"Ach! NEIN! *Ten hours* under a purse?! What the hell are you *thinking*?!" Emma jumps at the snarling German voice shouting from the storage compartment. Without a second thought, she grabs her purse and throws it on her seat, looking around to see if anyone else heard the outburst.

Two days. She just needs to keep it together for two more days.

She slips into her seat and lets out a breath. Finally, she can rest. There's nothing left for her to do now but wait.

The last passengers are finally on board, crammed into the narrow aisle and banging into each other as they try to stow their cumbersome items and maneuver into their minuscule seats. A clean-cut young man standing two rows in front of Emma lifts his wheeled suitcase, but instead of placing it overhead, he stands it on the seat beside him and leans over to fasten the seat belt around it. Several passengers smile and raise their hands in the L symbol.

Two more days.

Standing in the aisle beside Emma is a brown-skinned man with deep-set eyes and wavy salt-and-pepper hair who's stuffing his briefcase into the crowded compartment over her seat. Emma looks away, hoping not to hear another cry of outrage.

The man takes the seat next to Emma. He looks to be in his fifties, and he speaks with an Indian accent when he introduces himself. "It's going to be a long flight, so it's nice to know who your neighbor is." He smiles warmly. "I'm Shakir Krimandi. And who do I have the pleasure of sitting next to?"

"Uh, Emma. Emma Parkland." Emma self-consciously extends her bandaged right hand and prays she doesn't have another irreverent bloodletting.

"So, where are you headed, Ms. Emma?"

Good question.

"Um, Mumbai."

"Mumbai! I lived there when I was a young man. Wonderful city. Smells like poop, though, in some parts. It can be a stinky place. But it's a cultural mecca, and the food is the best. The people, too. They're as kind as they come. And what will you do in Mumbai?"

"I won't actually be in the city. I'm going to a village near Matheran. To see a doctor."

"Ah, I see, I see. Matheran. Lovely town, up the mountain and in the forest. I'm a doctor, too. What is it that ails you, Ms. Emma? If you don't mind me asking?"

Because she's got nothing to lose, and perhaps also because Shakir is listening to her with such empathy and compassion—something she didn't realize she was starved for until just now—Emma tells her story. She omits some details, like the fact that her condition has progressed to the point where she's on the threshold of killing herself, because she doesn't want Shakir to have her blood on his hands for not preventing her suicide, if it comes to that.

Once she's done, Shakir nods gravely. "Makes sense," he says.

"What makes sense?"

"That Müller would come to India. You said he's an 'out-of-the-box thinker,' right?"

Beads of sweat break out on Emma's forehead and back, as she recalls wide-eyed Gregory in his satin-lined hearse.

"Yes. He's innovative."

"In India, we have a different approach to healing than you do in the West. Indian medicine looks at the whole— the whole person, and also the whole system they're a part of. Their relationships, the world they inhabit. Their past, the memories that shape their present. We don't just cut out a tumor, so to speak. We also ask what's wrong with the body, such that conditions were created in which a tumor could grow."

The flight attendant—a forty-something man with

bleached blonde hair and the kind of tan that went out in the eighties—arrives pushing a cart with foil-wrapped trays of breakfast. He leans toward Emma and Shakir, with a wide smile and dead eyes. "You have a choice of pancakes with chicken sausage or scrambled eggs with bacon."

'Cause if I were an Oscar Mayer Wiener…

"Pancakes and chicken sausage sound great!" Hopefully Emma's emphatic choice will encourage Shakir to follow suit.

The flight attendant picks up on Emma's cue. "For you, too, sir?"

"No, thank you."

That is what I'd never want to be.

"I ordered a vegan meal."

Two more days.

MUMBAI AIRPORT FEELS LIKE A SENSORY TSUNAMI. HIGH-INtensity LED lights, nonstop announcements and beeping transport horns, and wafts of incense and curry and perfume wash over Emma. The climate control system is apparently not working properly, and the air is muggy. Emma's unwashed hair clings to her neck, and her whole body is sticky, making the parts beneath her bandages itch. Dazed and jetlagged, she's swept along with the tide of teeming humans toward the exit.

After entering the densely packed arrival hall, she scans for her driver. Her eyes land on a diminutive man with a substantial mustache who looks like he could fit in her thirteen-year-old niece's clothes. He's holding up a wrinkled piece of lined notebook paper, the sides covered in tacky golden decals of trophies. In the center is written "Miss Ema."

Cautiously, Emma approaches him. "Hello, are you looking for Emma Parkland?"

He responds with a wobble of his head, somehow in three directions at once. It's neither a yes, nor a no, nor a maybe.

"Is that yes?"

"Miss Ema?" Wobble.

"I'm Emma Parkland. Are you here for me?"

Wobble. "Miss Ema. Okay."

Changing tack, Emma asks, "Who sent you here?"

Wobble wobble. "I'm sent from Touch and Go Healing, on behalf of venerable Dr. Hans Müller." Wobble.

"All right, then. I'm uh, Miss Ema."

"Ah! Welcome, Miss Ema!" The little man beams. "Congratulations, winner!"

***

STEVERINO, WHO WAS BORN ANNU, CHANGED HIS NAME after watching an obscure sitcom about nerdy teenage Italian American boys. He's driving his dinged-up little silver Hyundai like a bat out of hell, zipping in and out of traffic and slapping his palm on the horn like he's flattening a wad of pizza dough. Emma's stomach is doing backflips and every burp carries the threat of expelling more than just air.

"Miss Ema, it is very great honor to meet you!" Steverino is looking at her in the rearview mirror, instead of looking at the road.

"Thank you." Emma doesn't know what else to say. Plus, she doesn't want to encourage Steverino to keep his eyes on her rather than on his driving and risk an accident.

Then again…

"Winner gets an audience with esteemed Dr. Müller. You are very lucky. You are special!"

"So, um, Steve—"

"Steverino! I'm not Steve. Everyone is Steve."

"Steverino. Does Dr. Müller cure everyone he sees?"

"You are WINNER Miss Ema!"

"Yes, but I won a cure, right? Or the opportunity for a cure?"

Steverino laughs softly, shaking his head, as though Emma is a child who doesn't know better. "Miss Ema. What more do you need? You already won!"

An hour later, Steverino deposits Emma at the front steps of her hotel. It's a rundown little inn, but all she needs is a tub for a sponge bath and a bed so she can tumble into merciful unconsciousness.

Bidding her goodbye, Steverino reminds her to be ready by 5:30 a.m. the following day. "We have two hours' drive, then you take train, then two hours' hike. We take you the easy route for your injuries."

Easy?

Before Emma can protest, Steverino is trotting back to his car.

Turning toward the entrance of the inn, Emma heads to the room where she'll spend what could be the last night of her deadly condition. Or her life.

26

No Words

Day 34: Thursday

"**W**ake up, sleepyhead!"

As Emma pries open her sandy eyes, the echo of the dream voice fades away. The unfamiliar room is barely visible in the pale dawn light coming through the worn curtains. The plain walls, scratchy pillowcase, and stiff mattress flicker in and out of her awareness. Groggy and disoriented, she blinks to clear her vision and recognizes the hotel room she checked into yesterday.

"Get outta bed and make some bread! HAHAHAHA!"

Emma's heart leaps to her throat. Who on earth—? There's nobody in the room but her. She looks around the sparsely furnished space; there's only an old wooden bureau and a secretary desk. And—she notices with a start—the compact maroon suitcase standing in the corner, facing her. Feeling a wave of panic, she reminds herself that in just a few hours she'll be in the hands of the person who can cure her.

She reaches over to turn off her alarm, which reads

5:00 a.m., and pulls back the weightless covers. Sitting up, she gasps as stabs of pain radiate through her bruised ribs and aching shoulder and ankle. The hard mattress was not kind to her battered body.

By 5:25, she's standing on the front steps of the hotel, waiting for Steverino. The rising sun casts a sickly orange haze over the rubble-strewn driveway and patchy grass of the lawn, and the soupy air is already oppressively warm.

But Emma's heart is lighter than it's been since she came down with SOS. The hope she feels today isn't like the wishful thinking she had when Nick and her father talked or when she took the elixir or was on her way to meet with Gregory. It's an intuitive sense, a kind of knowing that she's right where she's supposed to be.

***

STEVERINO HAS BEEN MERCIFULLY QUIET DURING THE TWO-hour drive, which has taken them through city streets, past bucolic towns, and then up the foot of a steep mountain. When he first picked up Emma, he'd explained that "noble silence" is part of the treatment protocol and said he'd speak only when necessary.

"Today, you must be in state of readiness, Miss Ema. That mean no speaking, no singing, no thinking."

No thinking?

"Um, how can I not think?"

Wobble. "You need clear mind. You must be open to receive the healing."

"Uh, okay, but I can't just stop thinking."

Wobble. "Noble silence. Please, Miss Ema, for your

own good."

"It's just that—"

Steverino's head then started wobbling furiously, like the plastic laughing Buddha on a spring glued to his dashboard.

Emma bit her tongue. A wobble is worth a thousand words.

Steverino pulls into the Toy Train station, a dusty parking lot at the base of a forested, low mountain. Before slipping into noble silence, he had given Emma an envelope containing a one-way ticket for the Neral–Matheran Toy Train, a historic locomotive that traverses the narrow passageway through the upper parts of the mountain, where motor vehicles are banned. He'd told her she was to take the train for ninety minutes to Matheran, where she'd be met by a guide who would accompany her on the hike up the path to the village where the clinic is.

Steverino climbs out of the car to open the door for Emma and hand her her suitcase. Before getting back into the vehicle, he gives her one last wobble.

"Thank—" Emma catches herself and instead wobbles back, to the degree that she can, wearing a neck brace.

The morning sun is merciless, and Emma peels off her sheer, button-down shirt so she's wearing only a tank top, before heading across the parking lot.

Emma is one of about ten people waiting at the tiny station, which is little more than a couple of sheltered benches at the edge of the forest. Most of the people seem to be tourists, and they're eagerly snapping selfies as they pose in front of the askew wooden sign that reads "Toy Train."

Before long, a charming, heritage-looking steam

engine, painted in bright red, forest green, and burnt orange, is whistling its approach. Emma follows the other passengers inside and takes a seat in a booth. The train is largely empty, so she has the booth to herself and welcomes the opportunity to let her mind wander.

… no speaking, no singing, no thinking.

Or not.

Maybe she'll just sit and wobble.

"Tickets!" Emma hears the conductor approaching and opens the envelope Steverino gave her. Inside is a piece of lined notebook paper with handwritten text that reads "Ticket to Matheran Miss Ema" and which is ringed with the same little golden decals of trophies as his airport sign had been. Her heart races as she wonders how far she'd have to walk to get to the nearest station if she's kicked off the train for having a bogus ticket.

"TICKETS!" Emma almost leaps out of her seat. Standing six inches from her, the portly man with fleshy earlobes and suspenders hoisting his pants almost to his chest is as loud as he was when he was calling down the aisle of the train. Trembling, she hands him her paper. He narrows his eyes as he looks at the ticket, and then regards Emma with the same intense stare.

"MISS EMA?" he yells.

"Uh, y—"

"—SHHHHH!" The conductor cuts her off sternly. He puts a finger in front of his ample lips before repeating his question in a more reasonable tone. "Miss Ema?"

"Uh—" Emma cuts herself off and wobbles her head.

This seems to have been the right response, as a wide grin spreads over the conductor's face. "Remember, noble silence." Beaming, he adds, "Congratulations, winner!"

⁂

Emma tries not to let her mind wander as she looks out the window at the rich foliage the train is slowly passing through. The narrow mountain path is lined with giant Indian laurel and mango trees, their leaves thick and gleaming, and tangles of vines and ferns. It's like a lush, green cascade.

At 9:00 a.m., the Toy Train whistles its approach to Matheran, slowing to a stop. Nobody but Emma gets off at the deserted-looking station, which consists of a covered tunnel and a modest building with a slanted metal roof. The only other person in sight is a matronly woman standing on the platform, with dark brown skin, wide-set eyes, and gray hair pulled into a low, braided bun. She's wearing sandals and an orange robe, like Buddhists wear, and is carrying a sign made of lined notebook paper. The sign reads "Miss Ema" and, predictably, is ringed by gold trophy decals.

"Miss Ema?" The woman looks at Emma expectantly.

Obediently, Emma wobbles her head.

The woman's brow furrows. "Miss Ema? Is that you?"

"Oh, uh, yes?" Emma adds a wobble, just for good measure.

"Phew. You had me worried I was at the wrong stop." Wobble wobble. "I'm Adyanti, and I'll be your walking guide to Touch and Go. But before we get started, congratulations, winner!" Adyanti is beaming just as Steverino and the conductor had.

"Thank you. But I thought I wasn't supposed to talk?"

271

Emma rubs her temples. Her headache has returned with a vengeance, due at least in part to all the effort of trying, unsuccessfully, to learn Wobblespeak. Still, her newfound sense of hope hasn't waned.

Adyanti smiles warmly. "For this final part of your journey, you are to keep the noble silence but you may speak."

Emma shakes her head, trying to clear the cobwebs and make sense of what she just heard.

"Exactly." Adyanti apparently assumed Emma had just given a meaningful wobble. "So, we have about two hours to hike. We're taking the easy path so you don't do too much damage to your foot and other injured body parts."

Too much—?

"I'll take your bag." Adyanti reaches for the handle of Emma's suitcase. "Your appointment with Master Müller is at 11:00, but we'll arrive a bit early to get you checked in."

"*Master* Müller? Don't you mean *Dr*. Müller?"

Adyanti laughs amiably. "Master, doctor. Same difference. You may call him whatever suits you."

Emma feels the familiar bubbling of hysteria start to resurface.

Seeming to sense Emma's consternation, Adyanti adds, "Names are mere words. The fact is, Master Müller is a miracle worker. Why else would he be able to call his clinic Touch and Go?"

Adyanti leads Emma silently along a tight, twisty mountain trail. Perhaps because she's not engaged in conversation, or because she's using most of her mental energy to concentrate on not stepping on one of the jagged rocks or bulging tree roots in her path, Emma's mind is almost quiet. Maybe there's something to this noble silence concept, after all.

Adyanti takes her as far as the clinic grounds and then bids her goodbye. With a bow, she adds, "Now it's up to you to find your way." Emma bows back, and wobbles. As she turns to walk toward the buildings, she feels a little tap on her bottom that makes her jump, and she instinctively wheels around to face Adyanti. The woman merely winks and walks off as though nothing untoward has happened. Emma feels like a child being sent off to school. Or a patient being sexually harassed.

Sweat is streaming down her face and dripping off the ends of her hair as she limps along the slate walkway toward the entrance to Touch and Go, dragging her suitcase behind her. The small wood-and-stone building complex sits in a glade that's nestled in the midst of the forest. It looks more like a temple than a clinic, with a large fountain of the Buddha, his head flipped back at a ninety-degree angle and water spewing out of his gaping mouth, in the front courtyard and a curved roof atop decorative pillars.

The main doors to the clinic open into a large waiting room with a high ceiling and tall windows. A string of glitter-covered cardboard letters that spell out "CONGRATULATIONS WINNER!" hangs from the rafters and spans the width of the room. At the far end of the room is a booth under a sign that reads "Rezeption."

Emma approaches the booth and is told by the receptionist—a stooped, shriveled prune of a man with about twenty strands of white hair—that Master Müller is behind schedule. He asks her to take a seat and thanks her for being a patient patient, a phrase that's also printed on a sign standing on the counter. At this play on words, the old man tears up and presses both hands tightly against his mouth to prevent himself from laughing out loud. He's snorting and shaking his head while tears stream down his cheeks, as Emma turns to take her seat.

The room is almost full, with a diverse array of people and problems to rival those of New York—people of all races, ages, and genders. Some appear to have physical injuries or illnesses; others seem psychologically unwell. There's a downtrodden young woman with a third nostril, someone on a stretcher in a full body cast, parents fussing over a toddler sporting a thick mustache, and a man having a heated debate with nobody.

Every few minutes, the narrow door to the right of the reception booth opens, and a patient who's just been treated walks back into the waiting room. With each entrance, the hunched receptionist congratulates the individual and, with his hands raised above his head, claps loudly. The waiting patients join in the applause.

The first patient to come through the door is a woman clutching a heavily bandaged infant to her chest and holding a large bottle of medication. She's weeping openly and Emma is moved by her tears of joy. Next is a family of five, all of whom are also crying. The parents are arm-in-arm, kissing each other repeatedly, and the children are ringing them, grabbing their legs. Then comes an elderly man in a wheelchair with a scrawny, floppy-eared, hairless cat in his lap. Both man and cat have one leg in a cast, as does the androgynous-looking person pushing them.

During the ninety minutes that Emma waits to be

called, her sense of anticipation grows, and she feels almost ashamed of having doubted Dr. Müller. When she finally hears her name, her stomach is aflutter and she leaps to her feet, despite her injuries. She hurries to the reception booth to be met, like those who were called before her, by an orange-robed man with a shiny, shaved head. He leads her down a short hallway and ushers her into Dr. Müller's office. After bowing to the doctor, the monk quickly takes his leave.

The office has the cool, damp feel of a cave. The dark paneling, endless shelves of antiquarian books, and small, high windows give the dim room a feeling of gravitas. As does Dr. Müller's sizable wooden desk, which is strewn with folders and papers and what appears to be a collection of Hello Kitty figurines.

Like his assistant and Adyanti, the doctor is wearing an orange robe, but over it is a white lab coat. He's sitting at his desk across from Emma, looking at her with an intensity in his piercing, pale blue eyes that makes the back of her neck tingle. He has a wild mane of white hair and thick gray brows, one of which looks like it's perpetually raised. Hanging on the wall behind him is a framed quote by Thoreau that says: *It's not what you look at that matters. It's what you see.*

Without uttering a word to Emma, even in greeting, the doctor looks her over appraisingly and nods sagely, as though she's what he's been expecting. He opens a file on his desk that's labeled "Miss Ema," which contains the printout of the email she sent describing her condition and the documents she submitted, including her astrological chart. Notes are scribbled all over the pages, with question marks and arrows pointing in a variety of directions and words like *Ursache* (cause) and *Heilung* (cure), which Emma recognizes from her German courses in college.

After about five minutes of increasingly unsettling silence, Dr. Müller clears his throat and addresses Emma in a thick Austrian accent. "What is the sound of half a heart beating?"

Emma waits for the doctor to continue, but he doesn't. "Um, sorry, I—"

The monk who'd brought her into the office suddenly reappears. He quickly bows to the doctor and gestures to Emma to follow him to the door.

Hysteria rises in Emma's chest. "I just need to ask the doctor what—"

But Dr. Müller has returned the papers to Emma's file and is putting it on the pile behind him.

Tears begin flowing down her cheeks, and she rises mutely as the monk takes her elbow and ferries her back out to the main room, where she's met by congratulations and applause. Her heart freezes when she realizes that the previously released patients may not have been crying tears of joy after all.

Emma is desperate to flee the premises, but she stops at the reception desk to pick up her return ticket for the Toy Train, as Steverino instructed her. Dismayed and incensed, she can't help but point out to the receptionist that Dr. Müller didn't deliver on Touch and Go's promise. "Other patients were given medicine, bandaging, and—"

The old man cuts her off. No longer jesting, the look in his eyes is grave. "Miss Ema, every being is unique. Dr. Müller gives each individual what they need."

Emma has no words. She turns away, silently, to head back the way she came.

All hope of finding a cure is lost. She's as good as dead.

27

Faceplanting

✦

Day 37: Sunday

The tiny shards of gravel dig deeper into the side of Emma's face with every passing moment. Her head is pounding and her eyes, nose, and throat are burning, making it difficult to breathe. She blows out weakly to dislodge a pebble that's stuck on her bottom lip.

She can't remember when she fell. She's been existing outside the normal passage of time since the fleshy-eared receptionist at Touch and Go confirmed her worst fear: that Dr. Müller, her only remaining hope for a cure, is a quack.

Frankly, she doesn't care how long she's been lying atop this bumpy, pebbly terrain. There's nowhere more fitting for her to be, no metaphor more appropriate for what her life has become.

Even her view of the unspoiled blue sky is obstructed by a gnarly log lying directly in her line of sight.

It's not what you look at that matters. It's what you see.

A sudden scratching beside the top of her head is followed by the sound of streaming water. Emma chokes on the burning ammonia of Annie's urine, and coughs spastically. She manages to heave herself up just before the warm liquid makes its way into her neck brace, the window she'd been trying to peer through swaying as the blood rushes from her head.

She spent the past two days in bed after returning from Mumbai on Friday evening. Whether due to the jet-lag or the exhaustion from the trip or the fact that she'd run out of options to cure her SOS, she had neither the energy nor the desire to do anything other than try to stay unconscious. She got up only to feed Annie—and, a few moments ago, to finally clean his litter box, which she normally does twice a day.

Since the arduous journey, Emma's joints have been stiff and her muscles and wounds aching. So she had to kneel on the floor to clean the box. When she was lifting a hefty patty of hardened urine, her knee gave out and she fell forward face first, just managing to turn sideways to avoid a full-frontal faceplant.

Now, sitting beside the litter box, Emma robotically finishes what she started. Annie shouldn't have to pay the price for her dysfunction any more than he already has. Or will, given the progression of her condition.

After tying up the ends of the foul-smelling bag and depositing it in the trash, Emma climbs the wide, hardwood stairs to go back to bed. She stops in the bathroom to clean herself up, and almost doesn't recognize the face looking back at her from the mirror. Her light green eyes are sunken and ringed in purple, and her skin is a sickly yellow. Little pink dents cover the right side of her face, and stray granules of litter cling to the side of her mouth and her matted, frizzy hair.

Disgusted, she removes her neck brace as hard crumbs fall out, and kneels down to stick her head under the tap of the tub. There's no way she'll be able to sleep without washing at least her head and face. It's bad enough that she's still wearing the same flannel pajamas she put on when she got home on Friday.

How did the Touch and Go treatment fail so spectacularly? Müller was supposed to be a healer. Emma was supposed to be a winner.

She spent the long journey home stunned and dazed, feeling as though she was moving through a dream. It was like there was a thick piece of glass separating her from the world around and within her, muting sounds, blurring sights, and dulling her emotions. And those final, fateful moments at Touch and Go kept replaying in her mind, even while she hobbled through the airport terminal passing an unruly demonstration of protestors carrying placards of steel-blue suitcases and making the L sign with their hands.

Dr. Müller gives each individual what they need.

No matter how many times she revisited the ordeal at Touch and Go, Emma simply couldn't wrap her mind around what had happened. According to Müller's logic, what she needed was not medication. Or counseling. Or anything else that made any sort of sense. What Emma needed was, apparently, a koan.

Even when she'd been interested in Zen Buddhism, she wasn't a fan of the odd, paradoxical phrases that apparently bypass the rational mind to trigger deep insight. A practitioner is given a koan and is then supposed to "sit with it," allowing it to percolate, without analyzing it. Over time, the koan supposedly breaks through mental barriers and opens the mind to the true nature of reality. Emma's brain used to get twisted in knots when she'd hear things like "Does a dog have Buddha-nature?" and "What is the sound of one hand clapping?"

What is the sound of half a heart beating?

For the umpteenth time since leaving Touch and Go, Emma resolves to push Müller's koan out of her mind. She finishes rinsing her hair under the tub faucet and dabs it with a towel, checking herself in the mirror to make sure she hasn't missed anything, like a chunk of litter that may have gotten lodged in her ear. She gives a little head wobble of satisfaction and, with a start, recalls overhearing a passenger on the flight from India complaining that the wobble is contagious.

Once she's finally back in bed, Emma pulls the covers up to her chin. Annie, who has barely left her side since she returned, leaps onto her chest and headbutts her forehead, purring loudly. The cat has always been able to sense when Emma is distressed, and he knows what kinds of cuddles will comfort her. This time, however, his efforts are in vain.

There's nowhere to go from here. Nobody left to turn to. Emma had considered talking to Shana when the elixir seemed to be failing, but that was before she got the email from Touch and Go. At this point, there's nothing Shana could do. Emma's already covered all her bases. Plus, it's now exactly thirty-seven days since she woke up with SOS, the average life expectancy for SOS victims, according to Müller's calculations. Not that she should trust anything Müller says.

There's no hope left of finding a cure. That is, if the "cure" is to end her suicidality, rather than her life. What if she developed SOS because she's *supposed* to kill herself? What if her suicidal urge exists for a good reason, if it's a message from her psyche that it's time to move on from this life? Maybe Emma is clinging to her life the way some people cling to a relationship or job they've outgrown but aren't yet ready to let go. Maybe Emma's time is up.

She lets out a long exhale. Just the thought of giving herself permission to stop struggling, stop resisting, releases the tightness in her chest. Of course, the end of her suffering would be the beginning of others'. But she could make it low-drama, killing herself gently, beautifully, even. Poetically, like Sylvia Plath or Yukio Mishima or—

Even in her suicidal stupor, Emma knows that if she continues down this rabbit hole, she won't emerge alive.

But her will to survive is as fragile as the wings of a moth that have lost their powdery coating. Closing her eyes, Emma pulls the covers over her face and slips back into her deadly fantasies.

28

"I'm done."

Day 38: Monday

"I don't deserve this life. I'm done."

Truer words have never been spoken.

"What?" Ricardo, whose usually pressed clothes are full of wrinkles and normally smooth face is covered in stubble, looks at Emma with his mouth ajar. He sits on the thick sofa, picking at the small, patterned throw pillow in his lap. Despite it being midday, the sky outside the window behind him is dark with gathering storm clouds.

Emma swallows when she realizes that she's again unintentionally verbalized a thought to Ricardo. What is it about therapy with this man that causes her to be so preoccupied and careless? Today, she's especially absentminded. She shouldn't have dragged herself into the office, when just yesterday she was face down in feline excrement. She'd rescheduled her other Monday clients—but she didn't feel right not seeing Ricardo when he's been going through such a difficult time, especially since he'd asked to see her today rather than wait for his usual Friday meeting.

"Oh, um, well—I just think you're being especially authentic today. Really speaking your truth." Thankfully, she doesn't have to lie.

"You're right." Ricardo's drawn face is sallow and his broad shoulders are slouched, emphasizing the creases in his Ralph Lauren button-down shirt. "Because I've got nothing left to lose."

Neither do I.

Did she just let another vocalization slip out? Horrified, Emma claps her hand over her mouth.

"What's wrong? Are you nauseous? Do you need to be sick?" Concern shows in Ricardo's eyes as his lip curls slightly, in disgust.

"Um, sorry. I'm a little unwell today, but I don't need to throw up." This is true. "And I'm not contagious." Also true. Most likely.

Speaking of which...

"Ricardo, before we talk more about what you just said, can you tell me if you've had any thoughts of hurting yourself?"

"You mean am I suicidal?" Ricardo snorts derisively. "As in, am I planning to do a swan dive off the Tobin Bridge after our appointment?"

Ricardo vaulting gracefully into the Boston Harbor— clad in a white unitard with large snowy wings affixed to his back and a long yellow beak fastened to his face— would definitely be on brand.

"I know you've got to ask this," he continues, "but it's awkward. Like, what am I going to say? Either I tell you I *do* want to kill myself, and then you have me locked up, or I say I don't, to keep you from preventing my suicidal success."

Suicidal success. That's got a nice ring to it.

Ricardo seems to deflate. "But honestly, no. I'm not planning to kill myself. What I'm planning to do is to quit therapy. I wasn't referring to ending my life, but to ending therapy." Ricardo locks eyes with Emma. "No offense."

If Ricardo terminates therapy, that would be one less loose end for Emma to worry about if she kills herself. She nods her head slowly, letting out a sigh of relief.

"I'm sorry, Emma. I can see you're disappointed." Ricardo's tone is earnest. "I want to make it perfectly clear that this has *nothing* to do with you. You've been great. I mean, maybe a little odd and gross the past couple of weeks, but overall, you're a great therapist. It's me, not you."

There's something embarrassing about the way Ricardo is taking such care with his words, which seem almost rehearsed. It's like he's breaking up with her and trying not to hurt her feelings.

Emma resists a sudden childish urge to tell Ricardo that *she's* glad to see *him* go. "I understand, and please, don't worry about my feelings. My job is to support you to follow whatever path is right for you. Why don't you tell me what led to this decision?"

"Phew." Ricardo squeezes his eyes closed and pinches the bridge of his nose, smiling faintly. His palpable relief embarrasses Emma further. Had he expected her to burst into tears and beg him not to leave her, like a woman scorned? "Coming here is making me hate myself even more than I already do. I feel like a hypocrite, paying someone to listen to me complain about how hard my privileged life is, when others are suffering so much more."

Emma has talked to Ricardo multiple times about his

use of the term "hypocrite," which is a judgmental way to describe someone whose values and behaviors aren't in alignment. A more accurate and respectful framing is to say that someone is living with contradictions. Which everyone is. Ricardo needs to understand that he, like all people, has to make imperfect choices in an imperfect world. What matters most is not whether he lives with contradictions, but how he relates to those contradictions. Does he reflect on them? Learn from them? Try to minimize them?

"After our last session, my depression got worse," he continues. "It was the guilt. I couldn't sleep, couldn't stop thinking about how I'm everything I've spent my life fighting against. Hypocritical. Entitled. Ignorant. *A bystander to injustice.*" He screws up his face, as though he smells something rotten.

Emma's stomach does a little flip-flop as she wonders whether she stinks of cat urine. Is it possible she didn't clean her neck brace thoroughly enough?

"Hell, I even have 'don't be a bystander' tattooed on my arm." Looking down, Ricardo shakes his head sadly. "And yet, after decades of activism, I discover that I've been directly contributing to suffering on a massive scale, to a fucking unimaginable injustice." He raises his eyes to meet Emma's, as if to see if she's siding with his inner critic.

Emma arranges her features so her face is soft, reflecting what she hopes is compassion and acceptance. If there's one thing that this man needs, it's to see himself through the eyes of someone who's not standing in judgment of him. To learn, through insight and skillful relating, to accept himself as a fundamentally worthy person. When

Ricardo understands that good people can and do participate in harmful practices and this doesn't mean they're less worthy of compassion than anyone else, he'll be able to respect himself, and others, as he works to make the world a better place. And, hopefully, he'll find peace.

Ricardo squints and leans slightly forward as he peers at the side of Emma's chin. He wipes his own chin, and purses his lips as though he's sucking on a lemon.

Emma feels the heat rise to her face. This is the second time Ricardo has seemed disgusted by her. Taking his cue, she wipes her chin, hoping to sweep away any leftover crumbs from the banana muffin she had for breakfast. But her hand rubs against a sticky lock of hair with gravelly lumps in it, that's poking up out of her neck brace. Her eyes widen in horror, but she keeps the rest of her features composed as she surreptitiously tugs at the strands, trying to pull the cat litter out.

Ricardo clears his throat. "I could almost justify my hypocrisy if I hadn't known better. But I could have seen the truth; it was all around me. I just didn't want to. It would have been inconvenient to have to care about another cause, not to mention to change my diet."

Even though she's caught up in her own, internal mortal combat, Emma feels her heart ache at Ricardo's self-recrimination. "And yet, you ultimately did see the truth. Why now? What was different about this time?"

"I have no fucking idea. I guess I just wasn't ready to see it before." Ricardo looks out the window on the side of the office.

"Can you think of another time you've had a similar experience?" Emma has been uncomfortably aware of the residual stickiness on her hand since she tugged at her soiled hair. Pretending she needs to clean her nose, she plucks a tissue from the box on the mahogany end table next to her, dabs at her nostrils, then rubs her hands with it.

"I've never thought about it. But now that you bring it up, yeah. Yeah. When I was with Xavier, my ex. Through pretty much our whole relationship, all three years of law school, he was putting me down. Judging me and telling me I wasn't good enough. Other people saw it, my friends and family. But not me. I couldn't see what they saw."

"And how is that similar to what you're experiencing now?"

"We took the bar exam at the same time, and Xavier didn't pass. He was in a total rage, which he of course took out on me. And then, suddenly, I saw how demeaning he was to me. It was like a light went on in my mind. And I left him." Ricardo is still gazing through the window, staring into his past. "I think I didn't see the truth sooner because, until then, I'd been convinced nobody else would want me, that I wasn't a good enough person, or successful enough. But after three years of law school I'd grown, and passing the bar showed me that I had what it took to accomplish my goals."

"So you couldn't let yourself see the way Xavier was treating you until you felt like you had the ability to leave him?"

Ricardo shifts his focus from the window to Emma. His gaze drops to her hands, which are still clasping the tissue, and he wrinkles his nose and grimaces.

Holding her breath, Emma follows Ricardo's stare and her stomach lurches at the brown smear across the crumpled white Kleenex. She quickly balls it up and shoves it in the pocket of her cardigan.

Ricardo is thankfully going along with her game of let's-pretend-the-client-isn't-noticing-what-a-disgusting-hot-mess-the-therapist-is. "Yeah, exactly. I was too afraid to even think about leaving him sooner. I guess I had to be ready to see the truth."

It's not what you look at that matters. It's what you see.

The blood drains from Emma's head, and the room tilts. Something inside her is moving, shifting, like tectonic plates sliding into a new configuration.

Ricardo doesn't seem to notice that Emma is clutching the armrests of her chair as she tries to steady herself. "I guess what you're trying to tell me is that I just wasn't 'ready' to see my hamburger as a dead cow and my hot dog as a dead pig?"

My bologna has a first name, it's O.S.C.A.R.…

NO!

"No? What do you mean, *no*? It sounds like that's exactly what you're saying." There's an annoyed edge to Ricardo's voice.

"Um, I mean, no, that's not the whole of it. But, uh, yes. Yes, people have to feel ready to acknowledge painful truths. They have to feel like they can act on these truths, and like they can handle the emotional pain that comes with acknowledging them."

"See?" Ricardo leans forward, looking intently at Emma. "This is exactly why I need to quit therapy. It's self-indulgent. Here I am, talking about how to handle the emotional pain I feel because others are in real pain. If you were on a sinking ship, would you talk about your fear, or would you try to bail out the ship and save all the passengers? Therapizing myself into complacency is just making me feel like even more of a hypocrite. I say I care about justice, and all I do is coddle my own bruised feelings, going on and on about my depression."

"So if you stop therapy, how do you imagine that will affect your depression?"

"I'm sure it'll get worse. Coming here was the only thing that took the edge off it. But I don't care." Ricardo's chin is raised, his tone authoritative. "I'd rather feel more depressed and less guilty."

"Can you help me understand why you feel you have to choose between depression and guilt?"

"Well, the guilt is depressing me so it's not like I wouldn't feel both. But I just can't handle the guilt of paying you to listen to me so I can feel better when there's so much suffering in the world."

"So, if *you* suffer more, *others* will suffer less?" So often, people think that throwing themselves under the bus on their own street will stop buses on different streets from running over others.

"When you put it that way, it sounds pretty irrational. But yeah. I guess on some unconscious level maybe I feel like I don't deserve to be happy as long as others aren't."

"Ricardo, hurting yourself is only going to bring about the opposite outcome of what you want. It's like shooting yourself in the foot when you're carrying someone with a broken leg. You end up stumbling rather than delivering them safely to their destination."

Ricardo pauses, seeming to be absorbing Emma's words. "Sort of like how you have to put on your own oxygen mask before doing the same for others, I guess?"

"Exactly. The more you hurt, the less you can give. So, consider sticking with therapy. Not only for yourself, but for the world you care so much about."

Seeing the light of understanding in Ricardo's eyes, Emma's own start to burn. These are the moments that have made her life worth living.

"So, if I don't take care of myself, I can't take care of others. Thanks, Emma. I'll sit with this."

Emma is giving Ricardo an affirming nod when the walls lurch and the room spins. The floor is rushing toward her face as she hears Ricardo shout, "Emma! You're going down!"

29

It's What You See

Day 42: Friday

Not all those who wander are lost.

Going, Going, Gone! is one of Emma's favorite places to window-shop. But today she doesn't pause beneath the travel agency's illuminated Tolkien quote and instead limps obliviously past the over-sized posters hanging in the window, of turquoise waters lapping white sand beaches; medieval European castles surrounded by verdant, rolling hills; and colorful, bustling Arabian bazaars.

Fading sunlight casts a sickly glow over the recycle bins along the sidewalk, lengthening their shadows. How long has Emma been wandering the streets of Arlington? It's possible that she's been walking—or, rather, hobbling—in circles for hours past the quaint storefronts on Main and State Streets. She staggers forward, passing the colonial buildings, budding trees, and green-and-white street signs.

Emma has never experienced such extreme disorientation. Perhaps Dr. Morelli was wrong about the spot that showed up on her MRI films being from a "dirty scan," and she does have a tumor after all. Or maybe she got brain damage from the carbon monoxide she inhaled this morning. She'd turned on the stove to cook a pot of oatmeal and didn't realize—for over an hour—that the flame hadn't ignited. Or perhaps the stupor she's in is just because, for Emma, these are End Times.

She would normally be in the office today. But after toppling forward and falling on her face on Monday during her session with Ricardo, she decided to cancel her sessions for the rest of the week—for her sake, and also for her clients'. She'll never be able to unsee Ricardo's bulging eyes and gaping mouth as she started her descent to the floor. Or how he gagged and dry heaved after her neck brace broke open and a piece of cat feces rolled out. Even though she hadn't lost consciousness and had assured him that she was probably just dehydrated from having replaced all the water she usually drinks with coffee, he was shaky and flustered and potentially traumatized.

Once home, she went straight to bed and stayed there, getting up only to take care of Annie and to eat or use the bathroom. Alternating between fitful sleeps plagued by nightmares she could never clearly recall and staring vacantly at the walls and ceiling, her mind at once empty and full, Emma lay waiting for death to take her.

Today, she dragged herself out of bed to roam the streets. For what purpose, she doesn't know. Perhaps it's to hasten her demise. Or maybe she'd just rather die limping than lying.

Exiting the boutique shop three doors ahead is an SUV stroller carrying two screaming toddlers. It's being pushed by a frazzled young woman with a high pony-tail and a Boston College sweatshirt who's probably their nanny. The last time Emma walked past Baby Thyme, which somehow manages to stay in business selling nothing other than outrageously expensive onesies to dress babies as plants or animals, they were having an Easter sale. They'd foolishly used a collection of live infants with real eggs and rabbits for their window display, inciting public outrage. Footage of overheated, screaming babies wearing fleece egg or bunny onesies with broken eggshell on their faces and yolks oozing into the necklines of their thick costumes was all over the news. The memory of those reports reminds Emma that she hasn't walked this same path since the day before she woke up with SOS.

Over the past six weeks, she's replayed the events of that day over and over. Nothing has struck her as strange. It had been just like any other day, with only a few minor exceptions. Now, retracing her footsteps, she finds herself again revisiting those final hours before she got ill.

SOS Eve day started out uneventfully, except for a traffic incident that caused Emma—who's always punctual—to be late for her first session. There had been a road closure due to what she later learned was an accident involving a cyclist. The rider had struck one of Boston's notorious potholes, causing him to fall onto the hood of an oncoming car and leading to a pileup of tailgaters. The cyclist lived but was seriously injured, and the road is still closed for repairs. Emma and Nick exchanged texts complaining about how roads in New England are falling apart, due in large part to negligence, and Emma sent him "It Takes a Tragedy"—a *Boston Globe* article about the incident, describing the harm that has to occur before problems get resolved.

During the day, Emma saw her usual Friday clients, who discussed the usual issues. The only thing that was out of the ordinary, and then only a bit, was that Ricardo, who was her last client of the day, had something of a breakthrough. She had urged him a few weeks prior to attend an event put on by the Cambridge Environmental Artists Society, or CEAS, which is pronounced "sees" and has a logo of an open eye. Emma had thought that being exposed to new, creative forms of activism might reinspire him—and, as he explained during their session, it had.

Ricardo told her of the performances he'd seen. There was a modern dance number choreographed to the Doobie Brothers' "Black Water," with naked dancers covered in black oil, slipping and falling all over the stage—which Ricardo assumed was intentional. Then there was a puppet show for children where a farmer and a pig engaged in a clever dialogue about how intensive animal farming contributes to climate change. Finally, there was a sweaty a cappella quartet in a closed, 110-degree greenhouse singing Gregorian chants and holding stalks of sugarcane, depicting harvesters in Brazil. Ricardo had been moved by the performances and, for the first time since losing his job, said he'd consider returning to activism.

After the session with Ricardo, Emma came here, to Main Street, to treat herself to takeout from The Dancing Buddha. The food was excellent, as always, even though they'd mistakenly given her the #39 pork dumplings instead of the #36 shrimp ones. Then she watched Netflix and went to bed early. The only unusual part of her evening was that she felt a little nauseous after dinner.

Once again, Emma's recollection of SOS Eve day has yielded no new insights. It's only made her feel worse. It's as though "Emma BS"—Emma Before Suicidality—never existed, like she's some figment of the imagination of "Emma AS."

Aching from all the walking, she decides not to turn down State Street to make another loop, but to continue on Main Street toward home. Fragrant spices and aromatic frying oils tinge the air as she approaches The Dancing Buddha, which is en route to her house. Despite her lack of appetite, her mouth waters. Maybe she should pick something up. If tonight is going to be her last supper, she should make it special. Plus, she can order the fattiest item on the menu and get the triple layer chocolate banana split for dessert without feeling guilty.

A poster-sized plastic menu is affixed to a sidewalk stand outside the restaurant. Judging by the silly cartoon graphics accompanying the photos of the dishes, you'd never know how delicious the food here is. There's a picture of bok choy, broccoli, and carrots, all with skinny legs standing next to the Buddha bowl; a hen squatting over egg drop soup; a smiling pig wearing an apron and brandishing a carving knife beside the pork dumplings, and—

Oh, I'm glad I'm not an Oscar Mayer Wiener. That is what I'd never want to be-ee-ee. 'Cause if I were an Oscar Mayer Wiener, there would soon be nothing left of me!

Suddenly, the sidewalk lurches and the world spins.

Emma's head is swimming and her vision is closing. She doubles over. Clutching her stomach, she gasps for air.

It's not what you look at that matters. It's what you see.

Bile rises in the back of her throat, and she's overcome by nausea. Pulling herself upright, she clasps a hand over her mouth, trying to hold in the vomit as she bolts toward her house to be sick.

Müller was right.

30

Mission Impossible

The backs of Emma's upper arms are the only parts of her body that don't feel wretched. She's torn off her long-sleeved T-shirt and cardigan and is just wearing her sweat-soaked, beige tank top. Sitting on the bathroom floor, she leans back against the cool tub, panting.

Tears and blood are streaming down her face and neck and onto her top, leaving watery pink streaks. When she skidded into her first-floor bathroom after running away from The Dancing Buddha, desperate to vomit, she slipped and hit her head on the side of the tub, and her forehead has been bleeding like only a head wound can.

It takes a tragedy for problems to finally get resolved…

A farmer and a pig engage in a clever dialogue…

#39 pork dumplings…

How could she not have seen what was right in front of her?

THERE WAS A HEAVY STILLNESS TO THE LATE SUMMER AFTER-noon, portending a New England storm. Thick, gray clouds hung low and clung to the sky, which was pregnant with the deluge to come. As she bounded toward Blossom's stall, twelve-year-old Emma took a deep breath, drinking in the aromatic mixture of ozone, ocean, and earthy sweetness.

After two weeks at art camp, she had just returned home, and she couldn't wait to be reunited with her pig. Camp was always a fun adventure, but without Blossom, Emma had no one to turn to for comfort, so she never felt fully secure. This year, she'd slipped and fallen during a bog jog, ending up with strings and clumps of algae hanging off her hair and face. The resident bully had dubbed her "Bog Beast," a name that left her crying herself to sleep for the first three nights. If she'd had her porcine friend by her side, she'd never have slid into such despair. Friends like Blossom remind you that no matter what happens, you're never alone.

Emma was so eager to see Blossom that the sprint from the house to the barn seemed to take forever. But after just a couple of minutes she arrived, breathless and sweaty from the muggy summer air. She entered the barn at a trot, slowed to a walk—and then stopped short. Something wasn't right. Instead of the rustling and grunting and stomping that always greeted her, there was silence.

Her heart racing and hands trembling, Emma bolted to Blossom's stall. It was empty, the gate hanging omi-nously ajar. Not only was the pig missing, but the dirt floor was bare, devoid of the piles of fresh hay that always covered it, and Blossom's food and water buckets were gone. As was the red, custom collar that Emma had made for him, which contained his contact information in case he got lost, and his name, "Blossom: Best Pig Ever." Only his plastic corn on the cob squeak toy remained, wedged in the far corner, an apparent oversight by whoever had removed all the other contents.

Emma instinctively grabbed the toy and pressed it to her chest, as though to protect it from whatever fate had befallen the rest of the items. She dashed toward the house, screaming for help.

"DAD! Dad! Help! Blossom's missing!"

Repeating her desperate cries, tears now streaming down her cheeks, she barreled up the porch steps and stormed into the old farmhouse, the screen door squeaking and slamming behind her. "DAD!"

Angie, the kindly housekeeper who was at the homestead twice a week, was standing in the kitchen rinsing a colander of freshly picked strawberries, strands of her salt-and-pepper, straw-like hair poking out from her bun. She looked at Emma with concern, but said nothing.

"Angie! Blossom's missing!" Emma couldn't stop herself from screaming even though she was just feet away from the matronly woman.

"Oh, hon." Angie's hooded gray eyes glistened, as though she was holding back tears. "I think you need to talk to your dad about that."

Before Emma could respond, Nick crept past the kitchen doorway and into the living room, looking like he was trying not to be seen. "Nick!" Emma screamed, running toward him, her heart pounding and voice shrill. "Blossom's gone! What's—" But Nick had scurried off.

What was going on?

The stairs creaked under heavy footsteps as Emma's father descended toward the living room, where Emma was standing, her whole body shaking. He was walking slowly, methodically, in no rush to heed her urgent cries. "Dad! Blossom's gone! He's missing! His whole stall is—"

"Emmie, Emmie. Slow down, honey." Her father stood before her, his face calm.

At the sound of her father's steady voice, Emma stiffened, flushing. Had she been overreacting?

"Dad." Her voice was more controlled. "Blossom's gone. I—"

"Honey, I know. Just take a deep breath, okay? Can you do that for me?" Her father took her by the hand and led her to the well-worn corduroy sofa, where they both sat down.

Emma tried to oblige, but the hysteria she'd felt just a few minutes ago had returned, as had her tears. "What happened, Dad? What's going on?"

Her father inhaled deeply. "There's been an accident. Honey, I'm so sorry. I didn't want to tell you while you were away."

At that moment, Emma left her body, barely hearing the rest of the conversation. She watched from afar, motionless and numb and dry-eyed, as her father explained that one of the heavy trenching spades that hung from the ten-foot-high rafters of the barn had fallen on Blossom's head at the very moment the pig was walking beneath it. It was a freak accident. Blossom had gotten out of his stall and wandered into the other side of the barn, where the tools were kept. The spade, which had come loose due to a rusty nail that had lost its grip, had caused massive internal bleeding, according to the emergency veterinarian Emma's father had called to the scene, and Blossom had been euthanized on the spot.

"Why?" Emma whispered, her tears returning.

"Why what, honey?"

"Why wasn't Blossom's gate closed? And who let him out to pasture?"

The latch to the gate had broken a couple of weeks before Emma left for camp, and had been slated for repair. Whoever let Blossom out for his daily walk in the pasture—which was almost always Emma and, if not, Nick—had to take extra care to secure the gate when the pig got back to his stall. Emma had been worried before going away, knowing that nobody was as concerned as she was about making sure that Blossom didn't end up on the side of the barn that had piles of tools with sharp ends protruding and other potential hazards. Nobody except Nick, who had assured her he'd keep an eye on the pig.

Emma's father looked down at his hands, perhaps realizing he should have made sure that Nick had been more attentive. "It must have been Jeremy." Jeremy was the orchard hand, who was notoriously unreliable. "He probably just forgot the latch was loose."

"WHY didn't Nick do it? You KNOW Nick was supposed to be taking care of Blossom while I was away!" Emma was screaming again. The sloppiness, the utter negligence that ended up killing someone, was too much to bear.

"I know, Emmie. But Nick was playing over at Robbie's, so he wasn't home."

Emma couldn't find the words or strength to respond. Her thoughts were jumbled, her feelings overwhelming. She slumped forward, defeated.

"It's gonna be all right, honey. You'll see. One of these days, soon, this'll all be just a bad memory, like a bad dream. It'll fade away and you'll eventually forget it ever happened." It had been less than twenty minutes since Emma had discovered Blossom missing, and her father was already trying to turn the tragedy into a banality.

"I want to see his body." Emma's chin quivered and her whisper was barely audible. "I want to bury him. He deserves a funeral." She had an irresistible urge to lay her eyes and hands on her pig. Even if he was dead.

Her father cleared his throat and looked away.

"Dad, I WANT to see his BODY!" The conversation felt like an undulating ocean, with Emma riding crests of hysteria and sinking into wells of catatonia.

Her father shook his head slowly. "I'm sorry, Emmie. I didn't think you'd care about Blossom's body once he was gone, so I—"

"NO!" Emma's sobbing gushed out of her like a crashing wave. "You *didn't*! You couldn't have. You… you… Dad, please! *Please* tell me you didn't—"

"Emmie, you know the drill. We always—"

"The DRILL? Blossom isn't a farm animal! He's—he was—family! How COULD you?!" Emma was shrieking, shaking her head wildly and pounding her fists on the back of the sofa.

Her father's expression hardened. "All right, that's

enough, Emma." His voice was stern, his patience apparently worn thin. "Stop it right now. Blossom was dead. He died quickly, painlessly. There was no reason to let his body go to waste. It wasn't *Blossom* I sent to Meaty Mo's, it was his body. That's all it was. He——"

But Emma wasn't hearing any more of it. She leaped up and fled the house, vowing never to return.

She managed to stay away for two days, hiding inside a musty, damp little cave in the woods outside the orchard. She heard people in the distance calling her name, but the search team, if you could call it that, didn't include a dog and never found her. Knowing her father, he wasn't worried enough to put much effort into a rescue mission or to call the police.

During those forty-eight hours, Emma had nothing to do but think. And cry. Clutching Blossom's squeak toy to her chest, she was flooded with memories: running with the pig through wildflower-covered fields; walking with him through the forest, side by side; and scratching him behind his ears and under his chin while he grunted and wagged his skinny tail. Above all, she remembered Blossom's heart, the steady beating that had synced with hers and the unconditional love it always conveyed—during naps when they curled up together in the thick hay, both of them still babies; in the cold nights when Emma snuck out to the barn, frightened and alone, to sleep by his side; and on lazy weekend afternoons when she'd prop her head on the side of his belly like a pillow, to read aloud from her favorite book.

She also replayed the events surrounding Blossom's death. Which, she concluded, was her fault. Blossom never would have died if she'd been home taking care of him. She should have known better than to go away with the broken latch still unrepaired. She *did* know better; she'd had a bad feeling about it. But she went to camp anyway, selfishly.

During those dark ruminations, the cavern of grief inside her was flooded by a rush of guilt. Guilt that inundated every cell in her body. Guilt that threatened to drown her. Guilt that morphed into its toxic, debilitating counterpart: shame. Emma no longer felt that she'd merely *done* something bad; she felt that she *was* bad. Unworthy.

The Emma who entered the cave was not the Emma who left it. It was as if her father had thrown her heart on the ground like a glass vase, shattering it to pieces that could never be put back together. She'd never known such grief, or such shame. And because her young psyche was incapable of processing this trauma, it blocked it from her consciousness. She emerged from the cave with her memories of Blossom's life intact, and her memories of his death displaced. She would recall that he died in a freak accident and remember the memorial service they had in the pet cemetery, something her father no doubt arranged out of guilt. But she "forgot" the traumatic aspects of the tragedy: that her father sent Blossom's body to the butcher, and that the pig died because she failed to protect him. Nobody in her family ever spoke of the incident again, so it wasn't difficult for Emma to maintain her self-delusion.

When Emma crawled into the cave, she was sick with grief and wracked with guilt. And when she emerged, she was anesthetized and emboldened. She came forth with a mission that would shape the trajectory of the rest of her life: to be a healer, a protector, a caregiver; to always take care of those who needed her. No matter the cost to herself.

WHAT IS THE SOUND OF HALF A HEART BEATING?

How could Müller have known? Even Emma hadn't been aware of how the repressed trauma had affected her. She'd always maintained that she didn't eat pork because it was unhealthy, not because her father had her companion pig turned into hot dogs. She'd always believed she wanted to be a therapist only because she loved psychology and helping people, not because she also needed to heal others in order to feel like a worthy person herself.

As Emma leans back against the tub, the porcelain presses uncomfortably against her spine. Her legs are extended before her on the mosaic white tiles of the floor, her feet hanging limply outward. Exhausted from processing memories and emotions that had been lodged inside her for decades, she lets her head fall forward. Droplets of blood splatter on the floor. Her wound is still open.

Curling up on the bloody tiles, she falls into a deep, dreamless sleep.

31

The Secret

Day 43: Saturday

Wet sandpaper tickles the palm of Emma's hand. The itch isn't so uncomfortable that she needs to scratch it, but it's too uncomfortable to ignore.

Prying open her gritty eyes, she's assaulted by the glare of morning sunlight reflecting off a white obelisk just inches from her face. The toilet in her bathroom. Blinking sluggishly, she lets herself slip back into unconsciousness.

The light brushing on her hand continues, again rousing her from sleep. It's moved from her palm to the tips of her fingers. Emma looks down at the end of her arm and sees Annie's fuzzy orange head. His ears are flattened as he assiduously licks the blood off her hands, cleaning the sticky, viscous mess she wiped from her face yesterday.

Her head is throbbing, but it's not the headache she's had since developing SOS. It's localized to the outside of her forehead. She reaches up to feel the area, and is met with a golf ball-sized lump that smarts at her touch.

A growl from her stomach interrupts her exploration of the goose egg. She feels like she hasn't eaten in days. How can she be so hungry?

As the fog of her dawning consciousness clears, the memory of yesterday's events comes into focus. The perverse pig image at The Dancing Buddha. The triggering events on SOS Eve day. Slamming her head on the tub. Throwing up the entire contents of her stomach. Müller's koan. Blossom.

Blossom. Emma squeezes her eyes closed, struggling to hold back the flood of memories that are rushing in like a traumatic deluge—and with it, a stream of disturbing questions. What had Blossom's last moments been like? Her father said that the pig had died quickly. But had he? Or had he been lying in the barn, bleeding and in pain, terrified and alone, wondering why Emma wasn't there to take care of him?

A tiny tongue pokes into the corner of her mouth and snaps her out of her dark reverie. Annie is letting her know that he's done taking care of her and now it's his turn; it's time for his breakfast.

Clasping the top of the toilet seat with one hand and the side of the tub with the other, Emma hoists herself up. Once standing, she grabs onto the sides of the sink to steady herself, and catches her reflection in the mirror. The image before her looks like something out of a slasher movie. An angry, crimson orb resembling a cratered planet juts out from her forehead, which is framed by her matted, frizzy hair. Blood is streaked over her cheeks and smudged across her chin, and splashes of dried sweat and crimson blood stains mottle her beige tank top.

With shaky steps, she makes her way toward the kitchen. Glimpsing the litter box in the hallway, she realizes it needs to be cleaned and her breath catches. Better to refrain from scooping today, lest she have a repeat performance of last week's faceplanting, only this time with sticky smears on her face for the soiled litter to more easily adhere to.

After hobbling up to the cupboard where Annie's Stinkycat is stored, she retrieves a can and recoils as she opens it. Annie, on the other hand, is in a feeding frenzy, meowing and snaking around her ankles as though he hasn't been fed in days. And as though he doesn't have a full bowl of the dried version of the foul-smelling food right next to him.

Still groggy, Emma blinks in the morning sunshine that's slanting across the kitchen. The room is just as it had been when she left yesterday on her aimless wander. The glossy, round oak table and shiny white granite countertops are cluttered with piles of dirty dishes and takeout containers. The tall bay window opening to the backyard showcases the delicate red leaves of the Japanese maple and the fleshy, pale flowers of the two adjacent dogwoods. Nothing has changed in the past twenty-four hours. But it's as though she's looking at everything through different eyes. Has the koan shaken loose more than just her memory?

Since getting her memory back, Emma hasn't been able to stop returning to the scene of the accident, trying to make sense of what happened. What could she have done differently to protect Blossom, besides not going to camp? Should she have hung a sign on the gate? Talked to Jeremy to make sure he knew to pay better attention?

Asked Nick not to go visit Robbie while she was away?

And was the broken latch really as serious a problem as she thought? Yes, it was a risk. But it shouldn't have been a *fatal* risk. Emma's concern about Blossom wandering into the other side of the barn was that he'd step on a rake whose tines were facing up or cut himself on hedge clippers that weren't properly stored. Not that he'd die. For a trenching spade to fall down right at the very moment Blossom was underneath it… what were the odds?

In fact, the only thing she worried about while she was at camp exchanging ghost stories with her bunkmates and making cards with macaroni and glitter and running three-legged races against the boys' camp and—

Emma freezes.

Is it possible?

That freckled boy with the stick-straight hair in the potato sack who's hopping across her memory. Could that be who she thinks it is? Robbie Jenkins, from next door? The Robbie whose house her father said Nick was at when Blossom was killed?

Why would her father and Nick have lied to her? What were they hiding?

The blood roars in Emma's ears, as her pulse pounds in her wrists and throat and chest.

It's time for her to learn the truth—the whole truth. Snatching her phone off the table, she opens the chat with Nick.

meet me at warmer planet. Now

32

Emma AS Turns the Screws

Day 44: Sunday

"How *could* you?" Emma's voice is shaking, her green eyes dark. She's on fire, her energy driving out the stagnant, stale air of the small nursing home room. Her newfound rage breathes fresh life into the drab space with its conventional furnishings and predictable decor.

Her father is propped up in his adjustable bed, and Nick is sitting in a chair beside him. Dust motes float in the rays of weak, late afternoon sunlight streaming in from the little window behind them. The two men stare at Emma with mouths hanging open, brows raised, and eyes wide. It's striking how alike they look; Emma hasn't seen them side by side in years.

Emma called for this meeting yesterday, but Nick was out of town with his family. He'd immediately responded to her text request, probably thinking she was about to kill herself, by creating a group chat with her and their father. In it he asked what was so urgent that she needed to talk right away. Emma had simply responded *I know what you did.*

Nick and her father remain mute as they regard this new, unfamiliar version of Emma. The only sound in the stuffy room is Oprah's voice, on the television across from the bed in the upper corner. *And today on* Super Soul Sunday *we're talking about freedom after thirty years on death row.*

The men's silence speaks volumes, as do their expressions. Clearly, they weren't expecting that Emma would ever catch on to their deception, and they have no idea what to say now that they're in the hot seat. Nor did they think that the always-agreeable, levelheaded family mediator was capable of such outrage.

"Um, Em, what the…" Nick swallows, and rubs his hands on his thighs as he scans Emma's face and body.

"Honey," her father cuts in, looking her up and down, scrutinizing her as though she's hiding something in a pocket or her neck brace. "Honey, you look… you look terrible. What happened to you?"

"How *could* you?" Emma spits out, their attempted diversion adding insult to injury.

Standing at the foot of the bed, her body electrified by emotions reawakened after decades of slumber, she narrows her focus to Nick. "How could *you*? I understand how *he* could have done something so… so cruel. So deceptive and selfish. But *you*? And never coming clean, after all these years?" Heat pricks the back of her eyes and she steels herself, determined to hold back her tears.

Nick refuses to do battle. "Okay. Okay… I know we need to talk about what happened. But Em, holy shit. You look like death, and I think we need to talk about you first. I'm really worried you're—"

"NO!" The shout surprises even Emma. "No more

avoidance. No more denial. It's high time you—"

"We need to talk about Emma." Nick directs his comment to their father. Then, looking at Emma, he adds, "Em, I want to make sure you're safe before we get into this. I don't want you running off and—"

"STOP avoiding this, Nick! This is NOT about me, it's about—"

"Dad, Emma's going to kill herself." It's like they're kids again, and Nick is tattling on her, giving away her plans to sneak out her bedroom window at night. Emma has a sudden urge to stick her tongue out at her little brother and pull his hair.

"You *traitor*!" Despite all her efforts, Emma starts to cry.

A silence falls over the room as the family stares their collective trauma in the face, each seeing a different expression in its eyes and each wearing a differing one in their own. Emma's father is like a deer in headlights, as he sits frozen and mute. Nick's pupils are dilated, as he repeatedly wrings his hands. Emma's eyes are brimming, as she stands motionless.

The sliver of Emma that's able to think rationally knows that although everyone plays a different role in a trauma, everyone needs similar elements to heal: honesty, integrity, and empathy. Reconciliation isn't possible without authentic, compassionate witnessing. The remaining ninety-nine percent of her, though, doesn't care. She only wants justice.

Her father's voice is steady when he breaks the silence. "Honey, is it true what your brother's saying?" The gentleness of his tone and concern in his eyes, so different from those of the man Emma knows killed her pig, open the floodgates to her tears.

There's no point holding back now. No reason to hide the truth any longer. "Yes," she breathes. "I've been wanting to stop living for a while now, and I think I finally understand why."

"Em, maybe this is it!" Nick has suddenly perked up, his expression hopeful and his voice high. "The unresolved relationship issue that CouchGPT said was a cause of—"

But Emma cuts him off, refusing to be deterred. "I know you both lied to me." Her tears are again in check and her voice is flat. "You lied about the most formative and traumatic event of my life. If I do kill myself, my blood is on *your* hands, just like Blossom's is." Even in her desperate, wildly dysregulated state, Emma knows this was a low blow, utterly nonrelational and even cruel. It just goes to show that she's not the person she used to be. The very thought of saying such a thing would have been foreign to Emma Before SOS. Then again, Emma BS wouldn't have had the courage to speak so boldly, putting her own need for personal resolution ahead of the emotional comfort of her father and brother.

Addressing Nick, Emma AS turns the screws. "I expected more from you. I don't think I've ever been so disappointed by anyone in my life." Despite her outrage, Emma's heart clenches when she sees Nick's eyes redden and glass over.

"Don't blame him." Her father's voice is earnest. "He was only a kid. He was just doing what I told him to do." He's speaking candidly. Finally. "He didn't have a choice. I made him promise never to tell you."

Nick is looking down at his lap where he's picking at a loose thread sticking out of his jeans. Emma can't tell whether he's crying, until she sees a tear drop onto the back of his hand.

"It wasn't an accident that killed Blossom. I just made that up to make you feel better." Her father is looking at the wall across the room, watching a memory of an event long since passed but still very much alive. "I had always planned to get rid of Blossom. I told you that when we first inherited the orchard, that the animals were on borrowed time. I gave the chickens and goats to Meaty Mo's, once they were old. Old Ollie, too. Blossom wasn't supposed to be an exception. Do you know how much it costs to keep animals, especially a pig? Imagine how expensive a fat, gluttonous one like Blossom—" Biting his lip, he pauses, seeming to realize that any justification for the killing is not going to be helpful. "Blossom was older than the other animals I sent to Mo. But I knew you two were bonded, so I didn't want to take him away from you until you were old enough to deal with it."

How old is old enough to "deal with" the fact that your pet's been slaughtered and sold to people so they can eat his body parts?

"I waited till you were away at camp, and then told you a story I thought wouldn't distress you so much. I figured you'd get over it. Kids lose their pets all the time."

Emma's tears have returned with a vengeance. Now that the veil of deception has been lifted and the truth is out, she can finally feel the emotions she didn't have access to as long as the family maintained their collective denial. It's difficult, if not impossible, to grieve and rage and worry when the people around you are acting like there's nothing to grieve and rage and worry about—and when you, yourself, aren't ready to accept a painful reality.

On some level, Emma had known the truth all along. The truth about her father sending Blossom to the butcher, which she'd actively repressed, and also the truth that he and Nick had lied. But until she was ready to face these realities, she remained blind to them. Now, it's like she's pulled her finger out of the dam of feelings that had been held back for decades.

"Seriously, Nick. I can't believe you kept the truth from me all this time, when you *knew*." Emma is back on the summit of rage, as she rides a rollercoaster of emotions. "You may not be an active killer. But you're a passive bystander, which makes you just as bad."

Nick's bottom lip quivers, and his voice is hoarse. "I'm sorry, Em. I'm really, really sorry." Nick abhors conflict and bends over backwards to make sure the people around him are comfortable; he's way out of his element. "I thought about telling you, I really did. But I'd made a promise to Dad. And besides, what good would it have done? You'd just have felt worse."

The psychologist in Emma can appreciate Nick's rationale. But the psychologist in her also knows that secrets often have a way of infecting people's souls, becoming more harmful the longer they fester.

A familiar voice on the television interrupts Emma's train of thought. She glances up at the screen to see an ad for BuckleUp Airlines, where a flight attendant is strapping a steel-blue suitcase into a seat. A heavily made-up woman is standing behind the seat leaning forward with her arms draped around the suitcase, like a supermodel hanging over the shoulders of a playboy. Both the flight attendant and Olivia turn to face the camera and make an L shape with their hands as the words "No body belongs in cargo" appear on the screen. Of course BuckleUp has chosen Karl as their ambassador. Since he became the face of the #LoveThingsLove movement, countless companies have featured him in their marketing, attempting to make their brands seem more progressive.

"And… look at you, Em." Nick seems desperate to rescue his sister from the dark fate she appears to be heading toward. "You don't look like a person who's stuck in some past trauma. You're not a derelict or anything. Look at your life. You're the most successful person I know—your whole life is a mission to do good. All you care about is helping people. How can someone like you not be okay?"

"Have you never heard of masking?" Emma's father looks at Nick in disbelief. Oprah's had more of an effect on him than Emma had realized. The old man turns to Emma, his voice gentle. "Honey, if you wanna be mad at someone, be mad at me. Not your brother. He's a good man, and he was a good boy. He's always wanted what's best for you."

Nick is looking away, facing the empty wall with its faded peach paint, clearly trying to hide the tears rolling down his cheeks. Tears, most likely, of guilt for lying to his sister and of grief for the myriad tragedies his family has endured. From the killing of Blossom to the neglect of his and Emma's younger selves to his years-long estrangement from his dying father.

"I don't blame you for being mad, even for hating me

for what I did. Your feelings are valid," her father continues, sounding more like John Gottman than, well, himself. At least, himself of yesteryears. "I was wrong. What I did was wrong. I killed Blossom, and I hurt you. A lot. I won't try to excuse what I did, because I can't. All I can do is tell you how sorry I am. When I look back on how I was when I was young, and drinking… I can't believe how selfish, how reckless I was. Honey, I'm sorry. And please, you can hate me all you want; just don't take this out on your brother. Or yourself."

A tear rolls down her father's cheek, and he raises a frail hand to slowly wipe it away. Witnessing this simple act of humility and vulnerability, Emma feels like her heart is going to explode.

She knows that few acts are as relationally transformative as an apology delivered skillfully. Honest, raw, and humble admittances—where the person harmed feels truly seen in their suffering and reassured that the transgression won't be repeated—can repair years of damage and restore shattered connections. A skillful apology can even bring people closer than they were before the wrongdoing.

Emma's rage, once a tsunami, has all but evaporated.

She's now crying openly, and messily. "It's okay," she chokes out. "I… I understand. I forgive you, I do." She'll never be able to—nor does she want to—forget what happened to Blossom. And she'll never believe that what was done to him, and to her, was just. But she *can* forgive.

Emma almost always forgives people easily, largely because she knows that everyone is doing their best at any given moment. You can't have a solid understanding of human psychology and expect that people could have acted differently in the circumstances they found themselves in. So often, people look at their past selves through the eyes of their current selves—selves that have awareness and insight that their past selves lacked—and inaccurately assume that they could and should have behaved differently. Emma knows that each "self" is ever-changing, an idea expressed in one of her favorite sayings: *You can never step into the same river twice.*

There's a spaciousness inside Emma that she hasn't felt since she was a child. A lightness, as though she's lost emotional weight. It's like her psyche was a cluttered house that's just been purged of its heavy furniture and nonessentials, allowing fresh air to flow through open windows and circulate freely.

Could Müller's koan be the remedy that she needed, after all?

33

The Opposite of Trauma

Day 47: Wednesday

"U"ntil he has unconditional and unbiased love for all beings, man will not find peace.'"

Ricardo looks like a different person than he did just eight days ago. He's no longer unshaven, ashen, and disheveled, slouching on the sofa. Today, he's sitting upright and is neatly dressed, fresh-faced, and smelling of aftershave. His penchant for quotes, though, has remained the same.

"When I read this, it was like a light switch flipped on." Ricardo's eyes are clear, and he's addressing Emma with a composure and confidence she's never seen in him. He sets his mug of tea down on one of the clay coasters on the coffee table. "You once said that the Buddha was one of the first psychologists, and remembering that is what started me down the Buddhist rabbit hole. I mean, that's part of what started me down it. The other part was triggered by the blowup with Jesse."

Emma had called Ricardo to ask if he could move his

appointment up to today. She'd canceled all but her most urgent sessions this week, so that she could have tomorrow free, to kill herself. In fact, this evening with Ricardo will be the last session she has. Ever.

After her conversation with Nick and her father on Sunday, she felt as though a deep wound within her had been healed. She'd finally learned the truth about what happened to Blossom, and got the apology she needed. And she was able to forgive them—particularly her father, who was the true culprit. But although she left Warmer Planet with a lightness of spirit, the burden of guilt she'd been carrying was no less heavy. She could forgive her father and brother, but not herself. She'd known her father was reckless, alcoholic, and negligent. She should have known better than to go away and leave Blossom alone with him. She also realized that Nick had been mistaken thinking that the family trauma surrounding Blossom's death was the significant, unresolved relationship issue causing her SOS. After the "resolution" of the issue, her suicidality hadn't gone away. It had gotten worse.

For the past couple of days, she's been doing everything in her power to minimize the damage of her impending death. She's put together a document for Shana with all the relevant information about her clients so that they can be easily transferred, and she's met with the few clients she felt would need an extra session in order to have the necessary closure before learning that she'd died.

There isn't much left to do. Her will is in order, and she's left copious notes for Walter, who will inherit her house so that Annie doesn't have to move right away—or ever, if Walter wants to move in. She bought a year's supply of Stinkycat, as well as every toy and bed and scratching post Annie could ever want, turning her guest room into a storage space. She's also been writing personal notes for the people she's closest to, as well as for those clients and acquaintances she thinks will be especially distressed by her death and might take it personally.

Emma pulls herself back to the moment. "Wow, Ricardo. It sounds like there's been some really big change in the past few days." Since making her fatal decision, she's felt like she has one foot each in the world of the living and the dead, straddling two planes, unable to be fully present in either. She hopes her eyes don't look like those of an elderly person on their deathbed, staring into the afterlife.

"Yeah. The thing with Jesse, it was huge." Ricardo clears his throat and straightens his shoulders, like a minstrel about to regale the masses with an epic saga. The tall rectangular window behind him, opening to a pale, dusky sky, frames his head and shoulders so he looks like the subject of an oil painting. "So it all started Saturday afternoon, at Jesse's family's place. We'd been invited to their annual spring barbecue. Everything was going fine, until Jesse walked up to me with a plate full of spare ribs."

'Cause if I were an Oscar Mayer Wiener, there would soon be nothing left of me!

Emma jumps at the loud interruption in her head. But since there's no reason to fight it anymore, she simply lets the music play, nodding her head along to the beat.

"Right?" Ricardo responds. "I knew you'd get it."

He rearranges his large body on the sofa. "I couldn't believe what a hypocrite he was, knowing what he knows about the brutality of the meat, egg, and dairy industries. Whatever. Anyway, after we got home, I let him have it. I really tore into him, about how he has no right to call himself a progressive, how he's unethical and selfish, among other things. He didn't say much—not that he could've, since I was talking a hundred miles an hour—and then I left, even though he was begging me to stay home so we could talk things out."

Ricardo shakes his head, as if in disbelief at his own behavior.

"And what did I do? I went straight to the Trophy Room in Boston and got plastered. Jesse was trying to reach me but I ignored his calls and texts and turned off my phone. I knew he'd be a wreck, worrying about me getting hurt or doing something stupid like picking up some guy. But I didn't fucking care. I was just so enraged. And I did pick up a guy. I mean, we didn't have sex—but I kissed this young hottie I'd been flirting with all night, this fashion model."

Fashion. Emma hasn't thought about what she's going to wear at her funeral. She's sure her family will want an open casket, which is one of the reasons she decided to overdose on sleeping pills rather than borrow Walter's gun and shoot herself in the head. What could she wear that would comfort onlookers? Green is known to be a soothing color, hence the green furniture in her office. Her emerald dress with the high neck would be perfect. The only problem is that the fabric itches, but that won't matter. Remembering the last time she wore the uncomfortable frock, Emma automatically sticks a finger up into her neck brace to scratch her throat.

Ricardo blanches and stops his monologue, perhaps because he's all too aware of what could be lurking in the brace. His pupils dilate, and he lets out a little hiccup.

"Excuse me." He raises a closed hand to politely cover his mouth and pulls himself together. "Anyway, when I got home the next morning and had sobered up, I was horrified. I've never done anything like that to Jesse, to *anyone*. The way I talked to him about the barbecue, the fact that I walked out on him and got shitfaced and kissed another guy and ignored his messages... I was such a total asshole!" Tiny beads of sweat are glistening on Ricardo's clean forehead, and he repositions himself among the throw cushions on the sofa, his movements oddly comforting.

In fact, the more green at her funeral, the better. Maybe Emma could get a custom casket, with green lining? Would Gregory give her a discount? Recalling the coffin maker, his lips over-enunciating "SOS" from across the room, she shudders.

"I know. If even *you* have a visceral reaction to my assholeness, Emma, imagine poor Jesse."

Thank god this is her last session.

"So you know what Jesse did? Actually, lemme first tell you what he *didn't* do. He didn't yell or tell me what a dick I've been or toss my stuff in a suitcase and throw it out on the front lawn. Instead, he took me in his arms. He hugged me, and told me he loved me and that we're going to work it out." Ricardo shakes his head, incredulous. "*Jesse*. Renowned divorce attorney who won't take on a client if there's even a whiff of foul play from their end. If *my* issue is respecting animals, *his* is respecting partners in a relationship. I did exactly the opposite of everything he stands for."

"So, rather than judge you for not acting ethically, Jesse—"

"Responded with understanding. Compassion. With love." Ricardo rarely interrupts, and seems impatient to get to the point.

"And what was your response to his response?"

"I melted. Cried. Sobbed, actually. Jesse told me he knew what a hard time I'd been having, and he understood that I was acting out. Not that what I did was okay—I obviously need to get my shit together—but that *who I am* is okay. He treated me in the exact opposite way I'd treated him for eating spare ribs. And then I understood what you'd been trying to tell me, in so many words, all this time. That the opposite of trauma is love."

"Meaning?" Had Emma actually said that? Emma BS must have been good at her job.

"Meaning that if you want to get people to stop doing harmful things, you can't harm them in the process. Demeaning people, harming their dignity, to teach them that harming dignity is wrong just creates more of the same. The belief that some individuals are more worthy than others of being treated with respect and compassion is at the heart of every atrocity—from genocides to unjust wars to animal exploitation—and every harmful interaction. It's the core of trauma, collective and individual."

Ricardo leans over and picks up his mug. He sips slowly and deliberately, seeming to collect his thoughts.

"Jesse respected me. Treated me with compassion. That's what made me feel connected and secure with him, so I could open up to what he had to say. He didn't put himself in a position of moral superiority, looking down on me as though I'm less worthy of respect and compassion than he or anyone else is. He did the opposite: he practiced love toward me… Like you always say, practicing love means treating others the way you'd want to be treated if you were in their position, honoring their dignity. Jesse helped me feel worthy of being loved."

"Wow again, Ricardo. I feel like 'wow' has been my refrain this session. But really—you've been doing quite some work in the past few days. So you said your fight with Jesse was *part* of what sent you down the Buddhist rabbit hole?"

"Yeah. It got me started reading about Buddhism and partnerships. But then I got thinking about my future, what I should do with my life. So I googled 'purpose of life' and 'Buddha' and one of the first things that came up was an excerpt from this book called *Love Is the Way*. It was almost like the universe put it in front of me. I get goosebumps just thinking about it. I printed it out to bring here. Can I read it to you?"

Emma's not sure if she wants to hear this. All this pithy talk about love and healing and purpose is almost making her second-guess her decision to kill herself.

"Um, sure."

"*Love Is the Way*, by Thay Phap Nhat. Some people ask me… 'What is the purpose of life?' Then I don't hesitate and answer, 'This life shall teach us the lessons of love.' Love is not only a noun that we speak of, but we have to make it become a verb. We have to take concrete actions. 'Love' has to turn into 'loving.' To only talk about love is not enough. We have to behave in such a way that we express our love so that the energy of love can continue and spread out. When there is love in our eyes, our look becomes tender. When there is love in our ears, we listen without judging or reacting. We listen with calmness and concentration. Only then do we really listen. We will be able to hear everything the other person says and also what she doesn't speak out. When there is love in our words, those words will bring about forgiveness, peace, connectedness, empathy."

Ricardo puts the paper down beside him on the sofa. His eyes are moist. "This is why I've always been attracted to social justice movements. They're not just about making institutions more fair. They're about replacing trauma with love. They're about healing relationships. I never realized this point, or how important it was to me, until Jesse treated me the way I want people to treat the world, and helped me to feel worthy in the process. I... can't really articulate it. Am I making sense?"

More sense than you know. "Yes, yes absolutely."

"Phew." Ricardo smiles self-consciously. "And then when my searching pulled up that quote from the Buddha about unconditional love, it was the final—how should I put it?—the final nail in the coffin of Ricardo BS— Ricardo Before Sanity." He chuckles good-naturedly.

Ricardo's choice of words is unnerving. Suddenly lightheaded, Emma grips the sides of her chair in case she starts to fall over again. The last thing Ricardo needs is a repeat performance of their previous session.

Clearing his throat, Ricardo repeats the quote. "'Until he has unconditional and unbiased love for all beings, man will not find peace.' This just really nailed where I'm at. The practice of love has to apply not just to our relationships with humans, but also to our relationships with animals, which I only recently figured out. I mean, we know relationships affect us. But why don't we include animals in our definition of 'relationship'? Who hasn't had a pet that shaped their life in some way? Who doesn't know that kids who hurt animals are kids who will probably hurt humans? Who hasn't cried reading *Charlotte's Web*?"

Ricardo pauses and looks at Emma expectantly, giving her an opportunity to respond. But Emma remains silent. She's too busy trying to hide the fact that she's rocking out to the Oscar Mayer Wiener jingle.

"So to sum all this up, I've realized that I have to come to my activism, my life, from a place of love, not trauma." Ricardo exhales and stretches his arms out across the back of the sofa. "Anyway, Emma, I won't be coming back for therapy. I think I've gotten what I came for. Thank you. Thank you for helping me reclaim my life."

Emma's work here is done.

Now, there's only one thing left to do.

34

The Eulogy

Crisp flesh and sweet juice. Sticky fingers and straining feet. Earthy, fragrant ripeness. Plump bursts of warm hues against cool, open blueness. Enveloped in the branches of a Honeycrisp apple tree, seven-year-old Emma felt like the world had wrapped its arms around her, hugging her to its abundant breast. On the ground below was a young Blossom, also reaping the bounties of nature. The two of them were gorging themselves on their favorite fruit, whose tree in springtime yielded the soft pink petals and rich floral clusters that Blossom got his name from.

The weathered wooden bench Emma now sits on feels familiar, even though she hasn't been here in decades. As do the dark trunk, gnarled branches and bountiful flowers of the tree before her, which is framed by a twilight sky. Emma has come to the pet cemetery where Blossom was buried—or, rather, where what remained of the pig was buried. Her father had purchased a small plot for the pig right under a Honeycrisp apple tree, and Emma had turned a little white wooden box into a coffin. She'd filled it with Blossom's corn on the cob squeak toy, the bristle brush that he'd loved to be scratched with, a packet of the dried sweet carrots that were his favorite treat, and a photo that Emma's grandfather had taken of the two of them asleep together when they were both little, Emma's head on Blossom's chest, her cheek against the steady beating of his heart.

You are loved.

Emma had written the inscription for the headstone. She'd also written a eulogy, which she read at the memorial service that she, Nick, her father, and Angie, their housekeeper, had attended.

A chill runs up her spine, and she pulls her spring jacket closer around her.

She's come to the cemetery this evening to apologize to Blossom before she goes home to swallow the bottle of sleeping pills that's waiting for her next to her bed. She's going to keep Annie out of the bedroom tonight and she'll leave a voicemail for Walter asking him to come check on the cat in the morning, when he'll find a suicide note, so Annie won't be the one to find her body.

Everything is in order for her death. In fact, she's leaving behind what is surely one of the most well-organized situations a dead person could pass along. It's striking how many people have months, years, to plan for their deaths but nevertheless leave behind an administrative, financial, and emotional mess for others to clean up. Of course, when someone knows they're dying, they're often, understandably, in a state of desperation and don't have the wherewithal to focus on anything that doesn't feel urgent.

But still. If Emma weren't so miserable, she'd almost be proud. Just like people leave the way they loved—messy relationships usually end up in messy breakups—they tend to die the way they lived.

Emma hasn't looked at the eulogy she wrote since she stored it away right after the memorial service. It was one of those items that she brought forward through all her moves but never thought to look at. Today, she took it out of the cardboard box where she'd housed it along with the book of illustrated poems she'd created and the diaries she'd kept in childhood.

She carefully removes the fragile, yellowed paper from its envelope and unfolds it. The purple ink, from her younger self's special pen, is faded. But the rounded, swirly letters are legible. As are the hearts she drew all around the edges of the page. She'd written the eulogy in the form of a letter. She feels a sting of tears in the back of her eyes as she begins reading.

Dear Blossom,

Some people said you were only a pig. I always thought that was wrong. You weren't "just" a pig, like I'm not "just" a girl. You were someone, someone special. You were my best friend.

You were more of a friend than a lot of humans. You didn't tease me for being afraid to sleep alone sometimes, or ignore me when I was sad or walk away from me when I was lonely so you could do your own thing. Well, maybe sometimes you got distracted by your food but that's only sometimes.

You always knew when something bad happened to me. Even sometimes before I did! Like that night you kept pushing your nose against my stomach to make me laugh and at first I was annoyed and even sort of yelled at you but then I started to cry because Dad and Nick still weren't back from Vermont and it was 11 and they were supposed to be back 8 hours ago and nobody called me and I was really scared they were dead.

When I used to cry, people got mad or tried to make me laugh. Dad always said I was too sensitive and to stop taking everything so seriously. When I cried next to you, you just sat there and grunted the way you did when I was upset. You let me cry. Sometimes even for hours! I never felt like I had to be different. I could just be me. And being me, with you, made me feel like I was okay.

You were the best friend a girl could ever want. Or a boy. Or anybody. I woke up last night and wanted to come to your stall, to put my head on your chest and fall asleep listening to your heartbeat. But then I remembered you were gone and that I will never be able to sleep next to you again. Or scratch you under your chin and watch your tail wag or play hide and seek with you around the orchard or pile hay on your head to make those funny hairdos. It still doesn't feel real that you're gone forever.

Thank you for being my friend for all these years. I love you.

Emma's lower lip is trembling and her cheeks are moist. Her heart feels as bloated as a rising harvest moon in a hazy sky.

With shaky hands, she refolds the paper and slips it back in the envelope. "I'm sorry, Blossom. I'm so sorry I wasn't there for you." Her voice is husky. Even though it's been nearly forty years since Blossom was killed, her feelings are as raw as if he'd died just yesterday. Opening the Pandora's box of memories has brought her grief and guilt rushing to the surface.

"And you know," she continues, "Ricardo was right. Why do we think that meaningful relationships can only ever be between humans? I've spent my life trying to help people understand how to practice love—to honor each other's dignity, to be fair and compassionate. To be attentive. To be sensitive to each other, and to recognize that sensitivity is a gift, a strength, not a weakness to be ashamed of. To witness each other's pain and also their joy. How much of this did I learn from my relationship with you?"

A heavy sob wells up in the back of her throat, and she doesn't try to suppress it. She's not in any rush, and she allows herself the space to grieve. It's a relief not to have to stuff down her feelings and keep her chin up, not to have to put on a strong front for others—her clients, her family, all the countless people who depend on her. Right now, she can just feel and express what's true for her. She lets herself cry, until her tears finally abate.

Taking long, deep breaths, Emma steadies herself.

"If you were here now, I'd tell you that I'm going to be dead in a few hours. I'm going to kill myself. Because I've failed. I've failed to cure this SOS. Which means I've also failed everyone who depends on me. Just like I failed you. I tried to get better, I did my best, but I just don't have the energy to keep going. It's time for me to call it a life."

"You are loved."

For a moment it's as though the little headstone spoke to her.

Emma shakes her head to dispel the delirium that's been distorting her perceptions for weeks. Surely this is another SOS-induced delusion.

Still, that's exactly what Blossom would have said—communicated, through grunts and nuzzles—if he'd been alive. He would have loved Emma up until she stopped hating herself. And ultimately, that was his greatest gift to her, one of the greatest gifts anyone can give to another: to act as a bridge between them and their own hearts, to help them learn to love themselves.

The setting sun behind her radiates through the gathering clouds, illuminating the pale pink apple blossoms and transforming them into vibrant shades of crimson and fuchsia. Night is closing in.

It's time for Emma to go.

35

Love, PS

Day 49: Friday

The tears trickling down Emma's cheeks stroke her gently toward consciousness, while wisps of dreams dance across the backs of her closed eyelids: a golden statue of Ricardo-Buddha sitting cross-legged; Blossom rolling on top of a pile of fresh hay, kicking his hooves in the air and wagging his tail against the floor; her father whispering his apology, his eyes brimming with love; Müller juggling Honeycrisp apples and chanting his koan, over and over and over.

What is the sound of half a heart beating?

Droplets splatter on Emma's forehead and lips and stream down the sides of her face. Blinking her eyes open, she sees a gray sky above her, the heavy clouds just beginning to release their cleansing showers.

Wiping what she had thought were tears from her face, she slowly sits up, wincing at the sharp aches in her spine and hips. Her body is paying the price for lying on hard, wooden slats.

Judging by the light, it's shortly after dawn. She must

have fallen asleep on the bench last night, here at Blossom's grave.

At the sight of Blossom's headstone, Emma's heart sinks under the weight of grief that floods back in. Grief for her pig, for the people whose lives will be destroyed by her suicide, and grief for herself. For the little girl who wrote a eulogy for a dear friend who had been killed and butchered. For the sensitive child born into a violent world, who wanted nothing more than to create peace, to help foster more kindness and less suffering. For the girl who was taught to feel ashamed of that sensitivity, and of herself. And for the life she's about to lose.

Emma grieves, too, for the world. For the dysfunctional, nonrelational world that teaches us to believe that some individuals are more worthy of love than others.

Until he has unconditional and unbiased love for all beings, man will not find peace.

Ricardo's Buddha quote has been lingering in her mind and surfacing in her dreams, its truth impossible to turn away from. Love—the practice of honoring dignity, of treating others with respect and compassion—is the key to peace. Every time we practice love, we water the seeds of respect and compassion in ourselves and the world. And every time we act in a way that's not loving, we water the seeds of trauma and violence. Without love, there can be no peace.

The drops have turned into a drizzle, and the tips of Emma's hair are starting to drip. But she's unfazed. She remains seated on the bench, cradling her grief like a baby in her arms.

As she sits with the heaviness of loss, Emma realizes

that there's another feeling inside her, one she can't put her finger on. It's almost like a *lightness* of something she's lost. It's more the absence of a feeling than the presence of one. What's missing?

With a jolt, she realizes what it is.

It's her suicidality. The feeling of wanting to kill herself, to be dead, is gone. She's still sad, and tired. Her body still aches where she hurt herself. But her urge to die has been replaced by a will to live. By a genuine desire to be alive.

Her SOS has vanished. What happened?

In the same way she sought clues as to why she developed SOS, replaying the events of the day before she'd come down with it, Emma replays the events of yesterday. Her childhood memories of apple picking. The blossom tree, the eulogy. Her strange dreams, spotlighting Müller the juggler.

What is the sound of half a heart beating?

Her eyes well up as she remembers the silent void left by the absence of Blossom's heartbeat, and she looks at his headstone.

You are loved.

Emma gasps. Of course!

Müller's koan wasn't about her relationship with Nick and her father. It was about her relationship with *herself*. The significant, unresolved relationship issue was her inability to relate healthfully to herself, to practice love toward herself.

Suddenly, everything makes sense. The koan had broken through the fortress of Emma's psyche like a Trojan horse, its wisdom trickling out over time, creating a cascade of events in the process so that she could end up right where she is. It led her to remember and reconnect with her grief and guilt around Blossom's death, so she could remember and reconnect with the love and lessons about relationships she learned from the pig. And it led her to confront her family, so she could experience the powerful transformation that comes from the loving act of forgiveness.

Müller's koan, Emma realizes, is ultimately about love. It's about the need for holistic love, which Ricardo brought up when he shared the Buddha quote.

Until he has unconditional and unbiased love for all beings, man will not find peace.

Holistic love is love that has no limits, love that's not compartmentalized. Love that isn't denied to someone because of who or how they are—because they're a pig or a narcissistic parent or a girl who didn't protect her pet or a therapist who doesn't always make the right choices for her clients. All beings are nothing more nor less than the biology they were born with and every experience they've had throughout their lives. Everyone is doing the best they can with the cards they've been dealt. Emma knows that nobody is less worthy of love than anyone else, and it's time for her to stop acting as though she's the exception.

Some people, like Emma, are better at loving others than themselves. Some love themselves but not others. Some people love certain humans but not others. Some love certain animals but not others. The Buddha was right: the less we compartmentalize our love, the greater our sense of peace will be. Because whenever we practice love—no matter who it's toward—we strengthen the qualities that comprise it, like compassion, acceptance, and forgiveness. We also increase the chances that the other will practice love as well, because love begets love, just as violence begets violence. It seems like the Buddha and Müller are pointing to the same phenomenon. Holistic love creates holistic peace; like a heart, anything less than whole isn't enough.

Blinking to clear the fresh tears from her eyes, Emma tugs at her coat to straighten it and stands up. She takes one last look at Blossom's grave.

You are loved.

"Thank you," she whispers. She turns and heads toward the street, where she'll call an Uber to take her home.

The first thing she'll do when she's in her house, after making herself a decadent mug of organic coffee, is to cuddle up with Annie on the sofa and play an unlimited round of Candy Crush. Then she'll let Shana know that she's going to need the psychiatrist to cover for her next month when she finally takes that trip to Paris she's been fantasizing about for years. For which she'll bring only checked bags, just so she doesn't push her luck. She'll also treat herself to takeout from The Dancing Buddha. #73 chicken curry and rice. On second thought, that's what Emma BS would have ordered. Now that she's post-SOS, her tastes have changed. Emma PS will get the tofu version.

Finally, she'll update CouchGPT with new information on how to cure SOS.

Acknowledgments

I would probably never have written this book if not for the support of some of my wonderful friends and colleagues. I'm deeply grateful to my early readers: Sara Murray, who waded through a rough draft over many weeks and provided vital feedback; Tobias Leenaert, who guided me through the confounding twists and turns of the fiction-writing space and even came up with the title for the book; Tina Kaul, whose cheerleading and friendship was like a beacon leading me onward; Susan Solomon, whose psychological brilliance and incredible friendship improved both the book and my life; Robin Flynn-Joven, whose humor and insights and support carried me through more than just the writing process, as always; Camille DeAngelis, whose compassionate support and guidance changed the trajectory of my writing career; Jasmin Singer, whose wisdom and caring were like a life vest in the stormy sea of publishing; and my husband and muse, Sebastian Joy, who championed the book from inception to completion.

I'm also deeply grateful to my other readers and supporters: John Boland, whose belief in and support for my work probably means more than he realizes; Nina Stummvoll, who once again ended up buoying me and my writing; Evanna Lynch, whose keen listening and feedback helped catalyze my decision to write a novel and whose later support helped me through the process; Ria Rheberg; Leah Edgerton; Asheem Singh; Miriam Schafaczek and Wolfgang Hußmann; Vishwa Dave; Kati Radloff; Tainá Garcia Maia; and my mother, Nancy Hoinsky.

My sincere thanks to the amazing team I'm so fortunate to work with—Nirali Shah, Lucy Evans, Juyeon Shin, and Jessie Lingenfelter—and for the ongoing guidance and help from Dawn Moncrief, my trusted colleague and a true friend. A big thanks also goes to Rocky Schwartz, whose listening and encouragement gave me the ultimate push to write the book, which I likely would never have done otherwise; and to Owen Gunden and Sabina Makhdomi, whose Phauna retreat watered the seeds of my inner creative.

Finally, I'm grateful to Midge Raymond and John Yunker, from Ashland Creek Press, for taking the time to steer me in the right direction; Jo Hildebrand, whose editorial expertise and invaluable support I've had the honor of benefitting from for years; Donna Hillyer, for her thoughtful editorial feedback that helped turn the manuscript into a book; and Yasmine Schrey, for her editorial first aid.

About the Author

Melanie Joy is the bestselling author of seven nonfiction books, which have been translated into 23 languages. An award-winning psychologist, she specializes in relationships and the psychology of social change. When she's not running her international nonprofit, Melanie can be found strolling through the forest outside her Berlin home, whipping up creative meals to share with her husband, or speaking German with an unmistakable American accent. *A Half-Hearted Death Wish* is her debut novel. You can learn more about her at melaniejoy.org.